Madeleine was born in Hampshire, and lived there most of her life until she moved to Cornwall.

Her home now is a beautiful log cabin built in the remote and peaceful countryside near Bodmin Moor. She finds it a perfect place to write with its wondrous views and timeless sense of bygone days.

Madeleine has two much loved daughters, six grand-children and eight great grand-children in a close, ever-growing family.

THAT DAY IN NOVEMBER

Madeleine Orrick

THAT DAY IN NOVEMBER

by Madeleine Orrick

© Madeleine Orrick 2018

A catalogue card for this book is available from the British Library.

Paperback ISBN: 978-1-9996788-3-8

First published in 2018

Publication support
TJ INK
tjink.co.uk

Printed and bound in Great Britain by
TJ International, Padstow, Cornwall

Acknowledgements

Grateful thanks to all who patiently guided me. Without their help I would still be exploring the mysteries of my computer. Big hugs.

By the same author

Underwood
Anders Folly
Anders Full Circle
Anders Heritage

LIST OF CHARACTERS

Clare James	
Laura James	Clare's mother
Andrew Davenport	The country Vet
Alan Davenport	Andrew's father
Mark Carlyon	Cousin to Andrew
Kathy	Mark's wife
Luke and Emma	Their children
Connie Jarvis	Midwife in Cornwall
Jim Jarvis	Connie's husband
Ria (Victoria Kirby)	Andrew's ex fiancée
John Kirby	Ria's father
Jason	Television engineer
Arthur and Grace Carlyon	Grandparents to Andrew and Mark
Laurence Willerby	Family friend
Hannah	Housekeeper to Arthur and Grace
Peter	Gardener to Arthur and Grace
Chloe	Laura's pet spaniel

CHAPTER ONE

Listening to the hubbub around her, Clare was convinced she was the only one in the audience on her own. She should never have come. Never have used the complimentary tickets left on her desk a week ago, rousing a longing to relive the memory that still haunted her, tempting her to the same theatre, same play.

She pictured a blond head and clear grey eyes that held hers, sometimes softly, sometimes teasingly but always, she had thought, with love. She still yearned for his touch; how could her heart be so treacherous? He had walked out on her, and after all this time she still couldn't feel anything for anyone else. No one could possibly take Paul's place; that place in her heart could never be filled by anyone else.

She gathered up her coat and handbag, intending to leave, but at that moment the house lights dimmed and the customary hush fell over the packed auditorium as the safety curtain began to rise and the last musicians disappeared through the orchestra pit, leaving a blank where a moment ago there had been life and music.

Reluctant to disturb the tense moment she relaxed as the audience leant forward in their seats expectantly watching the heavy, gold fringed, royal blue curtain rise to reveal a lone figure standing on a dimly lit stage.

The scene was set for the murder mystery to begin. Then...

"Excuse me." The whispered words came again. "Excuse me. Sorry," the latecomer apologised, as a portly woman, having settled herself comfortably with coat, handbag and box of chocolates on her lap, gave a resigned sigh, struggled to her feet and smothered a gasp of pain as a tall figure added insult to injury by stepping on her foot.

Amid tuts of annoyance from behind, the figure settled in the vacant seat on Clare's right, apologising as his elbow touched hers resting on the arm between their seats.

She moved her arm and glanced sideways then drew away with a sharp intake of breath to stare unseeingly at the stage, alarmingly aware of the shoulder so close to her own.

The broad figure sat like a ghost from the past, completely banishing her concentration on the play. Could it really be? The one swift glance said the occupant of the next seat was Paul.

Without turning her head, she leant slowly back to view his profile, but it was too dark; she couldn't be certain. Her first instinct was to push past the rapt audience, rush home and lock the door behind her, but taking a tremulous deep breath, she forced her attention back to the stage.

She shouldn't have come. How could she have thought it would be all right? Painful memories came flooding back. Three years ago tonight had been the most wonderful night of her life. Paul had taken her to a small Italian restaurant and asked her to marry him. The restaurant was close to the theatre. This theatre; this play.

They had sat through the performance holding hands and afterwards, driven home to her bedsit where they talked until dawn planning their future together; and the following day they had chosen a beautiful engagement ring together.

Bitter tears stung her eyes as she recalled removing the

diamond solitaire from her third finger and placing it back in its black velvet lined box, only two weeks later.

Paul had told her to keep it, in the short note he put through her letterbox, saying he couldn't go through with their plans, but the hurt had gone too deep and she sent it back to him. He hadn't replied. She didn't even know if he got it. He gave no explanation; not even a chance to ask for one, because he had left the firm by the time she got to work that day and she had never seen him since.

Months of misery followed when she went to the office, returned home, cried herself to sleep every night and got up in the morning to repeat the day over again, without remembering anything clearly, except her work.

She heard much later, he had returned to his home-town, to be near his family, obviously abandoning all thought of their plans, by starting up a business on his own.

The yearning to see him and feel his touch lessened, but never went completely; the hurt remained.

Of course, speculation had flown around the office, but not knowing why Paul had left, and too miserable to talk about it, she left them to gossip.

Naturally quiet and reserved, she didn't make friends easily; Paul had been her world.

Paul, on the other hand, was a very popular Manager and had proudly announced their engagement at the office Christmas party, so her lack of communication led them to assume *she* had broken off the engagement.

Robbed of the exciting future they had been planning, her job at the insurance company became her priority, and desperately filling lonely evenings by working tirelessly and passing her accountancy exams, she earned promotion to Head Accountant.

A huge relief, that came with promotion, was a private office where she was surrounded only by files and paper work, affording her the solitude she yearned for, to avoid contact with the staff, except for work.

That, and the considerably higher salary which enabled her to buy an upmarket flat nearer to the office, gave her the boost her bruised ego needed most, and she continued to throw herself into the job; working late, returning home, too tired to do anything but put her feet up and eat her solitary meal in front of her new wide screen television, constantly hoping Paul would knock the door, take her in his arms and say he had made a mistake.

So, convincing herself he would come back sooner or later, after all the promises and plans they had made together, she stayed aloof and presented a business-like image by clipping her dark hair back into a severe chignon and wearing immaculate trouser suits and white blouses to discourage personal contact.

That was all three years ago now and she had given the other ticket to her mother thinking a trip to the theatre was something they would both enjoy. After all, her feelings for Paul were behind her now... or so she had thought.

The performance was due to begin at seven o'clock and they arranged to meet inside the theatre at half past six to allow time to order an interval drink, buy a programme, and get settled, but on arriving at the theatre her mother had phoned her mobile to say she couldn't leave Chloe, her two-year-old spaniel.

"The vet had to remove a huge thorn from her paw this afternoon. The Council were cutting back brambles in the park. I blame myself. I shouldn't have taken her there. Poor little thing; I can't leave her. I hope you aren't too upset with me, dear. It's a shame to waste the ticket. I'm really sorry."

Hearing her mother upset, she had quickly assured her that of course she couldn't leave Chloe, and not to blame herself because these things must often happen to lively young pups. "I'm sure she will be fine in a day or two and it doesn't matter about the ticket, I wouldn't have asked anyone else, anyway."

"No dear of course not." Laura sighed regretfully, wishing her only daughter did have *anyone*.

Returning her phone to her handbag, Clare had stared at the placard advertising the evening's performance and realised that not only was it the same theatre and same play, but also the very same date. November 30th.

Deep in thought, she was brought sharply back to earth as the house lights went up. It was the interval and she had missed the whole of the first act. Annoyed, she turned to look at the figure responsible and saw his eyes closed. Indignation mixed with relief swept over her as she saw it wasn't Paul.

Thank goodness," she murmured emotionally.

"Pardon?" The figure opened one eye and peered askance at her.

Startled she retorted, "I thought you were someone I knew."

"And you didn't want to see him?"

"It doesn't matter one way or the other." She shrugged and turned away.

There was a world of doubt in his, "Mm," and she sat forward again staring at him indignantly, about to tell him she had just missed the whole of the first act because of him and didn't wish to discuss the matter further, but on second thoughts remained silent and squared huffily into her seat, leaning as far away as possible.

What an insufferable man! How could she have thought he was Paul? He was nothing like him. Same size perhaps and blond hair, but Paul was always smartly dressed, in a suit; not like this man who wasn't even wearing a tie. No way to attend the theatre in the evening. No, they weren't a bit alike. She shot him a sideways glance. He was gazing intently at the stage, and his profile was a bit the same in the dimness. That was what she had seen. Well at least she could settle down and watch the rest of the play now. She had allowed her imagination to run away with her; that was all.

As she relaxed, her handbag slipped from her lap onto the floor with a soft thud, and with an impatient tut she reached down to retrieve it, as another hand reached simultaneously, and they both pulled back as their heads made painful contact.

"Sorry," the occupant of the seat on her right whispered, bending again to grope around in the dark for the bag.

Clare rubbed her temple and frowned, aware that people were looking round curiously. His hand accidentally touched her foot and she jerked it away indignantly, but in doing so she kicked the bag, and to her dismay heard it plop into the well under the seat in front. He also heard and sat up slowly, turning his head in her direction. Their eyes met and even in the dimness he could see her flash of annoyance and pursed lips.

Without a word, he returned his gaze to the stage and slumped back, seeming to shrink six inches, while Clare took a deep breath and leant back, forcing herself to stay calm and wait for the interval when she could retrieve it.

The curtain eventually descended again to deafening applause, and she fumed silently, realising she had also lost track of the second act. People in front vacated their seats, discussing the excellence of the performance on their way to the bar.

Rising quickly, intending to go round to the next row, she felt a sharp tug on her skirt, accompanied by a tearing sound and looked down to see her dress caught in the neighbouring seat, and a gap at her waist where the bodice had parted company with the skirt. Once again their eyes met, his filled with horror, hers cold and angry as she stood above him.

"What can I say? I really am very sorry."

Now that she could see him properly, he was younger than she had first thought, but she was in no mood to be placated. The whole evening had been disastrous. She should never have come.

"Don't say anything. Just be good enough to release my skirt," she answered coldly.

He got up quickly. "Of course. Sorry. At least let me get your bag for you. I can step over the seat; it won't take a minute."

Clare hesitated, reluctant to accept, but glancing along at the number of people still in seats, she agreed with an unsmiling, "Very well."

He stepped over the back of the seat, his long legs spanning the gap with ease and with another swift movement picked up the bag and held it out to her with a triumphant grin. "Forgiven?" he asked, and softening slightly at his effort to make amends she took the bag, with a small relenting smile that froze as the contents emptied between the seats.

With groans of, "Oh no," they both dived to retrieve them and it took the rest of the interval for Clare to satisfy herself nothing was missing and demand furiously, "Did you really have to hold it upside down?"

"I am really, really sorry." His contrite tone belied the faint glint of humour in his eyes that said he was trying not to laugh, and thoroughly dishevelled from her foray under the seats and aware that nearby onlookers were also finding the mishap amusing, Clare glared at him.

"If I hear you say sorry just once more, I won't be responsible for my actions. Just leave me alone," she snapped, in a tight-lipped undertone.

"I really am dreadfully..." He stopped at Clare's warning look.

"How can I make up for my stupid clumsiness?" he asked.

Clare's only answer was a scathing look and with only five minutes to go before the curtain went up again for the third and final act, she gathered up her short evening jacket and handbag and left, ignoring the concerned look that followed her.

Outside, in the overcrowded Festival Theatre car park, she breathed a sigh of relief.

It had been raining and the air felt wonderfully fresh after the auditorium. Wet pavements gleamed in lights from busy restaurants and bars and hundreds of stars shone between drifting clouds. Even the weather was as it had been.

She remembered walking to the restaurant, arms linked, Paul laughing, shortening his stride to match hers and with a sudden irresistible urge to see the Italian bistro again, turned her steps towards North Street. She had never been able to bring herself to visit this part of town since.

She wended her way past a newly opened wine bar and a

Chinese takeaway, expecting to recall memories, but everything was different, even the Bistro, which although still there, didn't look at all like the same romantic hideaway, where waiters came and went like shadows and spoke in melodious voices to couples at secluded tables.

Red candles in raffia-covered bottles throwing soft light onto red tablecloths, had disappointingly been replaced with small electric lamps and bare tables with place mats decorated with wine bottles and fruit. The only thing that hadn't changed was the black board with its boldly printed white chalk lettering, still standing outside, beckoning to passers by to try exotic sounding dishes.

Swamped with nostalgia she wandered past the softly lit entrance, then wandered back, drawn by emotion that closed around her like a dream as she entered and went straight to the secluded table where Paul had proposed. Ignoring the reserved notice, she sat down and fingered the leather covered menu. In her mind's eye, red tablecloths and candlelight reappeared, with soft music playing in the background. Yes, this was how she remembered it.

Oh no! What was that large table doing there, with a group of young people sitting around, waiting for their order to arrive? Where was the romantic love seat and perfumed bank of flowers, hiding a small desk where waiters discreetly prepared bills?

A waiter appeared carrying six huge plates of pasta, and she watched fascinated as he juggled them expertly onto the table, seeming to remember what each young person had ordered. The same waiter came over to her and smiled, asking in a melodious Italian accent, "You would like to order, Signorina? This table is reserved for ten o'clock, but we have another."

9

She shook her head absently. "Just a glass of wine."

About to say they only served drinks with food, the waiter spread his hands with a sympathetic smile as she leant back, overcome with nostalgia.

The youngsters on the big table were laughing loudly and she could hear smatterings of French and Spanish as well as English. She found herself smiling at their efforts to communicate, and when the waiter returned with the wine, he nodded with approval.

"You have a beautiful smile, Signorina. Don't be sad."

"Buona sera, Luciano," a voice hailed, as a figure wended its way between the big table and the alcoves.

"I'll be at the bar until my table is free."

The figure continued on its way, hidden by the waiter who responded with a cheerful, "Ah, buona sera, Signor. I will be with you in one moment."

The waiter gave Clare a small bow before leaving and in her mind she pictured Paul exchanging pleasantries with a waiter, three years ago. She couldn't remember him; she had been too wrapped up in Paul. Could he be the same one? Would he remember them? She needed to know that someone else had witnessed their happiness; proof that it wasn't just her imagination. How could Paul have changed his mind just two weeks later? Did he have regrets that very night? What had she done to make him change his mind?

She put the red wine to her lips. It was pleasant; just the right temperature, as it had been that night. Music was playing in the background, as it had been then, and she relived the moment when Paul had slipped the ring on her finger; feeling his touch, hearing his promise to love her forever.

"Is your wine to your liking, Signorina?" Luciano's voice

broke into her thoughts. "You have stopped smiling," he scolded softly.

Her eyes filled with tears as she asked emotionally, "Do you remember me? Three years ago, I sat at this table, with a friend." Her eyes pleaded with him and he looked sympathetic.

"I have only worked here for two years, Signorina."

Realising she was embarrassing herself, she came back to earth with a bump and rose abruptly, sliding out from behind the table.

"I'm sorry. It was silly of me." He stepped back to allow her to pass, and watched her make straight for the door, leaving him waving the bill with a resigned sigh of, "Buona notte, Signorina."

The figure at the bar wandered over and took the bill. "My table is ready, I see."

That is one very sad Signorina; molto triste," Luciano crooned. "Do you know her?"

"We only met this evening, but I did manage to empty her bag between the theatre seats, and tear her dress on our short acquaintance."

Luciano pulled the corners of his mouth down and leaned his head sideways, as they watched Clare standing on the pavement trying to hail a taxi. Quite suddenly, the stars had disappeared and light rain was falling steadily.

"She will never get a taxi; the theatre has just turned out." Andrew gave a concerned tut. "I'll offer her a lift. Won't be long."

Luciano gave a knowing smile. "Yes? She is molto bella."

Andrew turned the collar of his coat up and dashed outside. "I can give you a lift. You will never get a taxi, now the theatre has turned out. You need to book."

Clare stared at him with startled deep blue eyes. Her dark hair was already clamped to her bare head and her light evening shoes were looking pretty wet, as was the flimsy dress clinging to her ten denier stockings, but she said haughtily, "Not you again! You are the very last person I would accept a lift from. I would die first."

He looked down at her inadequate attire. "In the circumstances, that is a distinct possibility; you are already soaked. My car is nearby. Let me drive you home."

"No. Leave me alone. I would rather walk."

He watched her disappear back past the theatre and out of sight.

It was raining steadily, and stamping with frustration she teetered along the wet pavements. Her mother was supposed to drive them back to the flat and stay for the night. Why hadn't she thought about getting home when her mother cancelled, she asked herself.

It was that impossible man! He was to blame!

Away from the town centre, it was quiet; and normally well lit, but fog was descending. She looked at her small gold wristwatch. Ten thirty. There was at least a mile to walk and she wasn't used to being out alone at this time of night without her car. Taking a determined breath, she began to stride out, but had only gone a few steps when her stiletto heel got caught in a crack in the pavement. Pain shot up her shin as she lurched forward, crying out as the heel of her shoe remained trapped, and she fell onto the wet pavement, with her knee taking the brunt. She knelt for a moment, too shocked to move, then with difficulty managed to get her foot out of her shoe and inch her way towards the boundary wall of a detached house, aware that no one would hear if she called out, on what was fast becoming a typical, foggy

November night. She would have to crawl to the front door and ask for help.

She attempted to move but agonising pain shot through her leg, which made her lean back against the wall to catch her breath, as a pair of arms lifted her and carried her towards a parked car, with its fog light blazing and the passenger door wide open.

Thinking someone was attacking her she struggled frantically, until a voice said calmly, "I'm taking you home. Where do you live?"

"You, again! Are you following me?"

"Yes. You were obviously heading for trouble, walking in those stupid shoes."

"I w-was n-not, and they are n-not stu-p-id," she shivered. All she wanted was to be left alone, in her warm flat. Obstinately holding back tears she told him the way. It only took five minutes and Clare put her hand on the door handle as he pulled the handbrake on.

"I can manage from here," she said firmly.

"Are you sure?"

"Yes. Thank you," she added curtly.

Andrew got out of the car, went round to the passenger door, held it open for her, and watched in silence as she put her foot to the ground and cried out in pain.

The silence lengthened as he watched her fighting obstinate pride until, without a word, he picked her up and carried her to the automatic door that opened as they approached.

"Second floor. Number thirty. The lift is over there."

A young couple followed them unsteadily into the lift and Clare's cheeks flamed as the girl laughed and gave an inebriated hiccup. "At least I'm still capable of walking."

Andrew stared straight ahead, as if he hadn't heard and

when the lift stopped, strode the short distance to number thirty.

She fumbled in her handbag for the key and managed to open the door.

"I can manage from here."

Ignoring her remark, he carried her into the small hall, and spotting the bathroom door ajar, took her inside and sat her on a chair.

"I suggest you have a warm bath while I make you a pot of tea."

He smiled and shook his head as he heard the door lock behind him.

Fifteen minutes later, Clare hobbled into the living room wearing a blue towelling dressing gown.

He was sitting in one of her armchairs with a cup of tea at his elbow and rose to push a stool towards the other armchair.

"That was quick. Hope you're warmed through?"

He poured a cup of tea from the pot on the breakfast bar and placed it beside her.

"I'll see to your leg when you've drunk your tea."

"There's no need for you to stay. I've seen to it." She raised the hem of the dressing gown slightly to show a foot that was rapidly turning blue. "The bruise is coming out, already."

"You should really go to A and E, but being Saturday you could spend all night there. I have painkillers in my bag. I'll fetch them from the car."

"You don't look like a doctor."

He gave a good-humoured smile. "How about a vet?"

"More so than a doctor," she murmured as the door closed.

CHAPTER TWO

Clare heard the front door open and close, followed by her mother's voice calling, "It's only me, dear."

Laura appeared in the bedroom doorway carrying Chloe, and Clare looked at the bedside clock.

"Mother, its eight o'clock, on a Sunday morning. What are you doing here at this hour?"

"I came to look after you."

She put Chloe on the bed and picked her up again quickly, seeing the alarm on Clare's face.

"Sorry. Your leg must be painful."

Clare was actually more concerned for her duvet cover.

"How do you know about my leg?"

"I had a telephone call, from Alan Davenport's son. Nice man. He removed the thorn from Chloe's paw yesterday." She held Chloe's bandaged paw up. "He was so kind. His father had been called out on an emergency and Andrew arrived at the surgery just as I turned up with Chloe. He treated her straight away, and wouldn't even let me pay, as I was a friend of his father's."

Clare tossed her eyes and pursed her lips as the penny dropped.

"So you gave him the theatre ticket."

"Yes." Laura beamed. "Wasn't it lucky I did, or he wouldn't have been there to help you, or let me know." Laura beamed again, and laid Chloe beside Clare's pillow.

"That's better, she won't touch your leg if she lies there while I get your breakfast. Won't be long."

"Just as long as I never have to see him again," Clare called loudly, frowning at Chloe, lying contentedly on her clean duck egg blue duvet cover. It was Sunday, and she liked Sundays to herself.

She could hear her mother busy making breakfast, on the semi circular breakfast bar dividing the kitchen from the living room, and thought how remarkably cheerful she was, considering everything. Chloe's paw; and now, her leg. What was going on? Had she come to stay? If so, how long? Another upsetting thought occurred. She wouldn't be able to drive, according to Alan Davenport's son, for at least a week and he appeared to know what he was talking about, she grudgingly admitted; but he was still impossible.

The telephone rang in the kitchen and she heard her mother speak briefly and tell the caller, "See you shortly then."

That sounded hopeful. She must be intending to leave as soon as she had made breakfast. She loved her mother to bits, but just wanted to be left in peace. Sunday was the only full day she had to herself.

As Laura breezed in with a laden tray she hauled herself up, trying not to wince at the pain in case her mother decided to stay. The painkillers that '*He*' had given her the previous evening were wearing off and she was sure she had some somewhere. When she was alone, she would hobble to the bathroom.

Her mother's next words instantly dispelled that hope making her groan out loud.

"Alan's son is coming with more painkillers. His name is Andrew, in case you have forgotten."

"We didn't actually exchange names," Clare said dryly.

Laura placed the tray across her lap, hesitating before adding, "And to look at your leg."

Clare's eyes opened wide in furious dismay as Laura hurried from the room and popped her head back round the door.

"He's coming for your benefit Clare, so be nice. You can see the doctor in the morning, and it will save waiting around for hours in A and E."

"I really don't want to see him, Mother," Clare called as she disappeared again.

"Eat your breakfast, before he gets here."

Laura's voice drifted away and next, the radio was playing loudly in the living room.

What has got into her this morning? Clare fumed. She tried to get out of bed but, hampered by the tray, fell back as pain shot through her leg.

She poured a cup of tea from the pale green, china pot and sat looking at the scrambled egg and two slices of toast, realising she hadn't eaten since lunchtime yesterday.

Why wasn't her mother hovering as usual, making sure she was eating? she asked herself. Now she came to think of it, she was definitely behaving differently.

The doorbell rang as she finished eating and she heard her mother greet Andrew, but several minutes went by before they came into the bedroom, during which time they appeared to be speaking in lowered voices.

Andrew greeted her cheerfully. "I've brought a crutch and more pain killers, and I'll come and take you to the doctors in the morning."

He actually had the effrontery to think she would allow him to, she bridled, answering coldly, "My mother will take me, thank you," expecting her mother to agree; but instead, Laura thanked him.

"That would be really helpful, thank you Andrew. It so happens, I am busy tomorrow."

Clare thought a funny look passed between them.

"I thought you couldn't leave Chloe," she accused.

"Andrew has offered to look after her for me. I'm going on holiday with my... friend. Just for two weeks... we leave tonight." Laura petered out as Clare's eyes widened.

"You never said. I would have gone with you."

"It was a last minute thing and I'm really looking forward to it."

She looked from Clare to Andrew, and he said quietly, "It will be marvellous for you."

Watching Clare's downcast expression, Laura capitulated. "I won't go if you don't want me to."

Clare brightened. "We can go together, as soon as my leg is okay."

Laura took the tray from her and left the room, murmuring that she must let her friend know, while Andrew stared in disbelief.

"She was looking forward to going; how could you stop her?"

"You wouldn't possibly understand," Clare said dismissively.

"You're darn right I wouldn't." He strode from the room and shut the door behind him, and she could hear him talking to her mother in a quiet urgent voice.

"But it's all arranged. You've packed. I'm having Chloe, and the car is booked to pick you up at two o'clock sharp. Your daughter will be fine. I'll look after her myself if necessary."

"I really want to go." Her mother sounded disappointed.

"Then go. It's only a sprain. Nothing is broken."

Peeved at being ignored, Clare threw back the bedclothes, struggled off the bed, and opened the door, anticipating her mother's usual reaction, when in a woebegone voice she called, "Go, Mum... I'll manage." Shocked when Laura's voice came back happily, "Well if you are sure, dear."

Andrew scanned the compact kitchen area, debating where to start looking for a saucepan. Everything was so immaculate and orderly. "Better not make a mess," he muttered.

Laura had brought crusty rolls, and home-made leek and potato soup from her freezer, for them. It was still frozen, and Clare's attitude was even more so.

Laura had entrusted him to look after her, but that obviously wasn't what Clare had in mind when she banged the door and locked herself in her bedroom after Laura left.

Having managed to track down a saucepan he was about to empty the soup into it, when the bedroom door opened and Clare appeared, looking very neat in a dark blue leisure suit. She was struggling with the crutch, but when he tried to help by advising her to try it under the other arm, she snapped, "*I've* never needed one before."

"Everyone makes the same mistake, first time," he said, the words *walking* and *eggshells* coming to mind...

"The soup goes straight into the microwave in its plastic container."

"Didn't know. I don't have one."

"Being dragged screaming through the twenty-first century, are you?"

She gave a superior raise of her perfectly shaped eyebrows and opened a cupboard door above the counter. "It's really quite easy."

"Very clever," he said when she produced piping hot soup less than ten minutes later, and poured it into two modern shaped soup bowls.

"Cutlery?"

She pointed to a stand of cutlery with black, shiny handles, and he raised his eyebrows.

"Something else you don't have? Still keep your E P N S in a drawer; the vintage way, no doubt."

He ignored the sarcasm, and suggested she sat in the chair with her leg up, while eating.

"I'd rather sit at the breakfast bar."

He sat down and watched as she obstinately perched herself on the high swivel chair, knowing from the way she fidgeted that she wasn't comfortable, but would rather die than admit it. She appeared to have everything: nice looks, good job, her own flat; so why so defensive? She certainly didn't get it from her mother.

"This looks excellent," he said companionably, picking up his spoon.

"Everything my mother makes is excellent," Clare responded, in a matter of fact tone.

He laid down his spoon. He really needed to eat, but Clare was watching him critically.

"What's the matter? Have I unwittingly offended you – again? Say now, if so, because I am very hungry. I answered a five o'clock emergency call at my father's surgery this morning, then came straight here. So I missed breakfast." He picked his spoon up again. "And in case you have forgotten, I also missed dinner last evening."

Without a word, Clare picked up her spoon and they ate in silence.

"There's cheese in the fridge," she said as he put his empty soup bowl to one side and started to butter another piece of crusty bread.

"Thank you," he said, viewing the range of identical doors, under the granite worktop. "And which door might that be?"

She pointed to the end one and he got up, asking if she would also like cheese.

"Not for me thank you. I'll just go and put my feet up."

"Good idea. You should have them up all of the time."

"I'm fine," she said switching the wide screen television on, and lowering herself carefully into the armchair.

Having eaten, he felt decidedly better, and suggested making them a cup of tea.

"I prefer coffee."

"Thought you might," he muttered, holding the gleaming stainless steel kettle under the high tap.

"What did you say?" she said, raising her voice above the television.

With a full stomach his good humour returned, and grinning to himself, he called back, "Black or white?"

"Oh, black, no sugar."

He raised his eyes to the ceiling, murmuring, "Obviously sweet enough."

He placed their cups on the coffee table between the two armchairs and sunk down with a sigh. This was going to be a long two weeks; but hopefully it would be worth it.

He had made an early start that morning. The foal had taken a lot of persuading to leave the comfort of its mother's womb. Knows something we don't perhaps, Andrew thought, closing his eyes. The next thing he knew, it was dusk, the television was playing to itself and Clare was sleeping soundly, her dark head resting against the wing of the big, cream leather chair. In repose, she looked vulnerable, almost childlike.

As if aware of being watched, she woke and he looked away, stretching his tall frame, then relaxed, viewing his cup of cold tea with distaste.

"More coffee?" he asked, yawning widely.

"I think I'll have tea this time."

He spluttered with amusement, and covered it up by coughing and saying, "I need to go and see to Chloe. Your mother left at two, so she has been on her own for four hours. You could come with me if you feel up to eating out. The Bistro will be closed, but if you don't mind pub grub?"

He looked at her questioningly, relieved when, as he expected, she shook her head.

"I'm happy with something from the freezer."

"Ready meals? Never had one myself. What are they like?"

"There are ready meals, and then there are ready meals."

Clare was wearing her superior look again as she eased herself out of the chair and, using the crutch properly, made her way slowly to the kitchen and pointed to a door.

"There's plenty in the freezer. Help yourself. It's all home-made. I'll have lasagne."

He opened the door to reveal a neatly labelled stack of plastic boxes, each containing single portions of chicken, beef, or lamb cottage pies, and a varied selection of other dishes, just waiting to be heated up.

"My goodness you *are* organised. I'm impressed. However, I really do have to walk Chloe and feed her, so I'll make sure you have everything handy, then shoot off and come back in the morning to take you to the doctor." He produced a card from his wallet.

"Just ring my mobile if you need me. I'll be here in ten minutes."

"I'll be fine."

"I'm sure you will. There are painkillers on the coffee table. Sleep well and rest the leg."

Without more ado he left, breathing a sigh of relief, and Clare put her lasagne in her pristine microwave oven and waited for it to cook, feeling restlessly bereft, that her mother had gone away without her.

She pictured them sitting on the terrace of Cynthia's Villa in France, relaxing over a cocktail. They had been friends a long time. Cynthia loved France and went several times a year, and there was always an open invitation for her mother, but she was never included and that was why her mother didn't go more often.

Cynthia would never understand that of course, because she didn't have a daughter.

She rose painfully, as it occurred to her that her mother would be away for her birthday on December sixteenth. We *always* spend my birthday together, she thought resentfully. *Always*. She ran her finger down the calendar hanging on the wall over her bureau. Oh, she was actually due home the day before. She returned to the breakfast bar and continued to eat her lasagne, content that her mother had at least kept such an important day in mind.

CHAPTER THREE

Andrew arrived at ten past eight on the Monday morning.

"I managed to get you an appointment for eight fifty," he announced, when she answered the door in her blue towelling robe.

Clare looked indignant. "That is not convenient. I'll ring the surgery and make an appointment for this afternoon."

"It is the only slot they have all day, but in any case I'm not free to take you this afternoon." Andrew looked apologetic and explained, "I'm covering afternoon appointments. *And* I was *lucky* to get you an appointment at all today," he said pointedly.

Clare glared and he began to lose patience.

"I can take you to the hospital, if you prefer, but the nurse will be able to fix you up, and save a long wait in emergency." He shrugged. "Only hurry, someone else will be glad of the appointment."

Clare looked sharply at him and turned away, saying over her shoulder, "Anyway, how did you know who my doctor was?"

"Your mother told me before she left," he answered casually, recalling Laura's warning, as he followed Clare through to the living room, that her daughter would be very annoyed if she wasn't consulted. But knowing how busy surgeries were, it had seemed worth risking Clare's wrath, to visit the actual surgery at eight o'clock, in the hope of

24

getting an appointment, and luckily they had just had a cancellation.

Clare started to clear breakfast dishes into the sink and he took them from her.

"I'll see to that. Just get dressed, or we will be late."

She glared and he watched her hobble off to the bathroom, thinking how much nicer she looked with her hair down round her shoulders. But ten minutes later, when she left the bathroom and went into her bedroom, it was even more tightly drawn back than usual, and her make-up was perfect. Ten minutes after that she reappeared, in a smart trouser suit, looking as if she was ready for the office... except for her left foot.

"I can't go; I can't get my shoe on. I'll just ring the surgery and the doctor will have to come here," she said in a business-like tone.

"Good luck with that," he said as she hobbled to the telephone.

He wandered into the bedroom, listening to the one-sided telephone conversation, knowing full well what the answer would be, as he returned and gently slipped her slipper on her foot as she replaced the receiver, looking mutinous.

"Come on, or we will be late, and you will miss your appointment."

With a face like thunder, she hobbled after him. As Andrew had predicted, the doctor referred her to the nurse, who dealt with the wrenched ankle and warned that the shin muscles would take longer to mend if she didn't rest, before sending her home, armed with a supply of painkillers.

"I need to ring the office and tell them I will be in shortly," she said firmly, as he held the front door open for her.

"Not a chance," he said even more firmly. "*I* will ring and tell them you won't be in for at least a week."

She gave an obstinate stare, leant the crutch against the breakfast bar, and took her mobile phone from her pocket.

He heard her telling someone, very briefly, that she had been delayed and would be in at ten thirty before, without further explanation, switching her phone off.

"You should have arranged for someone to come and get you," he said quietly.

She regarded him with sharp surprise that quickly turned to an expectant raise of eyebrows.

"You told my mother you would help me."

"Yes, and that is what I am doing. You've been told to rest. I'm not taking you. Now if you have everything you need, I have things to do, so just sit in the chair and I'll be back in a couple of hours."

For once Clare seemed lost for words, and silently watched him leave, shutting the door firmly behind him.

Fuming with frustration, she picked up her mobile and ordered a taxi, explaining that she would need the driver to help her down in the lift. Within ten minutes, a driver arrived at the door and took a step back on seeing her pale face and bandaged foot.

"Have I got the right address, Miss?"

"Absolutely," she snapped.

Andrew gave a resigned sigh when he arrived back at the flat to find it empty.

No prizes for guessing where she is, he thought grimly, walking back to his car.

Laura had told him where Clare worked, and the office was on his way back to his father's clinic, so he drove past slowly, in the hope of seeing that she was all right, but there

26

was no sign, and he decided to park in their small car park to check.

A woman looked up from behind a highly polished desk, and he asked to speak to Clare James.

"Miss James isn't here at the moment; perhaps I can help?"

He looked surprised and she added, "Was she expecting you? Did you have an appointment? Only, she would have been here, but unfortunately she fell getting out of a taxi, and has been taken to the local hospital."

Andrew groaned, thanked her, and left. Making his way to the hospital, he debated what to do about his father's afternoon appointments starting at two o'clock, and decided he would have to ask the secretary to rebook. Fortunately, it was an annual injection clinic, and he should be able to reorganise them for tomorrow morning if the owners could make it. Little had he realised what Ria's last minute change of heart would escalate into.

On arriving at the crowded reception desk, he was informed that Clare was in X-ray. His stomach rumbled as he settled down to wait. She was having a serious effect on his eating habits, he thought with a long-suffering sigh. Breakfast had been a rushed bowl of cereal, and it was long past his twelve thirty lunch.

Three quarters of an hour later, Clare appeared, in a wheelchair, pushed by an orderly. She looked chastened, but when she saw him waiting, her chin went up defiantly and they left the hospital in silence.

He made her comfortable on the back seat of his father's car and drove her home, looking in the driving mirror frequently, wondering what she was thinking.

Once settled into her armchair in the flat, she sat staring

into space, whilst he put the kettle on to boil. "Tea or coffee?" he asked, breaking the silence at last.

"Whatever," she said briefly.

He put a cup of black coffee on the table beside her, and sat down with his tea.

"What happened?"

"I caught my good foot against the stupid crutch as I got out of the taxi," she said sulkily.

"Well, at least nothing is broken but it will take longer."

"There's no need to rub it in. If you had done as I said in the first place, and taken me to the office, it wouldn't have happened."

"You don't think you should have taken the doctor's advice to rest, then?"

"I never neglect my duties."

He suddenly felt sorry for her, wondering why she was setting herself such rigid standards, both at work and home. "I'm sure your colleagues know that, and will understand," he murmured sympathetically, realising in the next instant that it was completely the wrong thing to say, when she tossed her head and retaliated with, "I don't need sympathy, thank you very much."

"Sorry. Look I need to go and attend to a few things. Is there someone I can get to stay with you for a couple of hours?"

"It won't be necessary. I'll be all right. In fact I would appreciate being on my own."

"How about if I sleep in the chair tonight? I could bring Chloe."

Her deep blue eyes registered uncertainty. "I'll think about it."

"Okay. Promise me to stay where you are, though. I'll

bring Chloe, in case. Now I must run. I'll take the key, to save you getting up to let me in."

Left alone she relaxed. The strong painkillers were making her sleepy and just looking at the ham sandwich Andrew had picked up at the hospital café made her feel sick.

Apparently, she was going to be off work for weeks. If only her mother was here. Dare she send her a text? She imagined his reaction, and decided to go and get into bed instead, asking herself as she struggled out of her clothes, why it had anything to do with him anyway.

When Andrew returned two hours later, his jaw dropped when he saw the empty chair. "Oh no," he groaned, but seeing Chloe go straight to the bedroom wagging her tail he followed and saw with relief that Clare was sound asleep.

"Well done, girl, you just saved me from a nervous breakdown."

He looked in on her several times but Clare didn't stir all evening and she was still sleeping soundly at ten thirty.

"Looks like we're sleeping on the settee tonight, Chloe."

Before six o'clock, the next morning they were both woken by Andrew's mobile phone, and half asleep, Clare forgot her leg and fell back with a cry of pain as she went to get out of bed.

Andrew was at the door instantly. "Sorry," he mouthed, with his ear to the phone as Clare opened her mouth indignantly, but his lengthening face and look of alarm stopped her, as she watched him listening intently to what was obviously bad news. "I'll be there as soon as I can; this afternoon hopefully. Thanks for letting me know."

He switched his phone off and stood motionless for a full minute, staring into space.

"Problem?" Clare asked curiously, breaking the growing silence.

"Mm? Oh... yes... trouble at home. I'm going to have to go home." He spoke absently, obviously thinking about the call.

"I'll put the kettle on. I need a cup of tea. I expect you do too." He disappeared and she could hear him on the phone again, apparently arranging for a colleague to take over for him at his father's clinic. "Thanks a lot, Kevin. I owe you."

He took Clare a cup of tea; his mind working overtime. "You'll have to come to Cornwall with me."

"WHAT! You must be out of your mind." She glared at him. "I'm not going to Cornwall or anywhere else with you for that matter. So you can forget that, *right away*."

"Then I will have to hire someone. I have to leave as soon as possible."

"I'll text my mother. She is only in France. I'm not having a stranger in my home."

"Your mother is having a well-earned holiday, from running around after you. I said I would look after you, and so far I haven't made a very good job of it. No more arguing. You are coming."

Clare opened her mouth and shut it again, before giving a triumphant little smile. "I can't with my leg like this."

"We'll take your car; it has a reclining seat. My father's car needs to stay here anyway."

Clare's triumphant smile disappeared. "How do you know I've even got a car?"

"Your mother told me."

"Mm! She obviously talks too much. I'll have to have a word with her."

"I imagine that's how you get your own way. Now will you please get moving?"

Clare pouted. "I don't manipulate her, if that's what you're thinking."

"It had crossed my mind." Andrew strode to the door and on looking back was surprised to see a shocked expression instead of the expected anger.

"Look, I'm sorry. I've got a lot on my mind. Please get dressed. Wear something warm and loose, none of those tight suits, and I will make you as comfortable as possible. It is really important, or I wouldn't ask; and I need to make sure I have left your mother's house safe, first."

Clare pursed her lips at him. "Just go so that I can get dressed. You are wasting time."

Totally bemused by the sudden change of attitude, Andrew raised his eyebrows, and said meekly, "Yes of course."

They finally got away by mid morning, with a large suitcase, packed with what Clare considered suitable for two or three days in a country house. Now that she had given it careful consideration, it seemed the lesser of two evils. Sitting around the flat all day, with Andrew popping in every few hours hadn't promised to be very entertaining, and she had never been to Cornwall before. She had heard a lot about it, eavesdropping on the staff's holiday stories. Most of them went camping or caravanning. Not her cup of tea at all.

Sitting on a beach all day, ruining her complexion, was her idea of self-torture. And then there was all that sand in your toes, and screaming children everywhere. She definitely didn't want to go to the beach. Not that it was likely to be suggested with the weather as it was, thank goodness.

It was a long journey and he drove fast, wanting to get home as quickly as possible, but he stopped once to walk Chloe round the car park and buy chicken and chips from a takeaway café, because Andrew considered they needed something warm. But when it came to eating in the car, for quickness, she considered it the height of indignity and was very glad nobody could see her eating with her fingers. Andrew guessed her thoughts as she pulled the hood of her anorak up, but after the early morning phone call, he was too concerned about what he was going to find when he got home, to worry.

They were driving through narrow lanes now, with just room for two vehicles to pass each other, and every now and then, Andrew had to brake and either pull in or back up to allow the occasional car and even the odd tractor to pass. Propped up in the passenger seat, Clare could see her wing mirror brushing the hedges and became alarmed at the damage it would be doing to the bodywork.

"Do we have to drive so close to the hedge?"

"Fraid so."

She tutted impatiently. "Just bad driving."

Although only three o'clock, it was almost dark, and the weather had got progressively worse on the journey down. Sleet started to hit the windscreen and Andrew switched the wipers on. Without street lighting, all she could see in the headlights was a muddy track, bordered by high hedges.

"You're lost," she accused, picturing them stuck in the middle of nowhere overnight.

"No. We are nearly there."

His anxiety was evident and she was convinced he wasn't telling the truth, but minutes later a five bar gate with 'The Haven' carved into the top bar, came into view.

He stopped the car and got out, and she watched him walk through into a large paved area to hook the gate back, before driving up to a long building, outlined against the darkening sky. Welcoming lights at the far end, glowing from latticed windows on the ground floor, promised warmth and Clare's spirits rose, until a figure appeared, silhouetted in a doorway, and for the first time it occurred to her that Andrew had a wife.

He hadn't mentioned a wife; he had let her assume he was single. Her opinion of him sunk even lower. He really was impossible. She would demand to go straight home tomorrow. All she wanted at the moment though was a cup of tea and some warmth; and then she would insist on being taken to a hotel.

Andrew went over to the figure, spoke briefly and returned to the car.

"Connie is going to take care of you, for a while. There is something I need to attend to, then I will take over." He went to pick her up, but she pushed him away.

"I can manage. Why didn't you say you were married?"

He looked taken aback, before giving a tired, resigned smile.

"Connie isn't my wife. She is married to Jim. She has offered to put you up for the night, until I get sorted in the morning."

"Oh." She tossed her head and eased herself out of the car. After two faltering steps, he bent and scooped her up, and she started to object.

"Do be quiet. It's been a long day," he said, wearily. She held herself stiffly in his arms to show her objection, as he carried her over and introduced her to a comfortable looking Cornish woman.

"What you bin doin to yersel then?" She asked in a broad accent, hovering until Clare was settled in a comfortable chair. "Teas made. 'Elp yersels ta scones."

"Thanks, Connie." Andrew sat down at the table, on a chair next to an armchair, where an elderly man was sitting, smiling with obvious pleasure as Andrew touched his hand and introduced Clare.

"Jim likes to paint. You must show Clare your paintings, Jim."

Connie stood behind his chair and put her hands on his shoulders. "She be pretty anuff ta paint."

Jim looked up at her and they smiled fondly at each other as Andrew realised he should have mentioned Jim's poor health. Another slapped wrist, he thought dolefully.

After demolishing two scones, thickly coated with cream and jam, and two cups of tea, Andrew thanked Connie and rose reluctantly.

"Otpot 'll be ready fer six, mind," Connie warned sternly.

Andrew gave her a fond smile. "Fantastic. See you in a while, Jim."

After he had gone, Connie cleared away the tea things, peering out of the window with a worried frown, chatting about how much worse the weather was getting; her mind obviously on something else.

It was quiet in the living room and the log burner was throwing out a welcome warmth. Jim's head was jerking, in an effort to stay awake, but gradually sleep took over and Connie gave a satisfied nod, looking at Clare.

"Ye won' 'ave ta mind. 'E sleeps a lot."

"Are you sure you can look after me as well?"

"It's what I do," Connie answered cheerfully.

"Sorry?"

"I'm a nurse. I look after folk. Didn' Andy say?"

"No," Clare answered, pursing her lips. "Just one more thing he hasn't mentioned."

"Don' spose 'e reckoned it mattered," Connie defended, with a straight look.

"No I don't suppose he did," Clare sighed, realising that *Andy* could obviously do no wrong, in Connie's eyes.

"You 'ave forty winks, me lovely, while I get dinner on."

She disappeared and Clare could hear her moving about in the kitchen across the narrow hallway. She found it comforting. It reminded her of her childhood, when her mother, after putting her to bed and reading the nightly story, went to do – what? Prepare for the next day? It had never occurred to her to wonder before. She wished she was back in her flat. Why had she agreed to come?

Jim grunted, half waking, and Connie appeared instantly, saying softly, "Connie's 'ere."

Clare watched as she smoothed his brow, seeing the bond that existed between them and her eyes filled with unexpected tears.

CHAPTER FOUR

Andrew looked around the empty rooms. Connie warned him Ria had moved out, but he hadn't been prepared for the complete removal of his home. She had taken everything; things that were his, years before they met. Treasured furniture given to him by his father, treasured because it belonged to him and mother. Too shocked to take it all in, he went from room to room, his footsteps echoing on bare boards. Even the curtains had gone. How could she have done this? And why?

A sudden thought struck him, and he hurried downstairs to go along to the surgery, where he had expensive equipment; fearful she had stripped that as well. To his relief he found the door locked, and both keys were on his key ring.

When Ria said she wanted three weeks off to prepare for the wedding, he had happily agreed with whatever she wanted and employed a young student for that time, just to book appointments and answer phone calls, so when he left for Hampshire, looking forward to their wedding and a two week cruise around the Greek islands, everything was going smoothly.

He hurried back to the cottage, thinking about Clare. The plan had been for her to have the cottage, where she could have privacy. He knew Connie would be happy to have her stay, but what would Clare think.

He sunk down onto one of the wide, low windowsills in the sitting room, head in hands. His well planned future, in ruins. And to top it all he had taken on Laura's spoilt daughter for two weeks. Two weeks!

"And it's only been two days," he groaned aloud.

Overwhelmed by the endless problems he forgot the time, until he heard the front door shut and saw Connie, in the doorway, staring at him.

"What you doin', sittin' there gettin' cold? Dinners on table." She looked around. "My god, she made a proper job."

Wide eyed, she walked through, surveying the empty dining room and kitchen, then returned to stand and stare blankly at him, before saying that he was to come and eat. "You'll stay at mine the night."

The evening had turned icy cold, and sleet was falling steadily as he followed her out into the dark courtyard, taking her arm, hurrying her back to her warm cottage, glad to leave the depressing sight of his empty home.

Jim was already at the table and Clare was sitting where he had left her, with her meal on a table across the chair and her leg up on a rest.

"You look happy," he commented, bending down to hide his feelings, by stroking Chloe, asleep on the hearthrug in front of the log burner.

"Is everything all right?"

"Just a few things to sort out, before I take you home," he said giving Connie a warning glance.

After they had eaten, Andrew helped to carry the dishes out to the kitchen, where Connie asked why he wasn't telling Clare what was going on.

"She wouldn't understand," he said, shaking his head disdainfully.

"Mebbe. Mebbe no."

He gave her a questioning look.

"Miserable, I'd say."

"Huh! I don't know what she's got to be miserable about. You should see her immaculate flat, perfect job, *and* a mother she twists round her little finger."

"Don' sound perfect, ta me."

He gave her a puzzled look.

"Twenny five? No bairns? No man? Father and grandparents died when she were a bairn." She raised her eyebrows at him and he raised his back with a glimmer of a smile.

"You know more after an hour, than I do after three days." She gave a big grin and was relieved when he grinned back. She loved him like a son, and hated to see him feeling so low.

He started washing the dishes. "I know *one thing* you don't," he joked.

"She don' trus' men?"

He looked over his shoulder and pursed his lips at her.

"'Er leg were 'urtin'," she said simply, as if that explained.

"Thanks for phoning. I wouldn't have known anything for two weeks, if you hadn't."

"Saw van leavin' as I came 'ome from Jane's, 'alf five this mornin'." She gave a big smile. "She 'ad a boy. Eight pounder 'e were. An' 'er such a little thing. Nothin of 'er." Andrew glanced round questioningly and she reassured him, "Kathy listened out fer 'im."

He put his arm around her as they were about to go back into the sitting room.

"I'll take Clare home tomorrow. I promised her mother I'd look after her. Can't think what she'll say about me bringing her all this way with her bad foot, especially as Clare blames me for refusing to take her into work."

Connie tossed her eyes. "Tek no mind. Early night for us all, I reckon."

Andrew suddenly realised she hadn't slept last night. "You must be exhausted."

"I 'ad a couple o' hours, but I'm ready fer me bed, now."

She finished filling the hot water bottles and he tightened the stoppers as she passed them to him.

"I'll be back to help with Jim, as soon as I can," he promised with a concerned look.

"'E misses ye," she admitted. "Ye make 'im feel useful, even if 'e can't do much."

"The animals love him. Especially the dogs. He calms them."

Clare was dozing in the chair and Andrew offered to help her to bed, fully expecting her to refuse, but she nodded.

Noting her look of dismay as she saw the single bed and he said the bathroom was along the landing, he said quietly, "I'll take you home in the morning."

Left alone she inspected her surroundings. Although not large or modern, the room was pleasant enough. In keeping she supposed with the countryside, with its lavender sprig curtains, plain cream bedspread and framed paintings of blue tits and owls, relieving the plain white walls.

The single bed, with its dark oak headboard, was higher than her double divan with its soft, padded head board, and she hadn't slept in a single bed since she was a child. Looking down at the bare, polished floorboards, with home-made rugs beside the bed, she yearned for her warm, carpeted flat. What on earth had made her think she would be staying in a country house, with an en-suite bathroom? Absolutely nothing about Andrew would even vaguely suggest that.

CHAPTER FIVE

Clare could hear Connie repeating herself. "Well I never! Well I never!" Her voice came closer and then the door opened and Connie appeared with a cup of tea, balanced on a small, round tray.

"Mornin' me lovely. You'll never guess what." She set the tray down on the dark oak, bedside table and threw the curtains back with a theatrical flourish. "Look at that."

She waited for Clare's reaction, as she hauled herself into a sitting position and looked out at the snow-covered scene.

"It been snowin' all night, 'parently. So it said on tele. We 'avn't 'ad snow fer years."

"Mm, it does look quite deep." Clare shivered and sunk down under the bedclothes again, tucking them under her chin, surprised by Connie's childish excitement. Snow was pretty but it did make a terrible mess. She wanted to go back to sleep; the painkillers had made her sleep, in spite of the flannelette sheets and blankets, and something she recalled her mother calling an eiderdown. The hot water bottle had been nice, but it would never take the place of central heating. She shivered again and wondered if hot water was too much to expect, as Andrew knocked on the open door.

"Can I come in?"

He was dressed in outdoor clothes and had obviously been out in the snow.

"At least Chloe enjoyed it. Completely forgot her paw; running around like a two year old."

"She *is* a two year old," Clare reminded him, reaching for her tea.

"Figure of speech," he grinned, then said tentatively, "It would be foolish to travel today; apparently the snow is worse further up country, and people are getting stuck. Perhaps it will have gone by tomorrow. It never lasts long does it?"

Clare looked crestfallen. She had been looking forward to being in her warm flat, but she had to admit that travelling in present conditions didn't appeal.

"I need to go out but Connie will be around all day, because the roads are blocked."

"How long will you be?" she asked anxiously, wondering what ever she would do if he didn't come back.

"I'll be back by lunch time."

Clare looked at the time on her mobile phone and groaned."Five or six hours?"

"Sorry. I've got to go. Text me if you need to, but if I don't answer immediately, it will be because I'm driving."

"Of course," she answered, feeling completely cut off and helpless. "Couldn't I come with you?" she asked, knowing it was impractical even as she asked.

"Really?" He pursed his lips and gave her a sidelong glance as he left. She heard him calling goodbye to Connie and Jim as the front door closed and shortly after that an engine started, and she listened to it fade away, feeling helpless and abandoned as the Jeep crunched its way slowly along the snow-covered lane.

What did one do in a place like this? she asked herself, looking up at the beamed ceiling, listening to the eerie silence that the pristine white world of snow seemed to create.

Connie appeared again, carrying two blue towels. "Stay abed til I've warmed the place up," she advised, and went bustling downstairs again, where she and Jim were listening to the news over their breakfast.

Clare continued to lay looking up at the ceiling, asking herself what on earth she was doing in this place that had every appearance of having stepped back in time.

Her thoughts were interrupted by the telephone ringing downstairs, and after a few seconds she heard Connie say, "I'll come an' see t' him Kathy; don't worry." And then there was complete silence as the television was switched off, and a door banged. She obviously doesn't have any trouble finding things to do, Clare thought, fighting to free herself from the well tucked in bedclothes.

Venturing out onto the landing, she found the bathroom. The spotless bath had a low side to it, and a strong handle fixed to the wall. She was nicely surprised by the modern Rain Shower and assumed the whole bathroom had been recently refurbished for Jim.

She faced a slight problem when it came to going downstairs, but by easing herself down on her bottom, was half way down to the flagstone floor of the square hallway when Connie came through the front door and gasped, "What you doin' lass?"

Clare looked pleased with herself. "No problem."

"Just 'ad to pop nex' door. Kathy's due in three weeks, an' little Luke 'ad wandered off down the garden. 'Is boots got stuck in the snow and she nearly got stuck as well, trying to get to him. He won' do that agen; proper frightened 'imself, 'e did." She laughed. "Full o' mischief, that one. Lovely little lad."

While talking, she helped Clare down the rest of the stairs, and to the easy chair by the wood burner. Clare expressed surprise at seeing Jim's empty chair.

"'E'll be in studio. Paintin' a snow scene, I shouldn' wonder. The snow'll 'ave give 'im an idea." She smiled fondly. "Don't know what 'e'd do without his painting, now 'e can't garden any more."

"If you don't mind me asking, what exactly is his problem?"

"Right as rain, 'til four month ago. Came in from garden an' collapsed. Twas a stroke, and 'e would've been a gonner, if I 'adn't been 'ere. It's affected 'is speech a bit but 'e's better than 'e was."

"How awful, and yet you seem so happy," Clare murmured, wondering how she would cope with the same situation.

"We are. At least I still got 'im." For a brief moment, Clare saw her underlying fear, and realised the suffering that had been dealt with and overcome. Her own problem suddenly seemed very small by comparison.

Connie straightened her shoulders and raised her chin, changing the mood by giving a bright smile that Clare suspected hid an aching heart; knowing she must be wondering how much longer she would have him.

"Now; what will ya 'ave for breakfast? There's fresh laid eggs, from our own chickens, bacon, an' sausage from local farm, 'ome-made bread. Fried bread – Andy's favourite."

Clare laughed, throwing her hands up in horror at the idea of fried bread, but agreed that a boiled egg with home-made bread would be lovely.

Connie went off, tutting, to return ten minutes later with two eggs and two thick slices of delicious looking crusty bread.

"Eat up my lovely. Jim'll be ready fer 'is morning coffee, so I'll be back dreckly."

Her homeliness reminded Clare of her mother. She was missing her, and hoped the snow would be gone by the time she was due to fly home. Christmas was less than three weeks away and she hadn't bought any presents yet. Not that she had anybody to buy for, except her mother – and Chloe of course; mustn't forget Chloe; mother would never forgive her. She suddenly wondered guiltily where Chloe was and called to Connie, in the kitchen.

Connie poked her head round the door. "She's with Jim. 'Ad anuff o' the snow; curled up on 'is sofa, she is. Dogs love 'im. Andy says 'e has a way with 'em. Dogs know good folk, don't they?"

"I can't say I've really thought about it," Clare admitted. "But you and my mother would get on famously."

"I'm lookin' forward to meetin' 'er." Connie went back to the kitchen.

Clare smiled picturing them exchanging recipes. "I must bring her down," she called, looking out at the falling snow and murmuring, "when the weather improves."

Jim ambled into the room, followed closely by Chloe, and his face brightened as he saw Clare. She was pleased to see him looking better. He had looked so frail last evening.

"Hello, Jim."

He pointed to the window. "Can't go home now."

Connie bustled in and started setting the table. " 'Ope Andy won't be long. Soup's ready."

She left and returned, carrying a framed canvas.

"Show Clare ye bluebell woods, Jim."

He took it from her and Clare gave a cry of admiration as he turned it to face her. Not expecting anything so professional, she was taken aback by the colour and brushwork. The bluebells looked as if they could be picked, and the woodland path disappearing into the distance had such depth and perspective, that she felt she could actually walk into the picture. She sat mesmerised. It was the perfect Christmas gift for her mother. "I want to buy it, Jim."

He shook his head vehemently.

"Really?"

He nodded and she looked disappointed.

"It's special, fer some reason, but 'e 'as others," Connie explained. She turned to the window at the sound of a car. "Ah, there's Andy."

She hurried to the kitchen and Clare's spirits rose as she heard the car door slam.

Andrew came in looking cold and tired and ate the hearty chicken soup hungrily, while Connie, Clare noticed, kept darting worried looks at him,.

Having eaten, he left saying he had work to do in the office, and Clare was forced to stay in the warm and rest her leg, frustrated and curious about what was going on. Snow started to fall heavily again from a leaden sky, turning to ice as fast as it touched the ground, and with it, her hope of it clearing by the morning faded completely as she settled back, wondering what they were doing in the office. Without doubt there would be numerous claims. Who was filling in for her? Sitting at her desk? She had left it immaculate and would be really annoyed if it wasn't so, when she returned. Her thoughts were interrupted by Connie, who having finished the dishes, was shrugging into a warm, blue fleece.

"Just goin' ta check on Kathy. School 'ad to close, so Luke's bin 'ome all day, an' she needs 'er afternoon nap. I'll just amuse 'im for a while." She looked at Jim and he said amiably, "Don't worry my love, I'll look after Clare."

Left alone, Clare could see Jim struggling to keep his eyes open and smiled as he finally gave in. He was such a big, comfortable looking man and she wondered what he had done before his illness. She had never known what it was to have a father. It had only ever been her and her mother. Men had never figured in their home life at all. She recalled a man coming to the house a few times when she was about eleven years old, remembered disliking him and refusing the expensive presents he bought her; seeing them as bribery, so that he could take her mother out, and leave her alone with a babysitter. She hadn't liked that woman either. For the first time she wondered if she had stopped her mother from marrying again? Was Andrew right? *Was she a little spoilt?*

Unwelcome thoughts flitted through her mind as she watched Jim sleeping; thoughts she had never had in her own world. What was it about this place that made her keep questioning herself? Or was it the irritating Andy?

Her eyes travelled to a clock on the wall, above a well-stocked bookcase. Its large round face, once white, now yellowing, showed the big black hand pointing to a large figure six and the smaller one to the three. It was an old railway station, waiting room clock; probably an antique now; not that it was something she would want in her own home. Her thoughts drifted on. Only three thirty, and already pitch black outside. Where were the street-lights? And although firelight was pleasant enough, the fire needed far too much attention. Her radiators warmed the whole flat; no bother at all. She wanted to turn the light on, but was reluctant to disturb Jim. How long would Connie be? Her eyes grew heavy from the warmth of the fire, her thoughts drifted, and she didn't hear Connie come back, or Andrew go upstairs to shower; in fact, she slept until Andrew shook her gently to say dinner was ready, and awoke feeling embarrassed.

"Jus' what ya needed," Connie said looking pleased, as she placed a roast dinner, on a blue and white Willow pattern dinner plate in front of her.

"Eat up. Local pork, and 'ome grown veggies," she said with a satisfied nod. And there wasn't a sound until Andrew sat back and sighed with satisfaction,

"No one can cook like you Connie. I suspect Clare is pretty good though, according to her freezer," he quickly corrected himself.

Clare looked at him. "You can stop digging that hole. I don't cook. My mother fills the freezer. I just microwave it."

"So, your mother cooks, a woman does your washing, ironing, and cleaning, your shopping is delivered; what do you do?" he asked sounding amused.

Clare looked at him with disbelief. "My job, of course. You're insinuating that I'm spoilt, aren't you?"

Andrew struggled to keep a straight face. "No. I am stating categorically that you are. You let me think all those carefully labelled meals in your freezer were your own doing."

"No I didn't, I just didn't contradict you."

"I don't know why; you did about everything else."

Connie shook with laughter. "Listen ta you two, goin' on' like an old married couple."

"Not knowing what old married couples are like, is that good or bad?" Clare asked.

"Bit of both, I suppose," Andrew replied with an amused smile.

"And more precisely?"

"Well, I suppose it depends on whether the couple like each other enough, between arguments, to want to stay married and reach old age together," he answered philosophically. "My grandparents seem to have mastered the art to perfection."

Thinking of Paul, Clare said, "Sounds a bit incompatible to me."

Andrew looked at Connie and Jim and smiled."Not if you meet the right one, it isn't."

"You'll know when the right one comes along," Connie interrupted, sensing things were getting tense, and although the rest of the evening passed pleasantly, Connie's concerned glances confirmed Clare's feeling that Andrew's light conversation was forced, and after a while, unable to keep her suspicion to herself any longer, she said boldly,

"Something is troubling you, and I get the feeling I'm the only one in the dark."

She looked from one to the other, as Connie and Jim looked at Andrew, expectantly.

"Just as well get it over Andy, accordin' ta forecast, weather's 'ere all week."

Andrew closed his eyes and sighed, looking thoroughly dejected; and the silence lengthened, before he admitted,"Ria has left me."

"Oh. I'm sorry."

"We were to be married, at eleven o'clock last Saturday. I travelled up on Friday with my cousin Mark, who was to be best man, to make last minute arrangements, tried to contact her in the evening to say everything was organised, got no reply, but assumed she was busy and just not answering her phone. When she didn't turn up at the registry office though, I thought she must have had an accident or something. We phoned the police but no accidents had been reported. They made enquiries and found Ria still here. According to them, she simply said she had changed her mind about getting married."

Clare sat quietly, trying to take in all that had happened to him since Saturday; *that day.*

"So – how come you were at the theatre on Saturday evening?" she asked in amazement. "Why didn't you come back here and tackle her?"

"I telephoned. She said it had all been a big mistake and she couldn't face any unpleasant goodbyes. She asked me to stay away until she had gone. I agreed because there didn't seem any point in an unpleasant show down, and at that point I don't know what I was thinking. I had to explain to everyone that the wedding was off and by lunchtime I couldn't take any more, so I went to see Dad, who I thought must have returned to his surgery, but he had taken a call. That was when I met your mother and she gave me the ticket." He shrugged. "I felt such a fool, I just wanted to escape and take my mind off the whole thing."

She stared at him in wonder. "And did it?"

"Did what?"

"Take your mind of things?"

He tossed his eyes. "Yes. I can safely say, without a shadow of doubt, it did that."

Connie looked intrigued, and Andrew explained what had happened.

"Oh dear," Connie and Jim chorused, trying to keep straight faces.

"Not your day, was it?" Connie gave him a vigorous nod. "Tell 'er the rest," she insisted.

Andrew looked down at his hands. "I feel such a fool."

"If it helps, much the same thing happened to me." Clare spoke quietly, surprising herself by suddenly admitting to being rejected.

Andrew looked up sharply. "Really?"

"Three years ago I got engaged and two weeks later, without any explanation, I got a note saying he couldn't go through with it; and I have never seen or heard from him since."

It became clear to Andrew why she was so defensive. "It's not knowing why, or if you're to blame, isn't it?" he said with a resigned shrug.

Clare's simple, "Yes," told him she was still wondering that, three years on.

"What did *he* take?" Connie persisted, seeing Andrew's reluctance to admit to what had happened since.

"My heart. That was enough."

Jim interrupted. "Bedtime." He knew Connie meant well, but it was up to Andrew to tell Clare his full story. Or not.

Connie took the hint and got to her feet. "Night my lovelies. See you in the mornin'." She gave them both a peck on the cheek, and followed Jim. Two minutes later, she returned carrying a bottle of wine and two glasses, put them in front of Andrew, and left without a word.

Andrew smiled fondly, poured two glasses and handed one to Clare. "I assume this is when I'm supposed to tell all."

"I wish you would, before I die from curiosity." She held her glass up to him and he did the same, before taking a large mouthful.

"And this is supposed to help loosen my tongue," he joked to cover his embarrassment.

"How long were you engaged for?" Clare gave him the

opening and gradually he told her that he and Ria first met at university, lost touch for several years, and met again shortly after he moved to Cornwall and started up his own business.

"She was looking for a job and happened to see my advert for a receptionist in the local business magazine. She didn't realise it was me, until she arrived, but then we both thought it good that we knew each other. At the time, the most important thing to me was that she took over the bookwork which I'm hopeless at anyway, and I was able to concentrate on the practice. It worked well and after a few weeks, she suggested moving into the rooms above the surgery, to save travelling each day. I wasn't sure at first, but it made sense. So she moved into the flat, and ten weeks later, we got engaged. That was when I took over the flat and let her have the cottage. It seemed the fair thing to do. She said she had never been happier. No one else was happy about it, but if anything, that made me defend her. We were together for fifteen months, so was it me, or country life she went off?"

Clare looked thoughtful. "Stepping back in time isn't everyone's cup of tea."

"Is that how you see it?"

"I would definitely miss my home appliances."

"Why would you have to? We have electricity, we also have clean air, views to die for, and a healthy way of life: that far out ways anything the city can offer."

She regarded him silently, recognising that he was completely content with his way of life and wanted a woman to share it wholeheartedly. How she yearned for love like that – but country life? Oh no! Definitely not.

"It obviously doesn't appeal to you?" Andrew's voice broke her reverie and she came back to earth with a bump.

"It sounds ideal, but you're talking to the wrong person. Realistically, *I'm* not cut out for walks in the rain, muddy floors and everything that goes with country life, either."

"It doesn't have to be like that." He sounded wistful, and Clare veered away abruptly. "This isn't about me. What did Connie mean when she asked what my fiancé had taken?"

Andrew took a large drink of wine and refilled their glasses before answering.

"The phone call on the morning we drove down was from Connie, to say that a self drive removal van had just left my house and Ria was in the van because the Daimler wouldn't start. Connie thought I should come home quickly. That was why I had to bring you. I hope your mother will understand."

"She will. More importantly, what has this Ria taken?"

"Everything not nailed down."

Clare looked shocked. "Was it hers?"

"No. None of it. And Connie said she overheard Ria, on her phone, telling someone she had packed the car, but the damn thing wouldn't start. Apparently, she was coming back today with a mechanic, thinking I wouldn't be here; and I wouldn't, if it hadn't been for Connie's phone call. As it happened, the unexpected weather would have stopped her anyway. I can only assume her clothes are in the car. Don't know what she was thinking. It's my dad's old Daimler. Wonderful car, but seldom used, because its so thirsty you need a BP tanker to follow it. Must have thought she could borrow it; but she most certainly can't."

"I'm afraid it all sounds rather planned to me."

Andrew emptied the last of the wine into their glasses and gave a sigh. "You don't need to listen to my woes; you've had your own."

"We hadn't set a day or arranged everything. You've been cheated and jilted."

She spoke quietly; guessing he had more shocks to come, and watching him as he sat staring into the fire, she wondered what his true thoughts were. He didn't sound angry, but then she knew *her* first reaction had been deep hurt, before heart ache and loneliness. Her next reaction had been to put on a business-like front, and avoid any personal contact.

"Maybe the family were right," he said ruefully.

"How so?" she asked curiously.

"According to them, I had a lucky escape."

He gave a derisive huh! and went off at a tangent. "Hope Mark gets home soon. He came up with me for the wedding, then had a meeting in Hindhead, on Monday. He was supposed to be coming home today. Hope he makes it. Their baby is due soon. The weather doesn't look promising but I'll get you home as soon as it's safe to travel."

He was sitting forward now, elbows on knees, the glass between his hands, still staring into the dying fire, talking as if to himself, sounding weary and despondent.

She sat forward, her tone brisk. "Don't worry about me. You need to sort things out here first. Right now though, I think it's time we went to bed. Help me will you please?"

"Of course. Sorry. Feeling sorry for myself." He gave a rueful grin.

"You have good cause; but it doesn't get you anywhere. Take it from one who knows."

He helped her up to her bedroom, where she was greeted by the warmth of an oil- filled radiator.

"Oh, wonderful!" She gave him a grateful smile.

I picked it up while I was out today. Being a soft townie, I guessed you would like it."

"You bet I do. Thank you."

"You're very welcome. Good night."

She reddened as he kissed her cheek and left, shutting the door quickly behind him.

She undressed slowly, wondering why this man, who obviously meant nothing to her, was consuming her thoughts. She was obviously just sorry for him; who wouldn't be?

As she hobbled along to the bathroom, she saw a light showing under the door of the other bedroom. There were only two rooms and the bathroom upstairs. So where did Jim and Connie sleep she wondered inquisitively, instantly realising that Jim would have difficulty in climbing stairs and knew they must sleep downstairs.

As she returned to her room, still mulling over Andrew's situation, she noticed his light was out, and wondered if he was laying awake worrying, and why it even mattered to her.

Fighting with the unfamiliar bedclothes, she finally got comfortable and her last waking thought was that he mustn't let this Ria get away with it.

CHAPTER SIX

Clare glanced across at Andrew, sitting at the table wearing a worried frown.

"Don't you think you should check on what is in the car? Ria could come while you are out and just drive it away?"

"That's my first job this morning. Don't worry, the car is safe enough until the weather lets up. The snow will have to be cleared from the garage door before it can be opened."

He nodded towards the window. Snow had started to fall yet again, quickly covering his and Chloe's footprints, from their early morning walk. He finished his cup of tea and took the cup out to the kitchen, where Connie was busy making bread. Clare heard him ask why Jim wasn't up yet, and Connie answer, "He didn't sleep much last night. He's woritting about ye Andy. You've so much on ye mind, ye can't think straight. Spend an afternoon by the fire with 'im. It 'ud do ye both good."

"I'll see what I can do."

"Good lad."

He popped his head round the sitting room door. "I'll be in the surgery. See you at lunch."

"How can I help?"

"Just stay warm. I need to get organised somehow." He pulled a long face. "It's knowing where to start."

"The first thing is to get your furniture back."

"I haven't a clue where she's taken it."

"Trace the van hire firm, and give them a ring."

He looked at her with new hope. "Good thinking."

"Go on then," she urged, as he stood staring at her.

He saluted her with a flourish. "Aye aye, Ma'am."

Connie's voice reached them from the kitchen.

"Most likely place is Truro. Daniel's van rental. Ask fer Ted. Tell 'im I said."

She appeared in the doorway with the telephone directory.

Andrew started looking through the yellow pages as Connie put a notepad and pencil beside him. Five minutes later, he came off the phone, with a set expression.

"Ted says she did hire one of his vans and also asked if he had two men who would move a house full of furniture. He didn't have, but told her who to contact. They were due to return his van today, but he had a phone call earlier to say that snow had stopped them travelling."

Clare looked puzzled. "Wonder where they were moving to."

"Ted didn't know where, but he got the impression it was some distance away."

Connie appeared wearing a grim smile. "The lads would know."

"No luck there. They were only booked for the removal. She already had a driver."

Andrew looked thoughtful.

"They won't get far until the weather improves, but I don't want to involve the police."

Clare looked dubious. "You might have to if you want it back."

"Oh, I want it back; most of it belonged to my parents. And there are paintings that have been in the family for generations."

"But at the moment, she's got possession, and I think I'm

right in saying that possession is nine points of the law, unless you accuse her of stealing," Clare pointed out.

Andrew looked worried. "If I could talk to her, I could sort it out without any fuss."

"Humph. Good luck with that." Connie bustled back to the kitchen.

"They didn't get on," Andrew explained.

"Well, it's up to you of course, but it would seem that *Ria* has planned this very carefully. It isn't a *last minute* change of heart."

Andrew sat down heavily in the armchair next to her. "You wouldn't think I could be so easy to fool would you?"

"We naturally trust those we love, but you should really go through your accounts."

He looked up sharply, stared for a moment, then left the house. Fifteen minutes later, he returned, admitting that he didn't know where to look.

"Ria is the only one who knew anything about the bookwork."

"I'll take a look, if you like."

Andrew looked eager. "Would you? Sure you don't mind? I'll fetch whatever I can find. Okay if Clare uses your sitting room, Connie?" He hurried out, suddenly filled with doubt, and as Connie called back, the front door was already closing. In the next minute Connie appeared, beaming at Clare.

"Am I glad you're 'ere lass; never did trust that one – neither did 'is Father, but Andy wouldn't 'ave a word agenst 'er. She 'ad 'im exaggly where she wanted 'im."

Clare looked thoughtful, wondering if loving someone always made you blind to their faults?

Connie hurried away as they heard Andrew kicking his

boots off, and a welcome breath of fresh air wafted into the warm sitting room, as the front door slammed. Clare hauled herself up straight and pulled the table across her chair, and Andrew dumped three ledgers in front of her.

"This is all I can find."

Connie came in with a cup of tea, and gave Andrew a satisfied nod as she put it beside Clare.

"Anything I can do?" Andrew asked anxiously, but Clare was already scanning the first page and didn't answer, so he just sat, waiting anxiously. She appeared to have forgotten he was there, until, without looking up, she said absently, "Shouldn't you be clearing snow, or something?"

Two hours later, he returned to find her still poring over the second ledger, and enquired how long she intended working. "Take a break, or I'll be in trouble with Connie."

She closed the book and leant her elbows on it. "When did you say your books were last brought up to date?"

"It will only be a month. Ria al-wa-ys ..." He petered off, slowly shaking his head from side to side, in time with hers.

"Was she actually a qualified book keeper?"

"Well, I left university before her but I assumed she was because she applied for the job. I suppose I should have asked for credentials." Andrew sat down abruptly. "We were friends. I trusted her."

"Naturally," Clare said briskly, reminded that she had believed everything Paul said.

"Don't blame yourself," she murmured sympathetically.

His shoulders drooped. "I've been such an idiot. Why didn't I realise?"

"Why would you?" she whispered as Paul's words: 'I will love you forever', echoed in her mind; but filled with self-reproach, Andrew didn't hear her forlorn question.

"She kept insisting we were short of cash, that I needed to inject more capital; that a new business takes time to get off the ground. I knew there was plenty of business, but I believed it when she said people don't pay their accounts promptly."

He spread his hands and looked at her. "I admit I've no head for figures. I just want to care for the animals. But I should be able to do both." He closed his eyes in helpless dismay and Clare brought him back to earth by saying in a business-like manner, "So did you invest more capital?"

"I had the seventy thousand my mother left me, so over the last six months I put forty thousand in the business account."

Alarm bells were ringing loudly in Clare's head, but she wanted to go through everything more thoroughly, before voicing her suspicions.

She put the books she had inspected to one side, and smiled reassuringly, even though she felt more than a little worried.

"I'll come along to the office in the morning and start on the filing cabinet."

He gave a concerned but hopeful look. "Sure you feel up to it?"

"Yes. Thanks to Connie."

"Well, the walkway is clear, but to be on the safe side I'll borrow Arthur's wheelchair."

In the morning it had stopped snowing and the wintry sun was melting the icicles hanging from the roofs and trees, and for the first time, Clare saw how high up they were.

"Breathtaking, isn't it?" Andrew took deep breaths, as Connie predicted pessimistically, "It'll be oright if it don't freeze agen, dreckley."

Andrew pushed Clare down the slippery walkway, past Kathy's cottage and his own, to the end of the terrace, where the surgery was.

After showing her around the large sitting room, which had been divided in two to make a recuperation area and a small reception, he took her into what had been the kitchen, but was now his surgery.

Obviously immensely proud of the well-equipped operating room, he would have spent time explaining what each instrument was for, but Clare was anxious to get on.

"So where is the office?" she asked, hiding her impatience with difficulty.

"Through there." He pointed to a door. "It was originally the dining room. Connie and Jim use theirs as a bedroom since Jim's stroke."

He wheeled her though to a light, pleasant room where a six drawer filing cabinet stood on one wall and a large, flat topped oak desk stood in front of doors leading into a conservatory running the width of the cottage.

"I've had a door knocked through, so that I can come and go into my cottage. Jim has his studio in theirs. Good light apparently. Mine will be a grooming salon, eventually."

Lost in enthusiasm he was in no hurry but anxious to get started, Clare cut him short and looked around the office. Other than the filing cabinet and the big desk, there was nothing else in the room, except for two swivel office chairs, and when Clare asked about a computer, Andrew said Ria didn't like them, so keeping suspicions to herself she suggested looking to see what was in the car.

Andrew worried that she would get cold, but she assured him she was enjoying the fresh air after being indoors for nearly a week, so he wheeled her outside to the carport between the surgery and the garage, where a side door led into the garage. She sat in the wheelchair, watching impatiently as he cleared snow away and disappeared inside. If she was right, he had more shocks to come.

He reappeared. "It's as I thought, just clothes and personal bits."

"Are you sure? Can I have a look?"

"Sure."

He pushed her through the narrow doorway and, as he said, it did appear to be just clothes, stacked with great care on the back seat; while the well of the spacious car was full of shoe boxes.

"Have you looked in the boxes?"

He shook his head and shrugged. "She adored shoes."

"What about the boot?"

Andrew went and opened it. "It looks like a beauty shop. Hair dryer, make-up cases, new clothes. Things she valued most. No doubt thought it safer than packing them in the van."

Disappointed, Clare looked thoughtful. "She will be pretty desperate to get them then."

Andrew looked downcast. "She thinks I'm still in Chichester, held up by the weather, so she won't be panicking, but she is extremely protective of her..." he wagged two fore fingers, "'Things' as she calls them, so she'll be back as soon as possible."

For a brief moment he looked sad and Clare knew Ria was still fresh in his mind and he was finding it hard to believe what was happening.

She looked away, uncertain of her own feelings, telling herself she was just sorry for him, as she looked in the passenger window. "What is that on the front seat?"

Andrew shrugged. "She called it her private brief case,

family letters etcetera. Nothing to do with the business, she said."

He opened the car door, and Clare opened the case, which wasn't locked. It was as he said: private stuff; letters, postcards and a supply of new writing paper and envelopes. She glanced idly at a photograph, tucked in the lid.

"That's just her cousin Jason. I was to meet him at the wedding. Didn't see him."

Clare closed the lid of the case, and ran her hand over the cream upholstery of the car seat. "Mm, real leather," she said appreciatively.

Andrew patted the gleaming bonnet. "My dad's pride and joy. It was due to go in for its yearly inspection after we returned from honeymoon in two weeks. I might delay it until the weather improves though."

"Of course. Mustn't get it dirty," Clare teased. "Even the carpet is immaculate; how do you manage that, living here?"

"She only gets used on high days and holidays." Andrew demonstrated how the front seat moved at the touch of a button and lovingly picked up an invisible speck from the chocolate brown carpet.

"Any hidey holes?" Clare asked, still convinced there must be something concealed.

"Only the one where we keep a spare key," he answered confidently. "You would have to know it was there, and even then, how to open it; only Dad and I know that."

He gave a derisive laugh. "He wouldn't even tell mother, in case she took 'My other Lady', as he named her, for a drive when he wasn't around. The only other key never leaves *his* key ring."

He bent to feel under the running board and his face lost colour as he straightened up. "It's open and the key is missing."

He went very still, realising how near he had come to losing his father's treasured car.

"Lucky she didn't know about the safety switch that disables the ignition. The mechanic would have known though. I need to check the safe in my bedroom. Won't be a minute." He hurried back to the house and Clare took the opportunity to go round to the driver's side, knowing that when she wanted to put something out of sight, it went under her seat. Disappointingly, there was nothing there and she closed the door just as Andrew came back, looking haggard.

"The log book has gone and the month's takings that I left. What can she be thinking of?"

"I'm afraid she has been planning this for some time."

Connie came towards them and noting Andrew's shocked expression and Clare's pursed lips, asked, "What you expected Clare?"

"Not exactly. But I know I'm right."

Andrew gave her a worried look. "What were you expecting to find?"

"I'll tell you when it turns up."

"Come away indoors. I've just made tea." Connie started pushing Clare back along the walkway, towards her cottage.

"Lock the door again and put my car against it," Clare called to Andrew, who looked startled and immediately moved her car from one side of the carport to the other, efficiently blocking the garage door.

With the snow melting slightly in wintry sunshine, the possibility of taking Clare home loomed large in Andrew's mind, and when they were settled by the fire, he said, "This is my problem; I must get you home. We'll need to leave early tomorrow morning, so that I can travel back here the same day."

There was a final ring to his words, and sounding dismayed Connie called from the kitchen, "Why not wait a day or two?"

"No, it's best this way. Clare needs her flat, and you have enough on your plate."

Connie came to stand in the doorway, hands on hips. "She's no bother; I'm glad of 'er comp'ny."

"I've made up my mind; she goes home tomorrow." He looked at Clare. "Okay?"

Clare raised her eyebrows and he tipped his head back, with a glimmer of a smile.

"What time would you like to leave?"

"Who says I want to go?"

Connie beamed. "I'll put kettle on, now that's settled."

Clare looked speculative. "Something tells me we will get company very soon now." Andrew's resigned smile disappeared as he remembered the surgery was unlocked, and Connie appeared in the doorway, when she heard him dash along the walkway.

"Thank 'eavens you're 'ere," she said and marched back to the kitchen, as Jim shuffled in, mumbled "Me too," and shuffled out again.

Andrew returned just as the five bar gate opened and two figures entered and made straight for the garage.

Clare gave a satisfied nod, as Connie and Jim joined them.

"Have you got a crystal ball or something?" Andrew asked.

"Just a shrewd guess that there is something more important than her things in the car. She doesn't know you're here, so stay out of sight and watch."

Andrew gave a disillusioned "Huh! Josh services all of our cars; and to think I took him for an honest man."

"Probably thinks he is following your instructions; you said it was due a service."

"Maybe," Andrew murmured doubtfully.

They watched as Ria caught sight of Clare's car blocking the only way in to open the double doors, which locked from the inside.

Clare and Andrew exchanged looks as they heard Ria say that some idiot had blocked the door and they would have to force the double ones.

"Don't rightly think we should do that, Miss."

Andrew gave a pleased, "Aah!"

"Mr Davenport will be annoyed, if he comes home to find his car won't start," Ria said.

"P'raps we should just ask someone to move the car," Josh suggested.

"All right, but it will take forever if it belongs to one of Connie's doddery patients."

She came towards the house and they remained silent while she hammered on the door several times, before going next door to knock on Kathy's door. Luke must have opened it, because they heard him calling to his mother. Then Kathy could be heard saying the car belonged to a lady staying with Connie and she had no idea where they were.

"The stupid woman has parked in front of the door. I can't get in the damn garage. You must know where Connie is," Ria demanded furiously.

"I don't and I need to shut the door. It's letting the cold in."

Connie turned to Andrew. "A side of 'er ye 'aven't seen; but we 'ave."

They watched Ria march back to the garage and heard her say, "We will have to break the door down."

"I'll come back when Mr Davenport comes 'ome, Miss."

"I insist you break the doors down now."

"Sorry, but no, Miss." He started to walk back down the drive.

"I'll give you two hundred pounds," she called desperately. He stopped in his tracks, and walked back, starting to look suspicious.

"I need that damn car started!" She stamped her foot, beside herself with frustration. Everything had gone as planned until this godforsaken snow came.

Andrew stood, staring out of the window, looking completely dumbfounded.

"Now might be a good time to show yourself," Connie suggested.

"Let's see just *how* desperate she is," Clare interceded quietly, putting a detaining hand on Andrew's arm.

Ria was speaking to Josh, pointing at his pick up truck, and sweeping her arm from the truck to Clare's car. They couldn't hear what she was saying, but it was obvious she was telling him to tow the car away from the door. Josh trudged reluctantly back to his truck and galvanised into action at seeing a tow rope about to be tied to Clare's car, Andrew went dashing out of the front door to speed across the courtyard.

Halted in the act Josh gave a relieved smile. "Oh, am I glad to see you, Mr Davenport."

Speaking to Josh but looking at Ria, Andrew said quietly, "I'll deal with this, Josh. The Daimler stays where it is."

"Right you are, sir." Looking nervously from Andrew to Ria, he jumped quickly into his truck and started to back out.

"Wait for me," Ria cried, before turning on Andrew.

"I'll be back for my things later. Don't touch them."

"That's rich," he said scathingly, following her to the gate and shutting it firmly.

When they had gone, he moved Clare's car, retrieved a length of chain and a padlock from inside the garage and secured the gate before replacing her car.

Clare complimented his caution, but pointed out that they really needed to know what was in the car, that Ria was so anxious about.

"She mentioned two hundred pounds. Why don't we take a proper look now? She will be back as soon as she gets transport."

Connie beamed as Jim said, "Good girl."

It was cold and dark in the garage, but Clare was too excited to notice.

"Just stand and watch if your conscience bothers you. I'll try the boot first. There *is* such a thing as being too much of a gentleman you know."

As Andrew said, the boot was full of beauty products and new clothes, still in their wrappers, as if she had bought them very recently.

"She seems to have set herself up very nicely and if my guess is right..." Clare was foraging and even lifting the floor of the boot to feel underneath, but her face fell with frustration as nothing came to light.

"It's got to be here somewhere."

She wheeled herself round to the back door, as Andrew asked, "What exactly are you looking for?"

"Evidence. She has either hidden cash in the car, or transferred it by computer."

"She doesn't do computers."

"So she says! I'm sorry Andrew, but she has been dipping into your accounts for months."

Andrew looked dazed and asked if she was absolutely sure.

"What is it going to take to make you see what is under your nose? Help me get these boxes out," Clare said impatiently, turning things over with careless abandon.

"Steady on," Andrew cautioned as he watched her removing rubber bands and emptying shoe boxes into the spacious well of the car.

"There is no time to be careful; help me look in these... hah! I knew it! Look!"

Andrew gasped and started to help, as they discovered money beneath each expensive pair of shoes; thirty boxes in all.

"One thousand in each; thirty thousand altogether," Clare said, quickly counting one bundle, as Andrew said ruefully, "Nearly all I transferred, a while ago."

She was repacking the shoes and replacing rubber bands as Andrew stood in stunned silence, surveying the neat piles of notes he was holding.

"You need to contact your bank, straight away. I checked and there are no receipts in the filing cabinet, only unpaid bills."

Andrew continued to stare at the notes.

"Now would be good," Clare said urgently.

"Yes, yes of course." He tossed the money onto her lap, then pushed her out of the garage and locked the door.

The bank confirmed Clare's suspicion. Money had been regularly withdrawn or transferred to a numbered account and the business one was empty, but fortunately his private account couldn't be accessed.

He returned the receiver to its cradle and sat staring into space, unable to grasp how he had been deceived. The dark eyes that he had trusted, had made a fool of him.

Clare watched conflicting emotions cross his face, and received a shrug in reply as she placed a pile of mail in front of him, asking, "Do you want me to deal with these? They need urgent attention."

They were in the office and sitting dejectedly at the big flat topped desk. He closed his eyes in despair, just as the sound of a horn broke the silence.

"Don't say we found the money; just let her take her things and find out for herself."

Andrew gave her a blank look and Clare spread open hands despairingly. "She can only give herself away if she says anything?"

"Aah!" He pushed her through to the reception and she watched through the window as he strolled slowly to the gate, while Ria hooted her horn impatiently and started moving the car before the gate was barely open, calling loudly, "I haven't got all day."

Ignoring her he opened the side door of the garage and Ria made straight for the rear door of the car, making sure the shoe boxes were the first things to be loaded into the vehicle she had driven over in. Once they were safe, she turned to him suggesting it would be quicker if he helped.

Andrew leant against a snow covered wall. "You told me not to touch your things. I wish I had said that before you walked off with mine."

"Oh, don't be so stupid," she said peevishly.

"I have been. But not any more. You have twenty four hours to return every last stick of my furniture, before I contact the police."

"Over a few old bits of furniture? What would Granny say?"

"We shall see. Perhaps I should keep some of your

69

things." He walked over to her car. "The shoes would fetch a good price, no doubt." He picked up two of the boxes, and she ran over with her arms full of the last of her clothes, to snatch them from him; then throwing them and the clothes into the car she slammed the door as Andrew walked round to the driver's side and removed the keys.

"I'll just keep these until my furniture arrives, and also the keys and log book to my father's car. Tell whoever is waiting round the corner you're finished here."

She looked frantic and started towards him with that little girl look he knew so well, but he put his hands up, warding her off, and waited while she got outside the gate before relocking it.

Watching from the surgery window and seeing his hurt, angry look, Clare sighed. For a moment she had wondered if he might give way to Ria's play acting, knowing all too well, as he walked towards her, how tempting that might have been. Ria had obviously captured his heart with her short, well rounded figure and Mediterranean looks. She felt a wave of jealousy. If only Paul had wanted her that much.

Still picturing Ria in her long, navy blue coat and three inch heel designer boots, to give her height, she wondered, yet again, what *she* had done to drive *Paul* away, as Andrew pushed her back along the walkway to Connie's cottage.

Sitting with Connie and Jim over a cup of tea, it was getting dark when they heard a large lorry stop at the gate, and watching from the front door as Andrew strode purposefully over and spoke to the driver, they saw two men get out to lower the tail gate on the lorry for Andrew to check that the furniture was his, as Ria appeared.

"It's all there," she snapped sulkily, tossing the keys and the log book to the Daimler at him and holding out her hand.

A duffel-coated figure watched from the far side of the road, as Andrew handed her the keys and watched her drive onto the road and allow the figure to take the wheel.

Minutes later, Connie, Jim and Clare went back to the fireside, to the reassuring sound of Andrew's home being restored to its rightful place.

Looking into the dancing flames, Connie said anxiously, "Wonder what she'll do when she finds the money missing?"

"We will just have to wait and see," Clare answered, with a determined look.

CHAPTER SEVEN

Ria flung the door of the flat open and marched in, carrying six shoe boxes, red faced with anger. Thoroughly fed up, John followed and dumped another ten boxes on the bare floorboards.

She had ranted and raged for most of the journey, and he was tired and hungry after driving for seven hours in atrocious weather conditions.

"Why are you complaining if you've got twelve thousand pounds you didn't expect?"

"I didn't *expect* to spend it on furniture; that's why I'm complaining," she snapped.

"But you told me you tried to take some of his home."

Ria pouted, and tears filled her big dark eyes as she spread her arms wide, indicating the empty room. "Because I needed it."

"But you couldn't just help yourself to his things without asking."

At the end of his tether, John felt helpless; unable to cope with Ria's tantrums any more.

"Let's empty the car and go and find somewhere to eat and stay for the night, then in the morning we'll buy what you need. I take it you didn't pack food?"

Ria glared at him. "I told you. It was all in the hire van. I had everything until the stupid snow came and the damn Daimler wouldn't start."

"You didn't mention a Daimler! What were thinking of?" John asked in a shocked voice.

"It would have been long gone, and on its way to Europe before he got back. I was just going to say I borrowed it and it got stolen. It was well insured. He would have got his money back. You don't understand. *He wasn't supposed to be there.*"

John felt sick with shock. "This wild behaviour has to stop. He could have you arrested for what you have done."

Ria sneered. "He won't."

"How can you be so sure?"

"Too afraid of upsetting his precious grandparents."

John looked around at the cheerless, empty flat. "Well you obviously can't stay here tonight and I've got a business to run, so leave this place and go back to your mother as fast as you can. I've never let you down yet, but this is the last time I get you out of a scrape. Don't involve me any more."

"But I've paid three months rent on the flat," Ria whined.

"You will probably get two years rent free accommodation, courtesy of her majesty if you don't see sense and go to your mother and get a proper job."

He started angrily towards the door.

"Don't forget my shoes," she cried in a shrill voice. He picked the boxes up, and she followed him back to the car, scowling at his retreating back. No way was she going to Malta. Share the money with her mother? No way!

Fifteen minutes later, they pulled into the car park of a Travel Lodge.

"Stay here while I book a room," John said abruptly.

Ria remained, fuming silently, until he returned ten minutes later, with a key.

"I've booked a twin room in the name of Johnson and the restaurant is just over there. Let's eat. I'm starving."

"There's no need for all this precaution," she said sulkily. "I keep telling you, he won't go to the police. His respectable family would have a fit. I don't suppose he will even tell them, and even if he did, they wouldn't do anything; they'd just be glad I'd gone."

"I wonder why?" John said under his breath.

The restaurant was quiet due to the weather and as Ria chose a table close to a window where she could keep an eye on the car, it was John's turn to jeer.

"How far do you think a thief would get in this weather?"

"It's not the car I'm worried about."

John's smile disappeared. "No, of course not, that's mine."

"I didn't mean it like that, Dad."

"Just get yourself over to your mother. You are going to get us both arrested if you stay here."

John got on with his T-bone steak and the conversation was dropped, but Ria went very quiet, and on returning to the car, said she would sleep on the back seat, in case someone broke in.

"Number seventy-five, if you change your mind," John shrugged.

"I won't," she answered sharply, but John was past caring about anything except a warm bed and a good night's sleep.

He had spent two whole days driving, since Ria phoned him in a desperate panic to say Andrew was being horrible and she needed to get away.

It had been a relief to be free from her constant demands while she was engaged to Andrew Davenport, and desperate to know if there was any chance of them getting back together, he made the long journey from his business in Winchester to learn that she had already rented a flat near Southampton.

Full of hate and resentment she had told him a convoluted story about Andrew being mean with money, how he expected her to work all of the time, and how horrible his stuck up family were to her. Knowing his daughter, and thinking he was reading between the lines correctly, John mistakenly assumed she had just got bored again.

Yawning widely he fell into bed. He needed to be in his office at seven, for an early delivery; and with luck, kill two birds with one stone, by helping Ria pack the mountain of luggage in his car, to her mother's address in Malta.

Let her have the worry for a change. He'd had his fill over the last twelve years, with university fees and supporting her high maintenance demands, when she got bored and dropped out without taking her degree. With Jason's expertise, he had plans of his own.

Wide awake, huddled beneath a blanket, on the back seat, unaware of his plans for her, Ria was making very different ones of her own as she climbed into the driver's seat, released the hand brake, and allowed the heavy Jeep to roll down the convenient slope leading to the road.

John pulled up with a screech of brakes, jumped out of the four by four and with long, angry strides marched up the path to the flat, rang the bell and thumped on the front door.

Several minutes passed before Ria finally opened the door, during which time he continued to ring and thump angrily. When he caught sight of her though, his anger melted and he forgot about waking to find himself stranded miles from his business, having to ring one of his men to pick him up and missing the important early delivery.

His first thought on realising his daughter had no intention of going to her mother, was to leave her to her own devices, but on second thoughts, she had his Jeep and could involve him in one of her wild schemes, so assuming she would be at the flat, he purchased a 4×4 and raced there, to give her a piece of his mind and retrieve his Jeep.

Without a word, Ria stood back and allowed him to pass into the empty flat, where he faced her, feeling uncertain. Her swollen eyes said she had been crying and hadn't slept, but there was obviously something more. He had never seen her this upset.

"So what's the problem? And why did you leave me stranded? After all I did..."

"The money has gone. He's taken it," she wailed loudly. "I told him not to touch my things."

At cross purposes, John shrugged, assuming she meant the twelve thousand pounds, that she told him Andrew had *given* her.

"He was entitled to take it back, after the way you treated him."

"I should have known you wouldn't see it my way," she snapped. "Well he isn't going to get away with it. I've got a plan he won't like at all."

John jumped in quickly. "I don't want to know. I was expecting you to pay me for the car I bought you, but I can see I've had that. Just stay away from me. I've had enough."

She gave a shrill laugh and caught the set of keys he tossed at her, saying in answer to his thunderous look, "Don't worry. I'm going to be richer than you can imagine."

She threw her arms in the air and twirled around lightly. "You'll see. I'm going to..."

John went quickly to the front door and let himself out to the sound of her laughter, saying sternly, "I don't want to hear."

CHAPTER EIGHT

"I think I'll go along and sort Andrew's office out for him this morning," Clare said firmly, expecting Connie to object, relieved when instead she replied, "Yes, it's time to start movin' a bit, and 'e can do with 'elp. Jim's with 'im now, 'elpin to unpack pictures."

She stopped massaging and inspected Clare's leg. "How's it feelin'?"

"It looks worse than it feels now."

"Mm, pretty bruised still, but the muscle's good. Do ye go to a gym?"

"No I hate that, all girls together in Lycra stuff."

"Well it's certainly healing quick."

"Your magic touch, I expect. I feel great."

"Good! All done; you can get up now."

Connie watched as she sat up, wondering why such a pretty young woman had allowed one bad experience to affect her so deeply. He must have been really special.

Twenty minutes later, Connie was pushing her in the wheelchair along the covered walkway to Andrew's cottage.

"I could walk now, with the crutches," Clare objected.

"No point in undoin' all the good for the sake of a few days. The snow looks as if it's goin'. Just be patient til ice 'as gone."

Connie smiled contentedly. This young woman was exactly what Andy needed.

Andrew's face lit up as they entered. "Well done," he said, giving Clare an encouraging look. "And am I glad to see you with your apron at the ready."

He beamed at Connie and she smiled back fondly.

"Guessed ya could do with 'elp, unpackin' the kitchen. I'll get started, while you see ta Clare."

"Sure you'll be warm enough?" Andrew asked anxiously, as he pushed her through the surgery and into the office.

"I'm well wrapped up, and Connie advises moving around more now."

"Excellent, as long as you don't knock yourself. No more bruises. I don't know what your mother is going to say. A thaw seems to be on the way, so hopefully you will be home before her."

"First things first," Clare said briskly, settling behind the desk, and producing her laptop from under the blanket covering her legs. "The bank has opened a new business account for you, so I will pay the outstanding bills, online. I'll need those details though."

Andrew produced a crumpled envelope from his back pocket, and Clare frowned.

"Somewhere safe, I said."

"I meant to put them in the safe," he mumbled looking suitably chastened as Clare tutted and smoothed the papers out.

"I did transfer cash into the new account though."

Waiting hopefully for a crumb of approval, his face dropped at her murmured, "That's something I suppose," as she opened up her computer, adding absently, "I've got everything I need. Don't let me keep you; I expect you want to get on."

"Er... right!" He backed away, waiting for her to look up,

if only for a brief moment, but she was already deeply focused on the job in hand.

By the end of the day, order had been restored to the cottage and Clare had made good headway with the accounts.

"When are you going to open for business again?" she asked as they were having dinner.

"As soon as I get you back home. The roads are supposed to be safe by the day after tomorrow." Andrew pulled a long face. "You've been a wonderful help. I shall miss you."

"We all will," Connie said ruefully as Jim nodded, looking depressed.

Clare covered his hand with hers, and raised her eyebrows at Andrew. "My mother isn't due home for another week."

Andrew looked hopeful. "The only problem is, Connie needs her rooms. A stair lift is being fitted tomorrow and her first two convalescent patients are booked in for ten days, the day after that. It's her retirement plan."

Clare looked surprised, as it became clear why the bathroom had been updated recently. "You don't look old enough to retire, Connie."

Connie brushed the comment aside. "I'm not. Just don't wanna be out these cold dark nights. Sooner be tucked up indoors."

Catching the soft, understanding look Jim gave Connie, Clare knew it was actually to be there for him, so changed the subject.

"That's a shame, it won't give me time to sort the office out properly or finish your accounts. Perhaps I can take them home with me?"

Andrew leant back in his chair looking serious. "That

would be great but," he hesitated, before saying hopefully, "if you aren't that anxious to go home, you could stay in my cottage. It's what I intended to begin with."

There was a small silence, before Clare said in a business -like tone, "Right. I'll bring my things along in the morning, after I help Connie prepare for her visitors."

She gazed around at their faces, that had suddenly taken on fresh hope and they gazed back, unsure of how she really felt now.

The silence of the night was broken by the telephone, that stopped after two rings. Clare heard Andrew's door open, and less than a minute later, whispered voices on the stairs.

She looked at the hands of the bedside clock, pointing to four o'clock, and out of curiosity, threw back the bedclothes to see what the problem was. As she opened her door, Andrew was hurrying back to his room, and quickly said that Connie was next door because Kathy had gone into labour.

"Can I help?"

"I think everything is under control, but a cup of tea would be welcome. Jim is awake, so I'm going to fetch Luke. He will stay with Jim."

While he was speaking, Clare was pulling on the warm dressing gown Connie had provided, in place of the thin silk one she had brought.

"Hold on, I'll see you down the stairs."

"I can manage with the bannisters."

"Sure? Don't want you falling."

"Go. I'm fine."

He watched until she reached the bottom and then dashed into his bedroom. Ten minutes later, Luke was settled in bed with Jim. He hadn't even woken when Andrew picked him up and carried him in.

Sitting at the kitchen table, Clare and Andrew were lost for words. It felt as if the world had come to a halt and was just waiting for this new arrival.

"I've been here a week and haven't even met Kathy, and yet I feel involved. Strange!"

Andrew was gazing at her, thinking how lovely she looked in the blue dressing gown, with her dark hair falling softly round her shoulders. It was good to see her looking soft and vulnerable, and not efficient and business-like.

Lost in thought, he suddenly realised she was waiting for an answer.

"The weather hasn't exactly been right for either of you to get about, but as for feeling involved; that's country life for you, and personally I wouldn't want it any other way."

Clare was silent, suddenly apprehensive of this 'Country life,' so different to her own, where women went to hospital to have their babies in sterile wards, surrounded by nurses; not just one midwife.

"Supposing everything isn't straightforward?"

"It will be. Kathy is in good hands," Andrew replied confidently. "I just hope Mark manages to get here soon. I rang him and he was already on his way, but no doubt the weather will delay him."

As if by telepathy his mobile phone rang on the table beside him, and he snatched it up quickly, seeing Mark's name on the screen.

Clare watched his face grow longer as he listened and said he would get there as soon as possible; then for a second or two stared at her speechlessly, before saying, haltingly, that Mark had been in a pile up.

"He's okay, thank goodness, but they have taken him to hospital for shock. His car is on its way to a garage, so I need to go and pick him up. He's about an hour away, so hopefully I won't be more than two hours and a bit." He looked at her anxiously. "Can you cope for a while? Jim and Luke will need breakfast. Cereal will be fine, and perhaps you would take Connie some tea? I hate to ask."

"Of course, and I'll make you a sandwich to eat in the car, while you get ready."

She gave a rueful smile. "Now I sound like my mother."

"What could be nicer?" he replied.

Spotting a large bread bin, she found two freshly baked cottage loaves inside and a cooked ham in the stone pantry. Prepared for the expected arrivals no doubt, but if it was for Andrew, Connie wouldn't mind, she told herself, as she wrapped two, well-filled rounds of sandwiches and put them beside his mobile phone.

Left alone, she got dressed, in case she was needed, then peeped in on Jim and Luke; closing the door quietly again when she saw them both sleeping soundly.

It was still only just after five-thirty but she decided to take Connie a cup of tea.

All was quiet as she let herself in Kathy's front door, and she was about to call out to Connie, when an agonised cry came from upstairs, so realising Connie would be busy, she edged her way upstairs, one at a time, and knocked on the door, from where loud gasps could be heard, accompanied by Connie's soothing voice.

"One more big push an' we're there."

Overcome by curiosity, Clare turned the handle, and poked her head round the door. The sight that met her eyes as Connie smiled and beckoned her in, was one she would never forget. Eyes closed in pain, a young woman was pushing as hard as she could. Mesmerised, Clare stood clasping the mug of tea, watching as the miracle of birth took place before her eyes: first a head; followed by a small pink body; then a lusty yell, that said all was well.

Filled with wonder, she moved closer, as Kathy opened her eyes and gazed dreamily at her new baby, a beatific smile lighting up her face. Becoming aware of Clare, she gave a tired smile. "You must be Clare. Connie's told me about you."

"Hello, Kathy," Clare said softly, watching in awe as Connie cut the umbilical cord, and wrapped the baby girl in a soft white towel before laying her beside her mother. Then, with a grateful smile relieved Clare of the tea and sat on the bed for a brief two minutes before attending to Kathy.

"Didn't take as long this time, did it my lovely? Mark'll be surprised. Better get you ready. He'll be home soon."

"We wanted a girl," Kathy said happily, gazing lovingly down at the baby laying contentedly in the crook of her arm.

Connie gave a broad smile and held her arms out. "Let's lay 'er down while I wash you an' change yer nightie. Then ye can do yer hair and make yersel all pretty for Mark."

Taking the baby, she casually passed her to Clare.

"Tek 'er while I see ta Mum."

Clare looked flustered. "I've never held a baby."

"Nothin' to it. Sit there." Connie motioned her towards a padded wooden rocking chair, then briskly set about changing Kathy's nightdress and tidying her bed, beaming at Kathy, as they both stole surreptitious looks at Clare, sitting bolt upright, eyes fixed on the baby, holding her as if she would break.

"I'm gonna make us a cuppa tea an get ye somethin ta eat, now. Ye mus be hungry, after all that 'ard work." She gave Kathy her brush and comb and a hand mirror. "Won't be long."

She disappeared, and as she brushed her hair, Kathy saw that Clare hadn't even noticed Connie go and was rocking back and forth gently, holding the baby comfortably.

She longed to have someone of her own age living close by; hopefully a friend this time. She had thought Ria might be, until she heard her call her, 'That slow witted, simple minded bumpkin', when the television repair van was outside Andrew's cottage.

It seemed to be there a lot after Ria moved in. She had walked along to ask the man to take a look at their television that had lost its sound, but as she knocked the door, she saw Ria through the glass panel, coming towards her with an impatient scowl and heard her say, "Oh, it's only that slow witted, simple minded bumpkin from next door. I'll get rid of her."

Without waiting, she had returned home, and Ria hadn't even opened the door. She never mentioned the incident, partly from embarrassment, but also in case it caused any awkwardness between Andrew and Mark.

Connie returned, interrupting her thoughts, and placed a tray across her lap. "Eat up my lovely; got to keep ye strength up."

She placed a mug of tea on a chest of drawers beside Clare, then checked on the baby, sleeping peacefully in Clare's arms. "You're obviously a natural."

Clare coloured with pleasure, and continued to rock gently.

"Luke can't wait to see his new baby sister. Jim'll bring 'im, soon as they've 'ad their cereal," Connie said, sitting on the end of the bed and leaning against the blue enamel bedstead.

Clare gave a guilty start. "I was supposed to get their breakfast."

"Jim can do cereal. I told 'im you was busy." She smiled broadly, recalling Jim's satisfied nod. His emotions ran high due to his heart problem, but she had never known him take to anyone the way he had taken to this young woman, or to be so concerned about Andrew losing her. The fact that Andrew had seen Ria in her true colours at last had been a great relief to them both.

Luke's excited voice and running footsteps came closer and Kathy held her arms open wide, waiting to hold him as he threw himself against the side of the bed. Connie helped him up and sat him against the pillow, before taking the baby from Clare and giving her to Kathy. Luke looked about to cry, but prepared for such a moment Kathy produced a box saying gently, "Look, Luke. Your baby sister has brought a really special present for you, because you are her big brother."

Looking through the cellophane lid his face lit up. His sister had brought him the thing he wanted most in the whole wide world. A red tractor!

Clare had to admire Kathy for the way she dealt with that moment. She was obviously a born mother, and no doubt a lovely wife. She felt a stab of envy, but immediately asked herself why, when she had everything she wanted, and wouldn't want to swap her life. She mustn't allow herself to be mesmerised by this way of life. She would be going home soon, and everything would be back to normal. Assuring herself of this, she rose abruptly. "I'll go and pack my things. Andrew won't be long now."

Connie nodded. "I'll be in to make lunch soon as Mark gets 'ere."

Clare left, making her way downstairs, looking to either side of the hallway, glimpsing a homely kitchen and cosy sitting room, wondering what this Mark was like, and why he spent so much time away from home; this perfect home, and his perfect little family.

Treading carefully on the wet surface of the walkway, she realised she had completely forgotten about her leg, and could almost walk normally. That was a relief; now she would be able to look after herself when Andrew took her home.

The quietness of the house as she let herself in the front door felt strange; she was used to Connie being in the kitchen and Jim sitting in his chair by the fire. How could she have become so attached in such a short while? It always took her a long time to decide whether she liked people, or not.

She wandered upstairs thinking about Kathy and how mapped out her life was. She had worked hard to get where she was, and she was independent. What would life have been like if Paul hadn't left her?

Defiantly zipping her suitcase up, and standing it on its wheels, she planted it purposefully at the top of the stairs. No danger of ever being jilted *again*; *that*, she was certain of.

At that moment she heard the crunch of wheels on the courtyard, and glanced out of the window trying to ignore the lurch her heart gave as she saw Andrew helping a figure out of the car. The figure was wearing a neck brace and moving stiffly, but in spite of that, they were laughing and obviously eager to get indoors.

She heard Luke shouting "Daddy," then Connie return to start preparing lunch, and deep in thought made her way downstairs, thinking that Connie never stopped working and yet she was the happiest and kindest person you could meet, so instead of going into the sitting room and waiting to have lunch brought to her, she went into the kitchen and offered to help.

She felt and looked self conscious, as Connie nodded and pointed to plates and cheese board on the table, where she was busy cutting thick chunks of crusty bread.

"Lay the table if ye like. Quick lunch, early dinner, then early night fer all of us."

Clare picked up the cheese board. "*You* most certainly need one; I don't know how you keep going."

"Good to be busy. I'nt that so, Andy?"

Arriving at that moment, Andrew looked pleased as Clare passed him in the doorway.

"What's that, Connie?"

"I were saying, it's good ta keep busy."

"Mm." He looked thoughtful. "Mark has a touch of whiplash, and can't do much. I think we should get you some help. You can't do it all, with your convalescent guests coming."

"They jus' need somewhere warm and comfy to sit and be waited on for a week. They won't be any trouble. Jim'll keep fires going, if we stack plenty of logs under verandah, an' it's only two more to cook for. I'll manage."

"But that will be nine of us you will be cooking for."

"I'll help if you tell me what to do," Clare offered hesitantly, returning to pick up the plates and bread.

"There ye are; help on the doorstep. Thank you, me lovely."

Clare saw Andrew's uncertainty and pursed her lips as she returned to the sitting room with a loaded tray. Huh! Thinks I can't cope.

Over lunch she was very quiet, and Andrew asked, "Are you sure it isn't going to be too much for you? I don't want you going home worn out."

"Ye know I won't allow that," Connie said quickly. "She'll be fine. Stop ya worriting."

"Got a good head on her shoulders, has Clare," Jim assured him seriously.

Clare gave them a grateful smile, appreciating their confidence, and Andrew quickly assured them that he knew there was nothing wrong with her head, it was her leg he was concerned about. "I'll really be in hot water with my... if any harm comes to her."

About to ask what he was going to say before he changed his mind, Clare was distracted by Connie yawning. "You need to sleep this afternoon, Connie."

"Hear, hear," Jim and Andrew chorused.

"Mebbe you're right," Connie confessed reluctantly. It had been a strenuous day since four o'clock that morning. "Soon as dishes are done."

Andrew got up and taking her gently by the shoulders, pulled her to her feet.

"Off you go. I'll see to them."

She allowed him to guide her to her bedroom, saying, "Why don't ya come too, Jim?"

"Aye; I'll come and keep ya company, lass."

He rose awkwardly and shuffled after them, wiggling his fingers at Clare. "See you later, sweetheart."

Hot tears stung Clare's eyes and she blinked furiously, as Andrew returned and stared at her curiously whilst starting to clear the table.

"You okay?"

"Yes."

"Sure?"

"Positive. Lets get these dishes washed."

"That's better."

"What?" She gave him a sharp look, but he just smiled and followed her to the kitchen.

"You wash, I'll wipe and put away," she said, taking charge, and as his smile turned to a wide grin, she threw the wet dishcloth at him, returning his teasing look, by putting her finger to her lips and pointing to Connie and Jim's closed bedroom door, as he started towards her holding it aloft.

"Later," he whispered, wagging his finger at her, as they laughed and quietly started on the dishes.

By the time Connie and Jim reappeared three hours later, they had transferred their things to Andrew's cottage and flat and Clare had stripped the beds and dusted before mopping the wood floors, in preparation for Connie's patients the following day; surprising herself with a small sense of regret that she wouldn't be sleeping there that night, as she gave a last look around, before closing the door.

She also helped to make an easy meal of jacket potatoes, pricking them as Connie instructed and rubbing them with a little oil and salt, before putting them in a hot oven.

"Makes em nice an' crispy, jus' like Jim n Andy like em," Connie confided, as she served them with the boiled ham and her home bottled beetroot and gherkins.

"Even my mother doesn't do all of this," Clare said, looking with astonishment at shelves full of preserves, in the large built-in pantry.

"Cos shops are nearby, I 'spect."

As she was speaking Connie brought a large bag of strong flour out of the pantry.

"Need ta make more bread in mornin', for me visitors. Best make some for Kathy, too. It'll be a while afore she can."

Quite daunted by the prospect, Clare offered to go to a shop. "I could get enough and stow it in the freezer for you. I've got my car here."

Connie laughed. "And 'ave Andy spend the day lookin for ya? It's no bother. I'll show ye in mornin."

It was strange sleeping in Andrew's cottage that night but very comfortable. His bed, she noted with approval, was a divan like her own, but the rest of the furniture was antique looking, and blended perfectly with the silver grey carpet and velvet curtains of the same soft shade. The bathroom was also tastefully decorated, in a delicate shade of aqua, with gleaming white, enamel fittings and suffused lighting. Lying awake, staring at the seascape picture on the opposite wall, she wondered who was responsible for the décor, and quickly turned the light off, asking herself what difference it made; she would be going home in a few days' time, and would never see it again.

Early next morning, Andrew knocked and called up the stairs, "Connie says she is starting on the bread."

Clare took a quick look at the clock and jumped out of bed. "At six thirty?"

"She had to be up for the baby's six o'clock feed and all that."

"The woman's a miracle." Clare groaned, slipping into her trouser suit and running a comb through her hair, before making her way down to him.

"Isn't she though? Hopefully Mark will be able to cope soon. I've just taken their breakfast in. He's already moving about better, and Kathy says she is getting up tomorrow, so that will ease Connie's load. Kathy has got plenty of food in, so no worry there. She is always prepared for emergencies."

He spoke of her fondly, and obviously admired her.

"She is a lovely mother," Clare said, recalling her way with Luke the previous day.

"Yes, and a lovely wife. Mark is a lucky man." For a moment he looked pensive. "Come on; mustn't keep Connie waiting."

After breakfast, Andrew said he was going to pop over and make sure his grandparents were all right, and with an amused smile, left Clare, wearing a fine layer of flour, energetically kneading a large pile of dough, under Connie's watchful eye. He prayed desperately that she would understand, when she learnt how he had helped to deceive her.

By lunch time, four large round loaves of bread were sitting on the kitchen table and Connie gave a contented nod as she saw Clare with a smudge of flour on her cheek, admiring their handiwork with a big smile.

"That sounds like my patients arriving. Tek one inta Kathy, will ya? An one fer you an Andy. 'E won't be long. Visits 'em every week. Near Crackinton 'aven; about alf an hour away." She went to the front door as an ambulance pulled into the drive, saying as she went, "Thank goodness, snow's nearly gone."

Clare picked up the two loaves of bread and made her way to Kathy's, smiling as she watched Connie help one of the elderly patients out of the ambulance. "Kettle's on, me lovelies. Let's get in the warm," she was saying.

Closing Kathy's front door quietly behind her, Clare left the loaves of bread on the kitchen table and started up the stairs to see Kathy and the baby, but as she got to the top of the stairs, she heard a man's low voice. About to turn away, her attention was caught by a reflection in Kathy's dressing table mirror. Kathy was sitting up and her husband was sitting on the side of the bed with Luke on one knee and the baby cradled in his other arm. They were gazing into each other's eyes adoringly, completely oblivious to anything but each other, and she heard him saying emotionally, "Thank you darling, for our two beautiful children. I love you with all my heart and always will. You are everything in the world to me."

Kathy gave a little sob. "I'm so glad. I've always loved you, but I've never been quite sure."

"Never doubt it, sweetheart." Clare watched, mesmerised at what should have been a private moment, as he kissed her tenderly and then kissed both of the children on their foreheads. "Never ever."

Sobbing with emotion, Clare turned and stumbled down the stairs.

It was late afternoon before Andrew returned home. There were no lights on, either in his cottage or the surgery, and assuming that Clare must still be with Connie, he went straight there, looking forward to the cup of tea that was sure to be waiting, at the sound of his car.

He smiled, recalling how at home Clare had looked that morning, with her good outfit covered with a white apron, and a lock of dark hair escaping her neat chignon. He couldn't wait to see her.

Connie called, as he was kicking his boots off. "In sittin' room Andy. Come on in and get warm. Tea's poured."

Grinning widely that everything was as he predicted, he pushed the door open expecting to see Clare, but instead, two strange women regarded him curiously, after hearing Connie sing his praises so highly.

"Oh! Hello ladies," he said hiding his disappointment, before turning to Connie.

"I thought Clare was with you. No lights on at home."

"She'll be in office; said she was goin' ta do ya books."

"I'll go and stop her; she's done enough for today." He grinned. "How did the bread turn out?"

"Fine! 'Appy as Larry she was."

Andrew gulped his tea, saying as he bowed out, "Thanks Connie. See you later ladies." But he was back in ten minutes, saying in a puzzled voice, "No sign of Clare in the office. Can't see her anywhere."

Connie looked delighted. "She took Kathy's bread into 'er; she'll be nursing new baby. Right taken with 'er she was. That's where she'll be oright."

Looking relieved, he headed for Kathy and Mark's, but they hadn't seen her at all.

"I assumed Connie left the loaves of bread," Mark said, rocking the cradle. "What's the problem anyway?"

"No problem. Just can't think where she can be, that's all," Andrew said looking even more worried.

Kathy was sympathetic, but at the same time pleased to see Andrew's concern.

"She can't have gone far. Don't forget she's been cooped up for a couple of weeks with her leg. Probably felt like a bit of a walk."

"But it will be dark soon, and she doesn't know her way around. She could fall into a ditch, or anything could happen, and I'm responsible for her."

"Perhaps she's gone for a drive," Mark said raising his voice above the baby's crying.

A ray of hope came into Andrew's eyes, and without a word, he left.

At four o'clock it was definitely too dark for her to go walking on her own, but even so he was pretty sure, knowing Clare, that she wouldn't go tramping about in the slush that the thaw had left behind. Even in the car, she would easily get lost in the unfamiliar, winding country roads, he thought, hurrying along the walkway towards the carport, his heart thumping as he saw her car was missing. Hurrying back to Connie he asked if Clare had mentioned going somewhere, but Connie shook her head. "She won't have gone far."

He poked his head into the conservatory, where Jim was painting, hoping she was there, but Jim hadn't seen Clare since lunchtime either, and he returned to Connie.

"She won't have gone far," Connie repeated, beginning to share his concern.

He went back to the cottage, as a thought struck him, and became even more concerned on discovering her clothes gone.

What on earth had made her leave without, at least, letting Connie know? Disappointed anger took over. Why hadn't she left a note or something? How could she be so thoughtless. She must know he would be worried, and that Connie and Jim would be upset. He debated whether to go and tell them and decided not to, for the time being, until he had tried to get in touch with her. She must have gone home. Heaven knows how long it would take her with present road conditions. The motorways were pretty clear, but she had to reach them first. Tormenting thoughts racked him as he wondered what had made her run away. Had she found out somehow? He should have insisted on her knowing.

Sad thoughts escalated. He had to speak to her. She couldn't possibly be home before sixish. He rang her number anyway and got what he expected; the answer phone.

Meanwhile, Connie decided to try Clare's mobile. They had exchanged numbers, when Clare moved into Andrew's cottage. 'Just in case', Connie had said, liking to be on the safe side, and now she was glad. After speaking to Clare, Connie put her phone down, feeling thoroughly puzzled, and walked along to speak to Andrew.

"Somethin's wrong. She left me, full o' beans, now says she can't tell me why she ran away. What do ya make of it?"

"Did she say where she was?" Andrew asked, thankful for Connie's forethought.

"On'y an 'our from 'ome, she said."

"I'm driving up there. I need to talk to her, about something I should have told her before now; something I can't tell her over the phone. Sorry. I'll tell you after I've told her."

Connie nodded, realising how important it must be, because this wasn't like Andy; he was always so open about everything.

CHAPTER NINE

Ria smiled to herself as she entered the automatic doors to the hospital and stopped to read directions on the wall just inside. Having found what she was looking for, she made her way along endless corridors and eventually located the crowded waiting room.

An hour later, she returned to her car, more than satisfied with her afternoon's work.

She had made a useful contact, even though the girl was unaware of how useful she was going to be. She watched as the girl made her way across the car park to a bus stop just outside of the hospital gates, then drove out and wound the window down to say casually, "See you again next visit maybe?"

"I expect so," Monica answered, looking unhappy.

As if as an afterthought, Ria said, "I'm going your way; I'll drive you home, if you like."

Monica got in gratefully. "Thanks. It takes ages on the bus and I'm longing to get home."

Home, Ria discovered, was a rented, ground floor, bed-sitting room, in a terraced three bedroomed house, shared by three other students.

"We share the kitchen and bathroom but I have a kettle in my room," Monica explained, inviting Ria in for a cup of tea.

The room was typically furnished for a student. Utility

table and two dining chairs in the bay window; a book case stacked high with folders and text books; a large chest of drawers in one alcove and a fitted wardrobe in the other, either side of a tiled fireplace with an electric fire. Apart from that there was just an uncomfortable looking settee, beside the fire, that obviously let down into a bed. Ria hid her disdain as she watched Monica switch the fire on and remove her coat, before leaving the room to fill the kettle. As soon as she left, Ria darted to the table, where she had already spotted a small pile of mail beside a laptop. Quickly memorising the surname and post code, she sat at the table and was watching out of the window when Monica returned to plug the kettle in.

Ria noticed her hands shaking and felt reassured. This girl needed help and that was going to make things easier for what she had in mind.

"Why don't I pick you up for your next appointment? I expect we will be on the same day as each other again. I'll be glad of the company; it's my first as well."

Monica nodded. "I'd like that, if you're sure it's no bother."

"Let's swap phone numbers, then you can let me know when your appointment is. Which doctor are you seeing?"

"Doctor Blake. Norman Blake."

"Oh me too. And which nurse?"

"Jenny Tompkins."

"*Me too!*" Ria opened her eyes wide with pretended surprise. "What a coincidence!"

Monica gave a tremulous smile and nodded hard, obviously feeling very emotional.

"There's nothing to be afraid of apparently; women do it all the time I'm reliably informed," Ria joked in an attempt to gain Monica's confidence, but Monica didn't smile. The prospect of being a mother was weighing heavily on her eighteen-year-old shoulders.

"How far are you? When is the baby due?" Ria asked seriously.

"Last week in August. I only found out today."

"Me too. This really is such a coincidence."

"I don't know whether to keep it," Monica confessed.

Ria panicked. "I'm told you always regret having an abortion."

Monica's eyes filled with tears. "That is such a horrible word."

"But is termination any better? The outcome is the same. I couldn't even consider it."

Ria shook her head vehemently, and Monica looked even more distressed.

"It's your decision of course, but don't do anything you might be sorry for later."

"My boyfriend doesn't want to know. He says he's too young." Monica gave a heartbroken sob, but Ria's mind was racing as an exciting new idea occurred, that would add weight to her plan.

"Something else we have in common. I'm going it alone, too." Ria tossed her head and stole a sly look to see what effect her words were having; pleased to see doubt on the girls face, as she dabbed her hazel eyes and tightened the band on her long blonde ponytail.

"My mother died when I was young and my father lives in France, with his new wife and their children. I can't bear to tell him. He'll be so upset. He has such high hopes of me becoming a foreign languages interpreter." Tears streamed down her cheeks and Ria touched her arm sympathetically. "Don't decide yet. Your boyfriend could change his mind."

They drank their tea in silence; each with her own thoughts; but Monica would have been very disturbed if she had known Ria's.

They exchanged mobile phone numbers before parting and Ria left with a clear plan in mind of her next step.

Once in her flat, she typed what she had astutely learnt about Monica into her computer, then set about arranging the furniture that had arrived that morning. Having picked it all up in a charity shop, she viewed it without enthusiasm. It was nothing like Andrew's, and she wouldn't get anywhere near what she would have got for his, she thought resentfully, promising herself with ruthless determination that it wouldn't be for long.

"Get Christmas and New Year over, then Monica's appointment. Perfect!"

On her way home, she had stopped at another charity shop, and now she eagerly tipped her purchases onto the settee and held up two shapeless dresses, regarding each one with equal disgust, as she remembered explaining to the surprised assistant that they were for her friend.

"Well I knew they couldn't be for you, even if you were pregnant," the friendly assistant said as they laughed together. "Far too old fashioned!"

"My friend won't mind; she hasn't got long to go. She said something cheap to tide her over the last few weeks. These look about right for her as well." She had picked up a pair of flat, beige shoes. "I'll take them as well."

Looking at them now, she grinned, picturing Grace and Arthur's disapproval.

CHAPTER TEN

Clare arrived home in a state of near collapse, after a harrowing journey. She had caught the teatime traffic and the last hour had been nose to tail. It had taken six hours to reach her flat, and she was shaking with cold. She turned the heating up and put the kettle on, before going to the bathroom to run a warm bath, all the time dwelling on her devastating discovery. Everything else in the past two weeks was as nothing compared to discovering that Kathy's husband Mark was none other than Paul Lewis. How was he keeping it from Andrew, Connie and Jim? Or was he? Perhaps they were aware of his double life, and didn't care as long as Kathy wasn't hurt. She was obviously very dear to them all, as was Paul, or Mark, as they knew him.

She took her cup of tea to her chair, waiting for the bath to fill, and picked up a photograph album, always kept on the shelf under the coffee table beside her.

Fresh, angry tears sprung to her dark eyes as she ripped Paul's, until now treasured, photograph out, reading the words, 'All my love. Forever yours, Paul. X'. "So much for forever," she sobbed, tearing it into four, and dropping it into the waste paper bin beside her chair. On second thoughts, she retrieved the pieces and took them to the kitchen bin, wiping her hands together with an angry gesture as she dropped them in and slammed the lid with a resounding clatter. Then straightening her shoulders and lifting her chin, she strode purposefully to the bathroom and sunk into the warm bath, but although the scented water eased her chilled limbs, her anger remained as she wandered restlessly back to the sitting room in her towelling robe, and opened a bottle of wine. Sitting in her chair again she glanced around the room, thinking how glad she was to be home, but finding the silence lonely, rose to switch the television on, picturing Connie and Jim settling down to watch the news after their dinner, probably with Andrew. Anger flared yet again. He must have known all along. She picked up her wine and took it to the breakfast bar. She wasn't hungry but realising the wine was going to her head she took a carton of her mother's home made soup and a bread roll out of the freezer. Andrew's remark about being spoilt came to mind, but it was no longer even mildly funny.

Thank goodness her mother would be home tomorrow, she consoled herself. Things would return to normal when she went back to work. Yes, that was what she would do. They were sure to need her, with the mountains of claims caused by the snow. She would ring first thing in the morning. "Or maybe I'll just turn up," she said aloud to reassure herself, dumping her bowl and plate in the sink with a frustrated clatter, as she remembered it was the weekend.

Connie would be cooking dinner and Jim would be painting, she thought restlessly.

"For goodness sake stop thinking about them," she cried aloud again, convinced by now that they too must have known, and kept it from her. No wonder she had seen a likeness between Andrew and Mark – *they were cousins, for goodness sake!* The more she thought about it the more she absentmindedly refilled her glass until the doorbell rang. Frowning deeply at the clock, she rose with a resigned sigh and went to answer it, wondering who could be calling at quarter to nine.

"Oh it's you," she said, going to shut the door, but Andrew put his foot in the way.

"What do you mean? Who else were you expecting? Is that why you sneaked away; to meet someone?"

She had never seen Andrew really angry before, and if it hadn't been for the wine, she might have chosen her words more carefully.

"So being underhanded is your prerogative, I take it?" she snapped coldly.

He calmed down enough to answer, "I wanted to tell you but I promised not to. I'm sorry."

"Well I'm sorry too, that everyone thinks its okay to lie to me. Now will you please go. I'm just going to bed."

Seeing that she was in no mood to listen, Andrew reluctantly removed his foot and she closed the door.

"I'll come back in the morning; and we *will* talk," he called through the door.

"Don't bother." Clare's voice receded and he heard the television turned up.

"Back to square one," he sighed, making his way back to the lift. Oh well, her mother would be back tomorrow. Things will get straightened out then, he consoled himself.

Clare waited anxiously to hear from her mother in the morning, realising that she had no idea of what time to pick her up. By lunch time she was feeling decidedly worried and considered phoning Cynthia, because on the rare occasion her mother had flown to France, she had always left flight times, but this time she hadn't mentioned a thing.

She recalled the whispered conversations between her

mother and Andrew and racked her brain for an explanation, but none was forthcoming. It was just too odd.

By mid-afternoon she was extremely worried and for a split second wished Andrew had called as promised. Don't be silly, she chided herself. How could he know where her mother was? Her shoulders drooped as she remembered Chloe was still in Cornwall. How could she have forgotten her?

The telephone rang and sure that it would be her mother, begging forgiveness, she ran to answer it, but on hearing Andrew, she said in a clipped voice, "I'm waiting for an urgent call," and replaced the receiver.

It rang again and this time Andrew said quickly, "Don't hang up, I've just dropped your mother home and she asked me to tell you she will be coming to see you this evening."

"Why? What are you...?" Clare began indignantly, but the line went dead, and livid with indignation, she glared at the receiver, frustratedly demanding, "Aagh! What's going on?"

Three hours later the door bell rang and Clare went to answer it, expecting her mother to be on her own, ready to demand answers, but was completely taken aback to see, not only Andrew but also an older man, both watching her anxiously. Her mother, on the other hand, looked radiant and Clare could only stare uncomprehendingly, for once completely robbed of speech as her mother greeted her gaily with a butterfly kiss on the cheek and ushered the two men into the sitting room.

Never having seen her mother looking so radiant and relaxed, Clare stared open mouthed as she followed her into the sitting room, searching for an explanation as to why she looked more alive than she had ever done. She had never returned from Cynthia's with a spring in her step before. Why, she hardly recognised her.

Finding her voice at last, she said faintly, "Your holiday seems to have done you good, mother." But still, curious as to why Andrew and this stranger were with her, she added, "You obviously enjoyed it."

"It was *wonderful*," Laura replied, looking fondly at the older man.

"Clare, dear, I would like you to meet Alan, Andrew's father." Adding softly, as she looked at Alan, "And my future husband."

"Your what?" Clare gasped, returning to earth with a sharp jolt.

"I asked your mother to marry me yesterday, and she said yes," Alan said happily, taking Laura's hand.

Andrew was watching his father with a happy smile on his face, while astonished, Clare glared at him. "I take it you knew?"

"Not until today. But I knew they were thinking about it and just needed to get away and have time to themselves."

"So why wasn't I told?" Clare asked in an offended voice.

"We needed to be sure," Laura said gently. "That is why, when his wedding fell through, Andrew suggested we should go instead... on his honeymoon cruise."

"It would have been a sin to waste it," Andrew explained.

"Well it certainly wasn't, son. Thank you." Alan put his arm around Laura. "Hope we can set the date soon, my love."

"As soon as possible," Laura replied, her eyes shining softly into his.

"How soon?" Clare asked in a dismayed voice.

Laura gave her a look that begged her to be happy for her, but all Clare could think was that she had been deceived yet again.

"You didn't even tell me you were planning on going anywhere, let alone where, or who with," Clare accused, standing stiff backed in Laura's kitchen.

"Because I wasn't. It all happened that Saturday, when Andrew was supposed to get married. I had to decide quickly. I knew you would get upset, and I very nearly cancelled when you hurt your leg, but Andrew assured me you would be all right. He wanted to tell you after we left, but I made him promise not to. I wanted to tell you myself."

"You actually shared a double room with this man, *and a bed?*"

Laura smiled at her daughter's shocked expression as she placed two cups of coffee on the table before sitting down.

"Nothing less than a honeymoon suite," she said happily.

"But you hardly know the man. You said yourself you only met Andrew that day, when Chloe hurt her paw; why the mad rush to marry his father?"

Laura lost her dreamy smile and looked sad. "I have known Alan for twenty years."

"What? Why have I never met him?" Clare was even more shocked.

"His wife, Rosemary, was my dearest friend." Laura's eyes misted. "She had lung cancer. I helped to look after her for her last five years; she died eighteen months ago; only forty-nine. Alan was heartbroken. Rosemary was his life. Just before she died she asked me to look after him, so I know we have her blessing."

Clare sat down abruptly and stared at her. She had always thought her mother's life was centred around her. There was walking Chloe, gardening, reading, watching television and cooking batches to fill their freezers of course, but now she was learning there was a part of it she knew nothing about; a completely separate part that had obviously taken a great deal of her mother's time, with people she hadn't known existed until now.

"You will always come first, dear," Laura ventured, recognising all too well the familiar look on her daughters face. Since Paul left her, Clare was so possessive and withdrawn, she hadn't dared tell her about spending time with Alan, or that he first asked her to marry him three months ago. And if Andrew hadn't offered them the cruise tickets, perhaps she would never have plucked up the courage, but as an amazed Andrew had pointed out, "Life is meant for living, not pandering to offspring who have left the nest."

Of course he hadn't met Clare then!

"Nothing will ever change between us."

Clare looked at her with a haughty frown. "It already has."

"I'm sorry you see it like that, dear, but I'm happier than I have been for a very long time, so I am going to marry Alan. Now are you staying for lunch? I know you like your Sundays on your own, but I get lonely and Alan has got used to coming over. We are glad of each other's company."

Laura rose collecting the coffee cups, feeling unhappy, but telling herself it was for Clare's own good; remembering Alan's tentative remark on the previous evening, when Clare couldn't be happy for them; that Clare needed to move on.

"She shuts everyone out – except you. Perhaps she needs to be told how much you have given up for her sake by staying a single parent and that you still have needs of your own."

He told her how different Andrew said Clare was in Cornwall, when she felt needed; helping Connie in the kitchen, and joining in when the baby was born; sorting his accounts out, and especially keeping Jim company, who had taken to her so amazingly.

"You have obviously been a wonderful mother, but perhaps my dear, she needs to think of what is right for you now," he had said softly, cradling her head on his shoulder, as they sat together, her happiness clouded by Clare's attitude.

Clare was taken aback by her mother's reproachful tone and didn't answer immediately.

When she did it was to refuse the invitation to lunch, muttering that she had things to do, as she intended going back to work the following day, expecting Laura to demur; surprised when she answered, "You know best. I was hoping we could go shopping in the morning, as it is your birthday today. I shall look for a wedding outfit for myself; best if I go on my own though, under the circumstances."

Clare couldn't believe, that even with the shock of finding out her mother had deceived her, so soon after discovering Paul was married to Kathy, she had completely forgotten her own birthday. Overcome with emotion, she ran from the house, got into her car and sped away, as Laura dialled Alan's number, too upset to wait for him to arrive.

Back at the flat, Clare flopped into the armchair, gazing miserably at her minimalist decor, trying to convince herself she preferred it to the homeliness of Connie and Jim's sitting room. If only she had never gone to Cornwall. She had been content with her life; why couldn't she just forget about it. But then she would never have found out about Paul and his cheating ways. Engulfed in self pity, she told herself that no one cared; not even her mother. She had even persuaded Andrew to lie for her. So had Connie and Jim known of her mother's plans?

She stood up, intending to ring her mother and ask, but at that moment the doorbell rang. She considered ignoring it but assumed it would be her mother come to make up;

perhaps she had even changed her mind about getting married she thought hopefully, prepared to be forgiving as she opened the door, but instead, Andrew marched in.

"We need to talk."

"We have nothing to talk about, after the way you have lied to me. I want you to leave."

"When I've said what I came to say. You have upset your mother."

"That is no concern of yours."

"It is when she has told my father that she can't marry him."

Clare looked up at him triumphantly. "Thank goodness she has seen sense."

"How can you say that? You saw how happy she was yesterday."

"Just a holiday romance. She'll get over it. Men never mean what they say."

"My father isn't like that. You can't judge all men by your one unfortunate relationship."

Andrew spoke sharply, but was sorry the minute he had, on seeing her misery.

"Let's sit and talk, like we did at Connie and Jim's. You've gone back to being angry about everything and making your mother unhappy, as well as my father."

"Why should I care about your father? He has never even been mentioned in the last twenty years. Why did she lie?"

"She didn't, she just kept it to herself, knowing you would get upset; and she was right wasn't she? This is all new to me as well, remember."

"Is it though?" she demanded accusingly, and he gave a deep sigh.

"What made you run away like that? You seemed so happy that morning."

"I don't want to talk about it. Go back to your cosy little life and forget about me."

"I can't. I care about you too much."

"So why are you still keeping things from me?"

"What things? I don't understand."

"Kathy and Mark?" she shot angrily.

Andrew gave a surprised frown and said quietly, "I don't discuss their private life; they are very happy now, and the past is in the past."

Clare stared at him, wondering how he could be so bare faced, taken aback when he just said, "We seem to be talking in riddles. Let's have a cup of tea and talk."

He strode over and filled the kettle, discovered used tea bags in the teapot and emptied them in the sink before taking them to the salvage bin. About to take his foot off the pedal to shut the lid, his attention was caught by a piece of photograph, and seeing a man's jacket he retrieved another piece from inside the bin, which had: All my love. Forever yours, Paul. X, written across the corner. By now totally curious, he delved into the bin again and brought out the remaining two pieces of photo, recoiling as Mark's face smiled back at him and it became mind-blowingly clear why Clare had run away as she did. He looked across at her, sitting quite still, staring out of the window, closing his eyes in sympathy at what she must be thinking. Tucking the pieces into his pocket, he forgot the tea and left; his one thought to get back to Cornwall as soon as possible.

CHAPTER ELEVEN

Mark looked at Andrew in disbelief. "You're saying you just happened to sit next to Clare in the same theatre that I took her to on the night I proposed."

"Well, it wasn't exactly like that. I didn't know when this lady gave me her theatre ticket, that my father wanted to marry her, or that I would be sitting next to her daughter; all that came later."

"It's unbelievable!"

"You are missing the point," Andrew said sternly. "After three years, she is still devastated; convinced no man can be trusted. Why did you lie to her?"

"I didn't; and I didn't want to leave her. I was desperately in love with her and hated myself for letting her down. *But I did because you were right.* I know it was cowardly, but we had made so many plans, I just couldn't face crashing her dreams." Mark buried his face in his hands, but jerked up quickly as Andrew asked tensely, "What about Kathy and the children? Are they enough now?"

"How can you even ask? They are my whole world. Clare, was the centre of the life I thought I wanted then: big house, sophisticated parties, smart clothes, eating out, but I know now that my roots are firmly in Cornwall; life as it is here."

Andrew had put the kettle on as Mark began to talk, and now he placed two mugs of tea on the kitchen table, sat down opposite, and pulled the pieces of photograph from his pocket.

"I rescued this from Clare's kitchen bin... when she wasn't looking. She thinks all men are liars, and is making life really miserable, not only for herself but for her mother and my father. You really need to speak to her and explain."

"What can I say that won't make things worse?"

"Tell her the truth; she may surprise you."

Mark gave a speculative look. "You sound as if you know her quite well."

"Not as well as I'd like to," Andrew admitted ruefully. "She is completely off men; thanks to you."

Mark's face fell and Andrew instantly regretted his remark when Kathy came in the front door with the children and passed the baby to Mark as Luke climbed on his other knee.

To make amends, he said, "By the way, I need to take Laura's dog back tomorrow, fancy keeping me company, Mark? There and back in a day and we could call in and pick your car up on the way home."

"Great! That all right with you, love?"

"Leave at sixish, get back for sixish?" Andrew said with a questioning smile.

Kathy nodded amiably. "If you see Clare, tell her we all miss her. Jim is certainly going to miss Chloe; she never leaves his side. Oh, and by the way, I've just seen Connie. She's pretty busy with her two patients, but Jim's feeling really low and she's worried about him; says will you have a chat, Andy?"

Andrew got up. "Misses helping in the surgery, I expect. I'll go now."

For once, Jim wasn't painting, he was just sitting on the sofa in his conservatory with Chloe beside him looking dejected, but he brightened when Andrew appeared.

"Hope you're going after that lovely girl. We really miss her."

"So do I, Jim. Hope to see her when we take Chloe back tomorrow."

"Good! Bring her back for Christmas; it won't be the same without her, tell her."

"Can't promise, but I'll do my best." Andrew pulled a doubtful face, wondering how Clare was going to react to Mark/Paul turning up.

"Can't understand why she ran off like that. She seemed so happy. I thought she would have told us if something was wrong." Jim shook his head sadly. "I really like her. You two would make a perfect match."

"If it's any comfort, I think so too. We just need to explain the situation to her."

Jim looked suspicious. "You know don't you? You know why she left without a word."

Andrew realised he had said too much. "Something came to light when I followed her, that I'm hoping to put right tomorrow."

"Tell me," Jim insisted.

"I can't; it isn't my place."

"Then whose is it?" Jim demanded angrily.

"Can't say; but you and Connie will be told as soon as possible. I promise."

"Fer goo'ness sake calm down, you'll mek yerself ill." Connie spoke from the doorway. She had heard Jim's raised voice, caught most of the conversation, and come running. "You'll not get any more out of 'im, 'e's obviously given 'is word."

Connie bustled around, straightening cushions unnecessarily, giving Jim concerned looks.

"Sorry Connie. I'll leave."

"Fer the best," she agreed without looking at him.

Andrew was devastated at having upset them both and left the house, for the first time ever, under what felt like a cloud.

Early next morning when he and Mark were setting off, Connie stood at her front door, hand raised, head nodding. Andrew stopped the car and ran over to her and kissed her cheek. "I'll tell you as soon as I can. Look after yourselves."

"Jim's still abed; 'ad a bad night; says come back safe. Can't 'ave bad feelin's atween us." She gave him a hug. "Drive carefully."

Feeling more at ease, Andrew drove off and they travelled in silence, both nursing their own thoughts, and only spoke when they stopped an hour and a half later to eat the sandwiches Kathy had packed for them.

The roads were fairly busy at that time in the morning and it was gone ten thirty when they arrived at Clare's flat. As he rang the bell and waited it occurred to Andrew, she could be out. In fact it was highly likely, now he came to think of it, so near Christmas.

His heart sank as Mark, sounding relieved, said, "She's not in," but at that moment a sound reached them and Andrew rang the bell again.

Within seconds this time the door swung open to reveal Clare in a blue towelling robe.

For a moment they all stared: Andrew apprehensively, Clare shocked, and Mark wide eyed, holding his breath.

Andrew was the first to break the silence, saying quietly, "May we come in?"

Lost for words, Clare shook her head violently and started to close the door, but Andrew held it. "Please, Clare, let Mark explain."

Clare recovered enough to ask in a trembling voice, "What is there to explain? He walked out on me."

She couldn't bring herself to look at Mark and he suddenly pleaded, "Please let me explain. I really loved you, but something turned up that I couldn't ignore."

"Like Kathy and Luke?" she asked bitterly.

"Yes, exactly that." His grey eyes looked straight into her hurt dark blue ones and she expected the long awaited longing to swamp her, but nothing came, and out of curiosity she stood back, saying in her most business-like manner. "I can spare a few minutes. Make some tea while I get dressed, Andrew – *you know* where everything is by now."

Recognising the old sarcastic edge to her voice, Andrew sighed to himself. This could be hard work.

Less than ten minutes later she emerged from her bedroom, in a black leisure suit with her hair in a tight chignon.

Ready for battle, Andrew thought. "I'll leave you to it."

"No. Stay," Mark said quickly.

Clare shrugged. "You are obviously party to his duplicity, so you might as well," she accused coldly.

Mark suddenly took over and defended Andrew. "I can't let you think that. Think what you like about me, but neither Andrew or the family knew about you. Before I could tell them we were engaged, Andrew came to tell me I had to do the right thing by Kathy. I had no idea I had a one-year-old son. If I had, I would never have allowed myself to fall in love with you or ask you to marry me. I lived with my grandparents from the time I was eighteen months. Lovely people, but they live in a time warp of a completely different era, so at twenty-two I left Cornwall to see what the world had to offer."

In spite of herself, Clare was interested.

"Why did you live with your grandparents? Are your parents dead?"

114

"No, they live in Jersey."

"And you didn't live with them because?"

"The grandparents didn't consider their life style suitable for me. My father was in show business."

"It's something Mark doesn't talk about; it has no bearing on why he left you."

Clare looked wistful. "I just wish you had been honest with me."

Mark looked embarrassed. "I didn't know how to tell you. We had such big plans. I told Kathy there was someone and she told me to go back to you if I really wanted to. I would rather not tell her who you are yet. I want you to be friends. She knows how much I cared and I don't want her to feel threatened, but I couldn't have lived with myself if I hadn't supported her."

Clare blinked rapidly and got up. "You did the only thing you could, and you know Kathy best, but I wouldn't leave it too long before telling her."

"Hear, hear," Andrew added.

Feeling pleased with himself, Mark smiled. "Let's enjoy Christmas first."

"We dropped Chloe off at my father's surgery. Your mother is going to pick her up later. Jim will be missing her dreadfully." Andrew hesitated. "He is also deeply unhappy about you leaving; blames me."

Clare looked concerned. "That won't do him any good."

"He said I was to bring you back for Christmas; says it won't be the same without you. How about it? We leave at three o'clock this afternoon."

"You're not serious?"

"I've never seen him more so," Mark said hopefully.

"Please come. Connie and Jim would love you there for

Christmas... so would I," Andrew added wistfully. Seeing her indecision, he lightened the moment with, "And don't forget you haven't finished my accounts yet."

Clare looked down at her hands. "I couldn't leave without seeing my mother. I was horrible to her on my birthday, and we haven't spoken since. You were right; I was being selfish and brattish... as usual."

Andrew put his arm round her shoulders. "You've been hurting for a long time. Don't be hard on yourself."

He led her back to the settee. "There is something I need to do. It won't take long."

Left alone, Mark looked sadly at Clare. "I am so so sorry. I know we could have had a wonderful life together and I wouldn't willingly have hurt you for the world."

He sat beside her and took both her hands in his, his grey eyes pleading with her. "Please say you can forgive me?"

Clare gazed back, smiling now at the likeness between him and Andrew.

"I can and do. Kathy is a lovely wife and a perfect mother. I only hope I can find someone as right for me."

"You don't have to look far. Andy..." His words were lost as Andrew breezed in, followed by Chloe.

"It's all arranged. I've spoken to Dad and they are travelling down on the twenty-third, to spend Christmas with us. Your mother is thrilled to bits with the idea; can't wait to meet Connie and Jim and we can take Chloe back with us until Jim is feeling better."

He rubbed his hands together gleefully and looked at Clare, who was staring open mouthed at him. "Let's get started then."

With just five days to go to Christmas day, everything was going well until the day Alan and Laura were due to arrive, when an early morning phone call changed everything.

Laura's bungalow, on the seafront at Hayling Island, had caught the full blast of a tremendous gale the previous night. The roof was badly damaged, fences were down, and the tool shed was demolished, with its contents scattered all over the garden; but most worryingly, nothing could be done to repair the roof properly until after the New Year. A team of roofers were making temporary repairs to all of the properties, but leaving the bungalow, even for three or four days, would be extremely unwise.

Clare spoke to her mother, suggesting she should come home and help, but Laura said there was nothing to do except house sit and keep watch for leaks.

"I'm glad Andrew took Chloe back with him; she would have been terrified. The noise was horrendous and I was really glad Alan was here. He is going to stay with me until the roof is repaired."

"Thank him for me, Mum; and I really, really mean that."

"I will, dear," Laura answered tearfully. "This will be our first Christmas apart, won't it?"

"Mum, I would like to buy your wedding outfit for Christmas... and help you choose it."

"That would mean the world to me, sweetheart."

"Bye, Mum. Take care of yourself."

"Bye, Precious. You too."

With fewer preparations to see to, Andrew and Clare relaxed and took time to go walking with Chloe. Now that the snow had cleared, Clare was surprised by the amount of ground surrounding the cottages and the number of outbuildings, with every spare space being used to grow vegetables.

"Until Jim's stroke, he tended all of this. He still organises, and tends the seedlings but a lad from the village comes in to do the heavy work."

"Was he always a gardener?"

"Apparently not."

"So what did he do before he retired?"

"Don't know; never wants to talk about it, even to Connie; so we don't ask. Her view is, he will say when ready; if ever."

"Amazing woman."

"Cornish," Andrew said simply.

They were walking downwards towards a river, through a wide meadow bordered by trees either side, marking boundaries between them and a large farm. The track was steep and uneven and Andrew held his hand out to her.

"In the spring and summer this is a mass of wild flowers. Jim grows them to attract the bees and wild life and there are beehives in the orchard. It is all rather beautiful."

The river when they reached it was clear and flowing gently. It only looked waist deep, but Andrew said it was deceptive. On a rough day it often ran fast and high.

He threw a piece of wood into the river and Chloe bounded in, swimming strongly to retrieve and drop it at his feet, before shaking vigorously, and spraying them both. Andrew laughed but Clare moved away, not amused.

Later as she was helping Connie with the evening meal, she voiced her doubt that she would ever get used to the countryside and Connie looked worried.

"Not easy if you haven't grown up with it I s'pose, but it's small price to pay for all the good things."

She sharpened the carving knife zealously, desperately hoping it wasn't going to stop Clare and Andrew getting together. It had become her own and Jim's dearest wish for him, but Jim was also very concerned for the young woman, they had known and become fond of in such a short while.

"That girl has big issues," he had said, shortly after they

first met her. Well they knew now, she ran away because Andrew kept her mother's holiday with his father secret, but they seemed to have got over that. So there had to be something else.

"Never can tell," she muttered.

Clare took the warmed vegetable dishes out of the oven and placed them on the table. "Pardon?"

"Oh, jus' talkin' to meself. You 'appy, me lovely?"

Clare wished she could tell her about Mark and herself, but she had told Mark it should come from him, after he told Kathy, so she just said, "Except for Mum not being here."

Satisfied, Connie carved the lamb, while Clare tipped vegetables into serving dishes, and together they took them into the sitting room, where Andrew and Jim were playing cribbage in front of the fire.

As they sat round the table and Andrew poured wine, Clare pictured her flat, reminded of how, until recently, all she wanted was to *be alone* in her self-contained world. Now, she wasn't sure what she wanted.

On Christmas Eve the traditional Carol Service was held on the village green. It was a bright, starry night with a slight nip in the air and everyone was in a holiday mood. Song sheets were handed out to the large gathering, and at the end of the service, when the local tavern provided mulled wine and minced pies, Clare found herself surrounded by the friendly community, who welcomed her warmly. And after that they gathered in Connie and Jim's warm cottage for supper.

Christmas day passed much too quickly and never having spent Christmas with children before, she watched Luke open his and Emma's sacks of toys, seeing for the first time the difference children made to Christmas.

At six o'clock, Kathy and Mark took the children home to bed and by ten o'clock, when Connie was falling asleep in the chair, Jim suggested an early night as it had been a long day for her.

Walking back to his cottage, Andrew said, "Would you like to come and meet the grandparents tomorrow? We always spend Boxing day with them. Connie and Jim prefer to stay home, so you won't be on your own, but I would really like you to come. Please? They live in quite a large house, overlooking the sea. I expect you will think it very old fashioned, but it's full of history."

"It sounds interesting. I'd love to, but will they be expecting me?"

"I phoned them and they are looking forward to meeting you. By the way, it's still early; do you fancy a night cap?"

She laughed and confessed she was hoping he would suggest it.

"Great minds," he quipped, opening the front door and standing aside for her to enter.

The sitting room was warm and inviting. Homely like Connie and Jim's but not so over furnished; and there was definitely a feeling of quality about the whole room.

"Wine or perhaps a brandy or whisky?" Andrew opened the doors of a drinks cabinet to reveal an array of crystal glasses.

"Wine would be nice, thank you." This was a side of Andrew she hadn't expected, and certainly hadn't seen on her first visit. She had assumed he would have a home with doggy smells and hair. Recalling how patronising she had been, she was embarrassed. No wonder he had thought her spoilt.

Andrew placed a coaster and a glass of wine on a table next to the deep cushioned, dark red settee where she was sitting, then sat opposite, in a matching chair, with his own drink.

Talking companionably. he told her about his mother; his soft faraway look saying how much he missed her loving ways and the lively interest she took in everything he did; and most of all what a happy family they had been. Then he told her what a wonderful friend her own mother had been to both his parents, when his mother was bedridden.

"I heard such a lot about her but strangely we never met until the day I met you." He gave a rueful smile. "Quite an eventful day, as it turned out."

"It certainly was, and I'm ashamed to say how little I knew of what was happening in Mum's life; too wrapped up in my own."

Clare buried her nose in her glass to hide her emotion, but looked up expectantly as Andrew said slowly, "I think I need to tell you about Mark. He has put it all behind him, thank goodness, and just avoids talking about his parents."

He rose to refill their glasses and, filled with curiosity, Clare waited.

"He had an unhappy childhood. His father was in the entertainment world and Mark was an encumbrance. His mother was my mother's younger sister. I'm told there were never two sisters so different. Jacqueline was wild and pleasure seeking; didn't care who she hurt as long as she got her way. She met Marcus when she was sixteen; on holiday in Jersey. He was a local boy, singing and playing guitar at the hotel and apparently they fell head over heels in love. To my grandparent's horror she brought him home, declaring they were going to get married. Apparently there was an almighty falling out, and she went back to Jersey with him. Eight months later she came home, repentant and pregnant, begging to stay, and after Mark was born she ran back to the father. Eighteen months later, the grandparents got a phone call, saying Mark was being neglected. It turned out to be the father's mother, who was worried about Mark being kept in dressing rooms. To cut a long story short, the grandparents went over to Jersey, saw the unsuitable conditions, confronted their daughter and without any argument brought him back here. They expected Jacqueline to follow, but she chose to stay with the father. They had apparently become a duo. 'The Leonardoes'. Did quite well we're told, but that is something else we don't talk about, because Grandfather has disowned her. Not that, I imagine, she cares."

"Poor Mark. Does he never see his parents?"

"He visited them when he was about seven, but never wanted to go again. Don't know what happened."

"How come you call him Mark when I know him as Paul Lewis?"

"I wasn't aware of that until I found the picture. I can only imagine, when he went looking for a new life, it seemed like a good idea. I don't know; we lost touch for a year. It must have cost him a lot to come back."

He looked at her long and hard. "And I mean a lot! But to answer your question, Mark has always been his first name. In actual fact, he didn't exactly change his name, he just took his two middle names. Paul after grandmother's father and Lewis after grandfather's. His own father is a Pendexter, but he hated it from the time he visited them and insisted, from then on, that he wanted to be known as Mark Carlyon; not Marcus Pendexter; so grandfather arranged it. They were already his guardians anyway."

The clock in the hall chimed midnight and picking up his glass he heaved himself out of the deep armchair.

"Enough about my family's dark secrets. Last one before bed?"

Clare nodded, not wanting the evening to end. So many things had been explained, and Andrew was…? She didn't know what; only that her first opinion of him had been completely wrong.

Andrew placed her refilled glass beside her and returned to his chair.

"I think you will like my grandparents and their home. Of course they will assume you are a prospective wife, but don't let that worry you. They can't wait to marry me off to a," he wagged his two fore fingers, "*nice respectable gel.*"

He smiled fondly. "They are 'old school'; both in their seventies and sticklers for respectability."

Clare giggled. "You're painting an alarming picture; are you sure I should come?"

"Definitely. I can't wait for you to meet them."

"Why?" Clare asked curiously.

"It will restore their faith in my judgement. It has been very low of late; but we won't go into that."

"Let's hope I pass muster then," Clare murmured.

"You will," Andrew said confidently, emptying his glass and standing up again.

"And now it's time I went, before I say too much."

She followed him out into the hallway, and with his hand on the latch, he turned to say goodnight, planting a light kiss on her cheek.

"I'm so glad you came."

"Me too." She looked up, smiling softly, and he bent quickly to kiss her on the lips before disappearing, leaving her staring at the closed door, confused emotions robbing her of clear thought.

Boxing morning dawned dull and misty with, according to

the weather forecast on the kitchen radio, promise of brighter weather later.

Unable to sleep, Clare was up by seven, wandering from bedroom to kitchen and back with a cup of tea, to sit on the bed wondering if she was making too much of a light kiss, which was more than likely due to three fairly stiff drinks. Whatever it was it caused her to sleep fitfully. Feelings she hadn't allowed herself for three long years had invaded her waking moments, leaving her helpless with yearning. Reliving it now, she was filled with longing again, just as the door bell shattered her reverie and Andrew's voice called, "Can I come in?"

She jumped guiltily and went to the top of the stairs.

"Heard you about. Thought we might share a cup of tea; and I think I owe you an apology."

Clare walked downstairs, tightening the belt on her dressing gown. "What for?"

"Thought I might have offended you?"

"How?" she asked, her eyes telling him all he wanted to know.

"I could remind you."

"I'd like that."

His arms enclosed her and his kiss was light and gentle as it had been the night before, but when she responded without hesitation, he clasped her to him with a contented sigh and kissed her ardently, until she laughingly begged for air.

CHAPTER TWELVE

The name on the granite pillars supporting tall, wrought iron gates said, 'TAMARISKS'.

"What a lovely name," Clare said as they drove along a winding, tree-lined drive, leading to a very substantial stone built house. "I thought you said it was quite big," she gasped.

"Well isn't it?"

"No. It's enormous!"

Mark, sitting in the back of Andrew's Jeep with Kathy and the children, laughed.

"Wait til you see the inside; nothing's changed since Victorian times – or there about."

The door opened as they arrived, and a smiling fair haired women in a dark green dress appeared in the wide doorway. Andrew greeted her with a kiss on the cheek and turned to Clare. "Hannah is grandmother's house-keeper, also Kathy's mother."

Hannah gave a friendly smile and took her coat, while Andrew returned to the car to help Mark and Kathy with the mountain of bags and the baby in her carry cot.

Hannah took charge of the baby and smiled at Luke's wide eyed expression as he stared at the eight foot Christmas tree, aglow with coloured fairy lights, tinsel, balloons and presents, standing in the corner of the spacious hall.

It was magnificent and Clare admired the whole setting but thought it rather over the top until Andrew explained it was in readiness for New Year's Eve.

"It's a good night. The grandparents support various charities, and about a hundred people attend every year."

Hannah led the way to a door near a wide oak staircase. "Your grandparents are in the sitting room, looking forward to meeting their first great grand-daughter."

"And your *first* grand-daughter, mum," Kathy said quietly.

Arthur and Grace Carlyon greeted them from their armchairs either side of the big stone fireplace, where a log fire burned brightly, giving off a welcoming warmth after the coolness of the entrance hall.

Andrew introduced Clare to his grandmother, then watched her adjust her gold rimmed spectacles and allow her eyes to travel upwards from Clare's high heeled court shoes, dark blue, calf length, pencil slim skirt, dusky pink chiffon blouse and on up to her well groomed dark hair, before travelling down again, head nodding constantly as he introduced Clare to his grandfather.

With a sigh of relief, Arthur also observed Grace nodding her head, as Andrew offered Clare a seat on the settee opposite the fire, where she sat ill at ease and tongue tied, under Grace's scrutiny, until Kathy put the baby on her lap.

"Don't mind do you? I need to give Mum a hand. Won't be long."

Thankful to be rescued, Clare missed the grateful smile Andrew gave Kathy as she hurried away, but able to recover her usual composure, now she was occupied, Clare thanked Grace for inviting her to share their day.

"I like to meet Andrew's," Grace hesitated slightly, "friends."

At that moment, Hannah came in carrying a silver tray bearing glasses of sherry, and the awkward moment passed, as Andrew handed Clare a glass and sat down beside her, saying cheerfully, "Happy Christmas everyone."

He clinked his glass against hers. "Happy Christmas," he whispered in her ear.

"And to you," she whispered tenderly.

Grace tapped the floor with her silver topped walking stick and gave Andrew a reproving frown for whispering, but Mark rescued the moment by showing Arthur how to control Luke's new electric car. Arthur was highly entertained by the way it kept bumping into the furniture and they all relaxed joining in the laughter, until Kathy came to say lunch was ready in the dining room.

Arthur rose immediately and offered Grace his arm to lead the way as Kathy took the baby from Clare. "Fall in. You aren't at Connie's now," she whispered with a grin.

"It's rude to whisper," Mark reminded her, grinning at Andrew, who bit his lower lip.

As they entered the dining room, Clare's interested gaze was drawn to a crystal chandelier suspended from a massive oak beam, above a long, solid looking table that stretched nearly the full length of the long room. Matching wall lights glittered on every wall, relieving the darkness created by deeply recessed, latticed windows and the polished table was set with silver cutlery, crystal glasses, white linen serviettes, and a long garland of holly, with glowing bright red berries, down the centre.

Impressed by the elegance, Clare vaguely heard Grace instructing Andrew to, "Kindly seat Clare on my right, Andrew, and you may sit on my left," as he held her chair for her at the far end of the table.

"Now, Clare you must tell me all about yourself," Grace said when they were settled. "Where do you hail from and what do you do?"

By the end of the meal, Grace knew most of Clare's history and Clare was feeling limp. Andrew kept looking across the table, mouthing 'Sorry', which didn't actually help, and neither did the more entertaining laughter going on at the other end of the table, where Luke and Mark, sitting either side of Arthur, were wearing paper hats and reading silly jokes out of silver and white crackers.

On leaving the dining room, Kathy caught up with Clare. "Sorry about that. She could have chosen a better time. Andrew is upset."

"Just looking out for him. Can't blame her I suppose," Clare said with a resigned shrug.

"Why don't you escape and give the baby her bottle?" Kathy whispered as Mark carried the carry-cot to a door on the far side of the hall.

"Andy said the kitchen; is that right?" he questioned with raised eyebrows.

Kathy took the carry-cot from him, asking if he had come to help with the washing up, and laughed as he turned and fled.

"They always play a very noisy game of snooker after dinner and grandfather must always be allowed to win."

Smiling tolerantly she pushed the door open to reveal Hannah, surrounded by dishes waiting to be washed, and Luke playing on the floor with his cars.

"I'll just settle you and baby in Mum's sitting room, then give her a hand."

She opened another door. "You'll be glad of some peace after your interrogation."

"No disrespectful gossip now, Kathy."

"Coming, Mum." Kathy twinkled her eyes at Clare. "Enjoy!"

Left alone, Clare surveyed her surroundings between watching the baby suck hungrily. The room was small and cosy, with a low beamed ceiling and exposed brickwork, over a fireplace taking up the best part of one wall. The furniture was old but comfortable, much the same era as that in the Carlyon's sitting room, she guessed, and like the rest of the house, deep window sills set in walls two feet thick made the room quite dark. Andrew's worried voice interrupted her thoughts.

"Where's Clare? Is she all right?" Kathy must have pointed to the door, because he appeared immediately and knelt beside her chair.

"That wasn't supposed to happen; I'm so sorry." He kissed her lightly and she warmed to the look in his eyes.

"I'm used to interviews, just wasn't prepared for the third degree," she joked.

"Mark and I thought a walk would be a good idea, are you okay with that?"

She nodded thankfully.

"Thought you might be. I know Kathy will have come prepared." He pressed a kiss on her lips, then another lingering one. "Won't be long."

Left alone again, Clare looked down at the peacefully sleeping baby and withdrew the empty bottle from her tiny rosebud mouth as tender unfamiliar feelings swamped her.

"That's better," Kathy laughed, taking a deep breath of cold, fresh air, stopping briefly to tuck the covers on the pushchair closer round the sleeping baby.

As promised the weather had improved and a wintry

sunshine held a surprising amount of warmth as they walked along a grassy headland, leading down to a small cove, where rocks dipped into the sea. Andrew and Mark were ahead, swinging Luke between them.

Kathy had, as Andrew predicted, come prepared and Clare was wearing borrowed jeans, a fleecy lined Parka and gum boots.

"Always come ready for outdoors, rain or shine," Kathy advised. "In summer, we spend full days in the cove. Luke loves the warm rock pools, and we quite often stay until seven o'clock in the evening. That's the time I like best."

Kathy glanced sideways at Clare when she didn't answer, and caught her lack of enthusiasm.

"You don't like the beach?"

"Can't say sand appeals."

Kathy laughed out loud and Andrew and Mark looked back, pleased to see them getting on well.

"Time we were heading back," Mark called. They had been walking for nearly an hour and the sun was beginning to dip behind gathering clouds.

"Here, let me take a turn." Mark passed Luke's hand to Kathy and took over the pushchair. "So tell us what the big joke was?"

"Nothing really. Clare said she didn't like sand and it just struck me as funny," Kathy said, swinging Luke in time with Andrew.

Mark smiled. "More an indoor girl. Never the outdoor type were you, Clare?"

Clare smiled and slipped her arm through Andrew's free one. "True," she agreed.

"Must show you what you are missing," Andrew said looking down at her fondly, making her heart somersault.

"You can try," Mark said cheerfully, striding on with the pushchair, blissfully unaware, as Andrew and Clare were, of Kathy stiffening with realisation.

Back at the house, Kathy went straight to the kitchen to help her mother lay sandwiches and cakes out for tea, before their journey home in time for the children's bed time, so her silence went unnoticed. And in the car she leant back with her eyes closed, claiming to be tired.

"Well it certainly wasn't a day off for you," Clare said sympathetically.

"Or my mother," Kathy said resentfully.

On reaching home, Connie greeted them at her front door. "Come in. I'll put kettle on."

"Need to get the children to bed, Connie. See you tomorrow." Kathy caught Luke's hand, as he would have run to her.

"Oh, oright." Connie sounded disappointed, but for once Kathy took no notice.

Mark picked the carry cot out of the car and started towards their front door where Kathy was fumbling with the key, but veered towards Connie when he heard her disappointment.

"Thanks all the same Connie. We need to get them settled. It's been a long day." He gave her a peck on the cheek.

"Is Kathy okay?"

"I think she fell out with her mother again. She'll be all right in the morning."

But Kathy wasn't all right in the morning. In fact, when Connie saw Mark and Andrew taking Luke and Chloe for a walk at eight o'clock and went round to see if she needed bread, she found the door locked. She went back again ten minutes later but Kathy still didn't open the door, and after the third time, convinced that something must be wrong went along and knocked on Clare's door.

"I'm worried. Mark says Kathy fell out with 'er mother again, but they do it all the time an' always make up before they go to sleep at night. She isn't answerin' 'er door to me, an' she's never done that afore."

Clare looked thoughtful. "I know she was annoyed that Hannah worked all day, yesterday, but that doesn't explain why she won't speak to *you*."

Connie shook her head. "Hannah worships that old couple."

Clare shrugged. "Not sure Kathy thinks too well of them."

"Well that's another story you'll 'ear about sooner or later."

"Do you want me to try?"

"Would ye?"

They walked back along the walkway together and stopped at Kathy' door. All was quiet as Clare knocked and after a few seconds called, "Are you all right, Kathy?"

Another few seconds passed before Kathy, sounding husky, answered. "I'm busy."

Connie and Clare looked at each other with raised eyebrows.

"You don't sound well. Shall I call Mark?"

"Oh, you'd like that wouldn't you?" Kathy accused.

Connie looked alarmed. "Kathy you're not makin' sense; please open the door."

Clare went pale and walked away, taking her mobile from her pocket.

"If she is thinking what I think she is thinking, Mark needs to be here. I knew it was a mistake," she said vehemently.

Connie looked even more alarmed. "What's goin' on for 'eavens sake? First you run away all upset, now Kathy. There's Mark talkin' nonsense all time and Andy changin' the subject. I dunno' if I'm comin' or goin'."

She went into her cottage and Clare heard her say angrily, "Somethin's up, but no one's saying," and then Jim's worried, "Don't fret, love," as she waited for Mark to answer his mobile.

It was nearly half an hour before Mark and Andrew hurried into the drive.

Clare had gone back to Andrew's cottage, unable to face Connie and Jim, but seeing them arrive she hurried out.

"Kathy has locked herself in and won't even open the door to Connie," she said in an urgent whisper. "Have you told her?"

Mark shook his head and handed the lead to Luke, giving him a gentle push to where Connie was waiting at her door. "Take Chloe into Jim, son."

Waiting until they had disappeared inside he tried his key in the lock but it was bolted.

"Kathy, love. Open the door. We need to talk."

"If you're going to leave us, just go. That's what she's come for isn't it?"

Andrew returned Mark's look of dismay with a resigned sigh. "You should have told her straight away. Why do you keep putting things off?"

Listening on the other side of the door, Kathy gave a loud sob. "So Andrew knows. I suppose everyone does except me."

"Knows what?"

"It was Clare you were engaged to, wasn't it?" There was another loud sob. "And you're going back to her."

Clare closed her eyes in dismay. "You certainly know how to complicate your love life," she said, glaring at Mark.

"Kathy, please open the door; I don't want Mark back. If I wasn't over that unfortunate episode in my life before, I certainly am now. Can't believe what an idiot I've been."

Mark opened his mouth and closed it again looking offended, while Andrew gave her a delighted hug, as the door opened slowly to reveal Kathy hugging the baby.

Connie also appeared in her doorway looking indignant. "There's tea in pot an' I'm makin' bacon samiches. What's goin' on?"

"Connie you're an angel. I'm starving." Andrew caught Clare to him and steered her towards the wonderful smell of grilled bacon, and gathered together round the log burner in the warm sitting room, Mark explained and made his peace with Kathy, while Connie and Jim gazed happily at Clare, curled up beside Andrew.

"Most importantly," Clare said seriously, pausing as everyone looked at her expectantly, "*when* is this lovely baby going to be given a *name*?"

"Can't decide," Mark said abruptly looking at Kathy, who just shrugged.

"Your baby. Your choice," Connie said adamantly.

"If only," Kathy murmured.

"What would you like to do today?" Andrew asked Clare, changing the subject abruptly.

"Quiet day I think. You?"

He nodded. "Need to spend an hour or two in the surgery, then I'm all yours." They smiled into each other's eyes.

"I'll give Connie a hand until then."

"There's nothin' won't wait. Spend an 'our with Jim."

Jim looked hopeful and Clare gave a big smile. "I'd like that, if you're sure."

Once in the conservatory amongst the paints and

canvasses, Jim wasn't content until he had Clare with a paint brush in her hand, and two hours later, when Andrew arrived, she had managed, under Jim's patient tuition, to produce a passable still life of a colourful china jug filled with bluebells.

"Eat your heart out Van Gogh," Andrew said, laughing at the amount of paint she had got on the blue smock she was wearing.

"Sorry about the smock, Jim, but I'm glad you insisted on me wearing it," Clare said remembering how she had lightly dismissed the need for covering her blue suit.

"And I'm sorry too, Jim, because I'm going to whisk your pupil away now."

Andrew undid the ties and she slipped the smock off, handing it to Jim with a kiss on the cheek.

"I've really enjoyed my first lesson. I'll come again, if I may?"

"Most certainly. You are an excellent pupil."

"Only because you are an excellent teacher."

Andrew slipped his arm around her as, walking back to the cottage, they stopped to watch two buzzards circling above the meadow.

"What a lovely man Jim is," she said leaning into him.

"Very special. They both are."

"I never knew my father. He died when I was a baby. It never mattered because my mother was everything I could want, but if I had a father, I would want him to be exactly like Jim."

"I'm told the feeling is mutual. Connie says he has really taken to you."

Clare blushed with pleasure.

"And he isn't alone. Connie feels the same, in fact everyone does."

"Not your grandmother, that's for sure." She gave him a mischievous grin.

"Most definitely Grandmother; didn't you notice how she kept nodding? That's her way of showing approval."

"I thought she had an affliction," Clare said seriously.

"An affliction! No such thing would even dare to approach Grandmother," he said in mock horror, before looking serious. "Everyone is keen for us to get together. Could you ever consider marrying me?"

"You're making it very hard for me to say no, but can we take things a bit slower?"

Her deep blue eyes looked into his earnest grey ones, longing to be sure of the passion he aroused in her.

"Sorry. Yes, yes, Forget I asked." His mood lightened. "Lets get back and settle in. I've got steaks out of the freezer and I'm cooking."

He caught her hand and hurried her along the walkway, giving a relieved laugh as she reached up and kissed his cheek, saying, "Promise you'll ask me again, though."

"Oh, *that* you can be very sure of." He stopped and wrapped her in a bear hug and she felt as if the world was spinning.

A week flew by in a dream, and too soon it was New Year's Eve, and time to attend the party at 'Tamarisks'. Connie and Jim were to baby sit for Kathy, and surprised at how unenthusiastic both Kathy and Mark were, Clare mentioned it to Andrew, who sighed.

"They have personal issues with Hannah. The main one being the baby's name. I'd rather Kathy told you about it. I don't agree with Mark."

The evening was in full swing when they arrived, and Clare was surprised at the difference in Grace.

Wearing a long, silver grey dress, shot with threads of lavender, and her silver hair immaculately dressed, she was the perfect hostess as, accompanied by Arthur, looking very dapper in his black bow tie and evening suit, they greeted guests warmly in the hall.

Clare noticed that all of the younger girls and women were wearing full skirts, and realised why when after the buffet supper at ten o'clock, they all left the hall and made their way to the big barn where a man, poised to play the violin, was already introducing 'Strip the willow', as couples gathered on the floor.

"Thought you might like to sit and watch," Andrew said, leading her to one of the bales of hay, dotted around the outside of the wooden dance floor.

The catchy music soon had Clare tapping her feet, and looking surprised, Andrew asked, "Want to have a go?"

"I don't know the steps, and my skirt is too straight. I didn't pack with this in mind."

"Did rather rush you away, didn't I?" He looked at her and eyes shining she whispered, "I'm glad you did."

"Come with me," he said, taking her hand and leading her back to the house, where Grace was waltzing sedately around the floor with Arthur. Waiting for the music to stop he led Clare over to them. "Clare would like to barn dance, Grandmother, but her skirt won't let her."

Without a word, Grace led Clare upstairs and into a bedroom, where she opened a wardrobe door and picked a bright pink skirt and matching top out.

"I would say this is about your size, but take your pick. I'll leave you to it."

She touched Clare's shoulder briefly. "I'm glad Andrew met you."

Nicely surprised, Clare just stared as Grace closed the door quietly behind her.

Left alone in the Victorian style bedroom, she decided to follow the good advice and slipping into the full, tiered skirt and peasant blouse, ran back down the stairs to where Andrew was waiting. His eyes glowed, and she just caught the nod of approval from Grace as she ran to him.

Following Kathy when they were separated from Andrew and Mark, she quickly picked up the square dances, and much too soon twelve o'clock arrived with everyone gathered in a circle for Auld Lang Syne.

Clare could never remember enjoying herself as much, and was very touched when, as they were leaving, Arthur kissed her cheek and wished her a Happy New Year, adding quietly, "Make sure we share New Year's Eve 2012, my dear."

CHAPTER THIRTEEN

Clare sat in her office wishing she could stop her mind from straying. She really needed to concentrate on the numerous claim forms waiting to be assessed.

She had been home three weeks. Her life was back to normal. Why had they been the longest three weeks of her life? Missing Andrew more than she thought possible was bad enough, but why did she keep thinking of Connie, and the painting lessons with Jim in his studio.

In the short time she had known them, they had become like family. And then there was Kathy, who had confided in her so indignantly about her mother insisting the baby should be called Grace. Like sisters would, she imagined.

"*Grace* of all names!" she had exploded. "*And,* Mark is prepared to agree because he hates upsetting Mum again after all the trouble we caused her; but *Grace*! That is just *too much*," she had ended on a high note with tears in her eyes.

It was unusual for Kathy to complain, so she had listened and murmured, sympathetically, "I'm sure she doesn't see you as a trouble to her."

"Oh, but I was. She nearly gave in her notice because I embarrassed her so much. Can you imagine? That job means everything to her."

Taking a deep breath and averting her eyes, she confessed, "I wouldn't tell her who Luke's father was. I didn't tell anyone. Mark had wanted a new life for a long time. He found living with his grandparents stifling. We grew up together at 'Tamarisks', and I loved him from when I was seven. I was seventeen and wanted to die when he told me he was leaving. We went for a drink with his friends the night before he left, and I had too much cider. I was desperately unhappy and threw myself at him; wanted him to make love to me just once before he left. We lived in the cottage in the grounds then. My dad was the gardener and it came with the job, but when Luke was a year old, Dad died. Mum and I were given rooms in the house because there was no way 'Milady' was going to lose her willing slave was there?"

This was said bitterly.

"But how else could she have supported you and Luke?" I asked.

This was met with a shrug. "Mum said if I didn't like it I must speak to the father. I hated living in the big house; I felt trapped, so I asked Andrew if I could have his empty cottage. He was fantastic, even though I wouldn't tell him who the father was; he even offered to marry me but I couldn't do that; it wouldn't have been right. I love him, but not like I love Mark. He eventually worked it out for himself, by talking to the village lads; that was when he tackled Mark."

Looking unhappy she had gone on to explain. "I just want you to know that it wasn't easy for Mark. The grandparents were horrified. They wanted a well educated girl from their own class; not the housekeeper's lowly daughter. So, as you have probably noticed, there's not much love lost between us, and Mum always seems to take their side."

Luke had run into the room then, and the conversation ended with, "Well you can't just go on calling her baby. What would you like to call your little sister, Luke?"

"Emma," he replied promptly, and Kathy brightened immediately.

"Emma! I love that, Luke; I really do. Clever boy! It's settled then. *Luke* has chosen his sister's name. Well done, Auntie Clare."

No more was said. Emma was baptised, with Hannah giving way to Luke's choice, on condition that Emma's second name was Grace.

She was glad that she and her own mother were back to their normal harmony, and still deep in thought, laughed lightly at the idea of no one ever being able take Paul's place, just as the door opened and Jane, the head clerk, walked in, hesitating in surprise at the sight of Clare, actually beaming and stretching her arms above her head in sheer joy; her eyes opening even wider as she placed a folder on the desk and received thanks with a cheerful smile, instead of the usual grunt while Clare carried on working.

"A miracle to equal the second coming," she commented dryly on returning to her desk.

Deftly guiding her tea trolley between the desks, Linda added, "Well the other day, for the first time since I've been here, she actually said how nice my home made cakes and sandwiches are, and how much preparation time it must take. Nearly fell over I did."

"Perhaps she hit her head when she fell over," Scott declared sarcastically, having caught the rough edge of Clare's tongue more than once, by making what she considered to be childish passes.

"Well, I'm glad she is happier. Who knows, she may even join us for a drink one night after work." Blonde and bubbly, Josie always jumped at any excuse to party.

"Don't hold your breath," Scott said sourly.

"Well if you will punch above your weight." Tony grinned, knowing Scott held a grudge because Clare had turned him down soon after Paul left.

"And you could do better, I suppose?" Scott challenged, going red in the face.

"Now boys, play nicely," Jane interrupted sternly.

"Well, you've either got it or you haven't," Tony taunted, smoothing his dark hair back with both hands; getting a last shot in before Jane called, "Enough!"

Unaware of the gossip she was causing, Clare left the office promptly instead of staying on until the cleaner arrived. Never anxious to leave before, she couldn't wait to get home now for Andrew's six o'clock telephone call every evening.

The weekend stretched invitingly and she considered driving down to Cornwall, but the weather was not good, and it would be pitch black along the narrow lanes by the time she arrived around ten o'clock.

As she arrived home, the telephone was ringing and she answered it breathless with excitement, but Andrew, sounding muffled, said the signal was bad and he would speak soon. Then the line went dead.

Disappointed she removed her coat and had started towards the kitchen as the door bell rang. Intent on waiting for Andrew to call back, she went to tell whoever it was that she was too busy to talk right now, but all she could see when she opened the door was a huge basket of red roses above a pair of familiar jeans and boots, until Andrew laid the roses down and swept her up into his arms, kissing her hungrily, whispering how much he missed her, and begging her to marry him soon. Between kisses she said, "Yes, yes, yes," and he released her to gaze in wonder and ask urgently, "When?"

Eyes shining, she hunched her shoulders and spread her hands. "You say."

He threw his head back laughing. "You actually mean I'm to choose?"

"As long as you choose Easter."

"That's my girl."

Tossing her head, she undid his coat, waved her hands at him to take it off, then pulled him down onto the settee and curled up against his warm chest, smiling to herself.

"Can't think what you mean."

The following day Andrew arrived early, having spent the night at his father's flat.

"Call me old fashioned, but I want to woo you first," he had said before leaving.

Chichester was having its usual busy Saturday morning as they made for the town to buy the ring and, gazing in the window of a jewellers shop in North street, neither of them saw Laura until she was standing beside them, eyes alight with curiosity.

"Hello you two." Waiting for them to say something, she looked purposefully at the trays of rings.

"Is there something I don't know?"

Clare laughed happily up at Andrew. "We didn't know ourselves until last night. We were coming to see you, afterwards."

"Afterwards being after we bought the ring, that is," Andrew explained, with a big grin.

"Your Dad and I are going out to dinner tonight, why not join us and surprise him? We must celebrate."

Clare nodded happily and Andrew kissed Laura's cheek. "Thank you. He will like that."

"We've booked a table at the Festival Theatre restaurant

for seven o'clock. Just turn up. I'll go right now and make it for four. What a lovely surprise it will be for him," Laura said happily, giving a cheery wave, already on her way to the top end of North Street to rearrange the booking.

An hour of much oohing and aahing followed with Andrew opting for a diamond solitaire, but reminded of Paul's ring, she chose a bridal 'ring set' of a dark blue sapphire set in a cluster of small diamonds with a matching white gold wedding ring.

On arriving at the restaurant they waited in a secluded corner until Alan and Laura were seated at their table, before casually walking over and sitting down. Alan's face was a picture of surprised delight, and they had to stand again to receive his warm embrace, as Laura's eyes filled with happy tears.

"This calls for champagne!" Alan said emotionally, as the wine waiter arrived.

A memorable evening followed, when, after admiring the rings and hearing their plan to get married at Easter, Alan and Laura broke the news of their own decision to have a quiet, registry office ceremony in five weeks time, on the 19th February.

"The work on the bungalow should be finished by then, and afterwards, perhaps we can come and visit Grace and Arthur. I'm sure they would like to meet your mother, Clare; they know what a good friend she was to their daughter."

"You must meet Connie and Jim, as well. You will really like them, Mum."

Clare glowed with happiness and her mother nodded enthusiastically.

Andrew smiled tolerantly. "I have a serious rival in Jim, for your daughter's affections."

Alan laughed and nodded agreement. "Nice people!"

The rest of the weekend flew by, and after Andrew left, Clare spent Sunday evening wishing the time away until Easter. Lonely and impatient, she decided to hand her notice in at the end of March, wondering how she was going to bear it until Andrew came back in two weeks' time.

The next few weeks were some of the happiest Clare could remember. Her mother and Alan got married as planned, and everything went without a hitch, with just the four of them at the ceremony. It had been a long cold winter and Alan and Laura decided to delay their trip to Cornwall for a month, in the hope that the weather would improve.

"The coldest we can remember," Connie and Jim assured Clare, desperately hoping she wouldn't change her mind about living in Cornwall, because to their completely unthinkable dismay, Andrew said he was prepared to move to Chichester and work with his father, rather than lose Clare.

"Have you decided where you want to get married yet?" Alan asked, as they shared Laura's Sunday roast at the bungalow. Clare hesitated.

"We hope you won't mind, Mum, but I rather want it to be Cornwall, so that the grandparents and Connie and Jim can be there. I know they would find the journey, and staying somewhere strange, too much."

She watched her mother's look of surprise turn to one of pleased approval.

"I think that is a wonderful idea, and very thoughtful, isn't it Alan?"

On seeing the change in her daughter, if Clare had said the planet Mars, Laura would have agreed, but Alan looked dubious.

"The grandparents will be over the moon, but you know you won't have any say in where the reception is held, don't you?"

Clare gave a questioning look, as Andrew said with quiet confidence, "Clare will think it perfect."

Mystified, Laura and Clare looked at each other.

"Tamarisks?" Alan volunteered.

"What Dad is saying is, having told the grandparents two weeks ago, Grandmother will have it all arranged by now; in fact, she has probably already spoken to the vicar." He frowned. "Come to think of it, I should have done that."

"Do you imagine you only have to say Easter Saturday, and by some miracle the church will be free at this late date?"

Alan tutted, as they all looked dismayed. "Don't worry. Grace will have it all in hand, but you both need to be in Cornwall to hear the banns read."

Clare went into overdrive. "I'll come back with you tonight," she said decisively, her mellow mood disappearing. "A reception at 'Tamarisks' will be wonderful. We must have a Barn Dance," she said eagerly, before looking serious again. "I must email work, telling them I won't be in this week, and I must also talk to your grandparents about cost."

"Oh dear, now see what you've done, Dad; she's wearing her accountant's hat again." Andrew rolled his eyes. "Next her hair will go back in that tight little bun; she won't hear a word you say, and those wonderful eyes will roll like a cash register."

"Just what you need, Son, you were definitely last in line when they handed out money management. Although I'm not sure about the hair. I like it as it is."

Laura smiled. "Me too."

"Oh, me too," Andrew said quickly looking into Clare's flashing deep blue eyes, where humour belied her pursed lips, as she said, "Remind me to have a word with you later."

"Yes, dear."

Unable to control her happiness, Laura burst out laughing. "Spoken like a perfect, future husband," she said, placing a treacle sponge pudding and steaming jug of custard on the table.

"That looks wonderful, Mum. You and Connie will get on so well," Clare said admiringly, surprising Laura yet again. She was used to her daughter taking her food for granted.

"This Connie seems to have made a deep impression," she said later to Alan.

"Mm," he murmured absently, picking up the Sunday Times crossword. "You'll like her... and him. One thing's for sure," he chuckled, "things will move fast if Grace and Clare work together."

They sat together in comfortable silence, reading the clue for one across and pondering, until she interrupted his concentration by asking, "Are you sure it won't be too much for Grace, at her age?"

He looked at her, in shocked amusement.

"Don't let her hear you say that. She's never forgiven Arthur for retiring from the navy so soon. She was self appointed Commander in Chief of Naval wives, had a hand in every function. Only time I ever saw her cry was the day Arthur retired. Big party on board 'H.M.S. Victory', in Portsmouth harbour. No expense spared. Marine band playing, and Grace looking absolutely splendid in a dark blue dress, with tiny gold anchors embroidered on the bodice.

"She certainly knew how to impress and they were both missed, but for her, life has never been quite the same. If they'd had a son, he would have been signed up for the navy the day he was born. They wanted Mark to enlist, but I can only think the discipline at home put him off. He would never have achieved a rank high enough to suit Grace, anyway. Anything for a quiet life, Rosemary and I always said. He and Andrew were like brothers, and we actually suggested he should come to live with us. The grandparents wouldn't hear of it though. He was all they had left of his mother, their youngest daughter Jacqueline. She was adventurous and very headstrong; should have been a boy, Arthur always said, before she broke their hearts. And then of course, that girl got her hooks into Andrew and that was the very last straw. Clare is the answer to all of Grace's prayers and the vicar is sure to be under her spell, so we can safely say an Easter wedding will take place."

He kissed her cheek, and they smiled contentedly at each other before turning their attention back to the crossword.

Alan's prediction was correct. Grace had rearranged the vicar's Easter Saturday for him, and the wedding service was now booked into his one o'clock lunch hour.

"So the poor man is to go without lunch?" Arthur queried.

"Yes but he *and* his wife will be invited to the wedding breakfast. He will love it."

Grace smiled at what she considered to be her clever solution to the late booking, and Arthur faintly agreed that it was, of course, the *only* one.

Arriving at 'Tamarisks' in time for lunch, Andrew and Clare were greeted fondly by Grace and, without preamble, handed a neatly written A4 sheet of information.

On hearing that Clare would be coming down for a few days, she had arranged for a catalogue of wedding invitations to be sent to Andrew's cottage, and a list of essential guests, on Andrew's side of the family.

Then Clare's ring was greatly admired, especially by Arthur, who said, "Perfect my dear; the exact colour of your eyes."

Clare blushed with pleasure as, looking peeved, Andrew wondered why he didn't think of saying that and decided he would have to get a few Naval tips from Gramps.

After lunch, while Andrew and Arthur played snooker, Grace listened to Clare's ideas. She admired her choice of the simple but elegant wedding dress and delighted at the idea of a Barn Dance, because it could be held in the barn, and leave the big hall free for the caterers.

By the time they left, Clare felt most of the important details had been covered, and she was looking forward to sharing the rest of the arrangements with her mother.

"Grandmother is getting on like house afire, with Clare," Andrew told Connie and Jim, later that evening.

"Why wouldn't she? Darned lucky, if you ask me," Jim bristled.

Worried by his uncharacteristic reaction, Andrew quickly changed the subject by asking how the painting lessons were coming on.

"She tries hard. Needs more practise, but on the whole, good effort!"

"Sounds like my school reports," Andrew laughed, yawning hugely, missing Jim's far away look as he said absently, "Mm, mine too."

Andrew yawned again. "Clare said she was having an early night after her bath. Think I might have one too. This wedding business is exhausting," he grinned sheepishly.

Unusually, Connie didn't reply; her attention was on Jim.

He had been behaving oddly since yesterday. Day dreaming was all she could put it down to, since Clare spent the afternoon in the studio with him.

"Sleep well, Connie. And you, Jim." Andrew was bending over to kiss her cheek, before she suddenly realised he was leaving.

"Sorry, love. Miles away. Early one for us as well I think." She got up and followed him from the room.

"Time for bed time drink; sure ye won't stay fer one?"

"I'm okay, thanks all the same. You're quiet tonight. Are you all right?"

She lowered her voice. "It's nothin' I don' s'pose. Bit worried 'bout Jim. 'E's usually bright as a button, after Clare's bin round, but he bin quiet 'n' moody since yesterday."

"Mm. Not like him. I expect he'll be all right after a good night's sleep, but if not I'll have a word in the morning. Don't worry, I'm sure he would say if it was serious."

They said goodnight and Andrew walked back to his flat, confident that if anything was physically wrong with Jim, Connie would be the first to know. His cottage was in darkness, and he smiled to himself, thinking how well Clare got on with his grandparents, wondering at Jim's reaction when he mentioned it. Jealous? Surely not. He was certainly very fond of Clare; had been from the start. Brushing the thought aside he let himself into the surgery and wended his way up to the flat, filled with anticipation for the future.

Over the next week a sudden rush of calls took Andrew to outlying farms, so with Mark working and Luke at school, Clare spent time with Kathy and the baby, as well as Connie and Jim, but with only two more days to go before she went home, Jim suggested finishing her painting.

He had been asking her questions about herself lately; suddenly curious, it seemed, about where her grandparents lived before they died. Unable to give him an exact location she could only say somewhere in Kent. Then he stared for a long minute, before asking, "Do I remember you saying your grandfather was in the Royal Navy?" And she had replied that she didn't recall mentioning it, but yes, he was.

She answered his questions as best she could, whilst painting, but explained she had been very young when they died, so she only knew what her mother told her, because she had no brothers, sisters or other family.

The fact that her mother had a brother killed in the Falklands war seemed to be of intense interest to him, and he became quite agitated when she told him her mother was, at one time, a private teacher, working from home, because her father was killed in the same Falklands war as her uncle, when her mother was pregnant with her.

This information seemed to agitate him further and he didn't ask any more questions. But as she was leaving to return home, he gave her a flat parcel, which she opened at home to find the painting of the 'Bluebell Woods'.

CHAPTER FOURTEEN

Ria drove up the winding drive and parked the shabby, red Ford Fiesta at the front door to 'Tamarisks'.

The long stone-built house, with its royal blue shutters and Union Jack flying from the barn, had always riled her, with its strict, Naval timetables and unwelcoming stares on the rare occasions when Andrew had brought her.

Well today they could jolly well sit up and listen.

A tall figure at the window told her her arrival had been noted by the mistress of the house, and before she had time to get out of the car another figure appeared, framed in the wide opening of the solid front door, waving her away, before the door shut again.

Without hurrying she eased herself cumbersomely out of the driving seat and with an exaggerated pregnant walk, rang the door bell.

She waited, happily anticipating the look of distaste on Grace's face when she saw her. She was wearing a cushion strapped to her waist, under one of the maternity dresses from the charity shop and the pair of worn down, flat shoes, relying on her appearance to achieve her purpose.

The Carlyon's wouldn't want any of their friends to see her calling and would certainly pay her to go away, which she would happily do... *if* they paid her enough. She rang the bell again and another full minute passed before quick, staccato footsteps rang out on the parquet floor of the hall;

a warning to a less intrepid caller that they were not welcome.

As soon as Hannah opened the door she pushed her way past, making Hannah gasp with shock and stare with indignation.

"How dare you barge your way in."

"Tell the old folk I want to speak to them... and hurry."

"Commander and Mrs Carlyon are not at home to you; now leave," Hannah said haughtily.

Ignoring her, Ria marched to the sitting room door and threw it open. "Listen to what I have to say, or you will be sorry."

"Sorry, Maam, I told her you weren't at home."

"That's all right, Hannah. English was never her best subject."

Sitting in her upright wing chair, Grace looked disdainfully at Ria. "Well, what do you want? I have heard how you robbed my grandson, and tried to steal his home. Say what you have to and go."

"In front of the servant?" Ria taunted.

Hannah half turned but Grace stopped her.

"Hannah is not a servant, she is a valued member of my family. Say what you have to."

"My my, you have changed your tune." She turned to Hannah. "Fetch the old boy, valued member of the family; he needs to hear this."

"I will decide what my husband may or may not need to hear. Now say what you must or I will call the local police."

"Oh you won't want them to hear what I have to say."

"Are you trying to blackmail us?" Grace asked incredulously.

"Now that's an ugly word, and also criminal, I understand."

Grace regarded her with bored disgust.

"All I want is fair recompense."

Grace looked faintly amused. "For what?"

"For your grandson forcing himself on me and making me pregnant."

Grace lost her temper. "Don't be ridiculous. Andrew would never do such a thing. Get out of my house!"

She stood up and tapped her stick, but Ria stood her ground and waved a photo scan in her face.

"Here's the proof, and the baby is due in September. Andrew forced himself on me two nights before our wedding day. That's why I ran away. And now I hear he is already planning another wedding. He certainly doesn't waste any time does he? But I bet she won't marry him when she hears what I have to say, in church, when the vicar asks if anyone knows any reason why they shouldn't marry."

Grace paled. "Perhaps you should ask my husband to join us, Hannah."

As Hannah hurried from the room, she heard Ria make another stinging remark.

"Oh, of course! She is your other grandson's mother-in-law; your family do seem to make a habit of getting girls into trouble, don't they?"

Seldom overcome by uncertainty, Grace sat down again, needing Arthur to answer the claim, which at the moment was playing havoc with her senses.

Arthur hurried in and went straight to Grace. "Are you all right, my dear?"

Hannah had only mentioned that Ria barged in and was being rude and unpleasant, so he was also shocked as she repeated her accusation and what she intended doing at the wedding.

Convinced now that her demand would be met, Ria was triumphantly embroidering her story.

"My father has turned me out and refuses to help in any way. I need to provide a home for my baby, so I must buy a house."

She stared at him, thickly pencilled eyebrows raised challengingly over her dark brown chocolate coloured eyes and, recovering sufficiently, Arthur answered in what he hoped was a confident voice, although in truth he felt anything but confident, when he challenged her with, "This sounds very much like blackmail."

Ria pretended to look shocked. "I'm merely asking for the means to provide your great grandchild with a decent home. Surely a roof over its head isn't too much to ask, from people in your position?"

Recovering her composure, Grace asked curiously, "What does your mother say about your father turning you out?"

"My mother died six months ago. I have no one."

Ria looked ready to cry, but changed her mind when Grace said firmly, "I must speak to Andrew and insist that he marries you."

She held up her hand as Ria opened her mouth to object.

"It is his duty. He must provide for you."

"He won't agree," Ria burst out hastily. "He's marrying this woman, from Chichester."

Grace settled back in her high backed chair, calmly placing one hand over the other, in her lap.

"He was, but now he must marry you, and provide a home for your child. The two of you must settle down in his cottage, and raise your child together."

Ria looked horrified as Grace continued, "The family name must be upheld. And in the meantime you must live here with us, so that we can keep an eye on you."

It was Arthur's turn to look horrified, until Ria suddenly stormed, "But I don't want to marry him; all I want is enough money to buy a house for me and the baby."

Arthur relaxed, realising that Grace was toying with her.

"So how much are you expecting from us?" he asked tentatively, wondering what Grace had in mind.

Ria dithered. She had been going to say one hundred thousand, but now she could make it more. "Enough for a house and furniture, plus baby needs?"

"So?" He waited while she pretended to add up in her head.

"Two hundred thousand should do it. And you will never see me again; one condition though: Andrew mustn't know about the baby. I never want to see him again."

Grace nodded slowly at Arthur.

"I'll get you a cheque." Arthur left the room and returned several minutes later to hand her a cheque and say, "I'll show you out."

Grace was looking out of the window and remained with her back to the room, as Ria triumphantly stowed the cheque in her Gucci bag and followed Arthur to the front door.

Watching from the window, they saw the ancient red car leave the drive, followed shortly after by their Land Rover.

"Need to make a phone call," Arthur murmured.

"Yes," Grace agreed.

It was dark when the Land Rover returned, and when Peter, the gardener, tapped on the patio door, Arthur went eagerly to invite him in.

"She went to a car park in Plymouth, left the red one and got into a four by four. A man was driving and I followed them to a hotel. I didn't get a clear look at him, but he looked about her age. I saw him sign the register and take one key, so I'm pretty sure they booked in together."

He handed Arthur a piece of paper with the registration number and the name of the hotel written on it.

"Good man, Peter. Keep a look out."

Grace thanked him as well, adding, "You must be hungry. We've only just finished dinner, so Hannah is sure to have some left."

Peter grinned. "Wouldn't say no, ma'am. Mighty nice cook, Hannah."

Grace pursed her lips in a smile, knowing how he admired Hannah. "Away with you."

Peter was in his forties and lived alone in the cottage vacated by Hannah and Kathy.

Kathy liked him because he made her mother laugh, and secretly hoped her mother would accept his shy advances, but Hannah only did things in her own good time.

"Think I might get Laurie on the job," Arthur said, when Peter left.

"He's in Plymouth at the moment isn't he?"

"Mm. And he always did enjoy a bit of sleuthing. I'll give him a ring."

Grace frowned. "Perhaps we should warn Andrew, in case she does come to the church?"

"Pretty sure she won't. I post-dated the cheque until after Easter. She'll no doubt have some heated remarks for me, but at least we have until after Easter, to look into things."

Grace smiled happily, confident that the wedding would now go ahead peacefully.

"That was very astute; but then you didn't get to be a commander for nothing, did you?"

"For one awful moment, I thought you were serious when you said Andrew must marry her and she must live here. So what was all that about?" Arthur looked curious.

"She was lying. She said her mother died six months ago, but Mark found it very funny and told me she was at the registry office *and* the hotel, loudly blaming her husband when Ria didn't turn up, because she had travelled all the way from Malta, at great expense and inconvenience to herself. Apparently after settling everyone down in the hotel, Andrew asked Mark to deal with them, and left them eating, drinking and gossiping, so he didn't hear that. But thankfully that was how he came to meet Clare."

She gave a satisfied smile, then winced.

"I've got to admit the hussy had me worried for a while, though."

Arthur looked thoughtful. "Mm, me too. What about the baby? Andrew's, do you think?"

Grace gave an adamant tap with her stick. "She can have the money... if it is."

"Ah well!" Arthur gazed mournfully into the dancing log fire, thinking how much this latest 'to do', plus the wedding, was going to cost. Keeping Grace happy was his mission in life, but there were times...

Ria threw herself onto the hotel bed, spreading her arms wide, elated at the prospect of taking the cheque to the bank as soon as it opened in the morning.

"I did it! I actually did it!"

She stretched, cat like, arching her back, long black hair spread out on the crimson coverlet, before kicking her shoes off and curling up, hugging herself. "I knew they wouldn't risk a scandal."

Jason was investigating the mini bar and stood up, hands full of small bottles.

"Not sure I believe they fell for it that easily. First thing we do is book our flight out of here, after you've changed the cheque."

Ria leant up on her elbow. "What did Dad say when you handed in your notice?"

Jason looked blank. "You don't imagine I gave up my job before I was sure, do you?"

"I told you it was a certainty," She flung herself back, stretching her arms again, laughing triumphantly.

"He will know when I don't turn up."

She gave him a mischievous look. "Wouldn't be in your shoes, if he ever catches you."

"Well hopefully he won't come looking for us in Italy."

She got up quickly and went to the bathroom, singing *Volaree oh oh. Cantaree oh oh oh oh*, as she turned the bath taps on full. Seconds later, the despised maternity dress came hurtling through the open door, to land in a heap beside the waste paper bin.

Watching from his car, Laurie saw Ria leave the hotel. Her quick walk, with the occasional skip, told him she was excited and impatient to get to the bank. It was five to ten and he had been sitting in the hotel car park since seven o'clock that morning, but his patience had been rewarded. He stepped out of his car. The picture of the well-dressed young woman Arthur had emailed him bore little resemblance to the pregnant woman, but the sleek black hair and dark, heavily made up eyes were unmistakable, so keeping her in sight, he entered the bank and went straight to a kiosk, close to where she was waiting to be attended to and pretended to fill in one of the forms.

He saw her look impatiently at the teller who inspected the cheque and went to talk to a supervisor, who followed her back to her position at the counter.

What followed drew the attention of everyone in the bank, before Ria left, clutching the cheque, close to hysteria.

Laurie followed her the short distance back to the hotel and waited in his car. Half an hour later he saw her stomp out of the hotel and get into a silver grey 4×4, accompanied by a foreign looking man, confirming the observations of Arthur's gardener.

He followed them at a distance, until it was obvious they were returning to Cornwall, then pulled into a lay-by to warn Arthur to stand by to repel boarders.

Rigid with disappointment and indignation, Ria's knuckles showed white on her clenched fists.

"He lied. He post-dated the cheque until after the stupid wedding. Well he'll soon see he can't mess me about. I'll be at that church; you see if I'm not."

"Then you can definitely say goodbye to any money," Jason pointed out calmly.

"We'll see about that."

Jason pulled into a lay-by and turned the engine off. "There is an easier way."

Ria looked at him with narrowed eyes. "How? And why haven't you said before?"

"I've only just thought of it. Tell the old folk that as Davenport's common law wife, you are entitled to half of everything he owns. If he owns that terrace of cottages it will be a lot more than what you are asking them for, so *if* they are as worried about scandal as you say, the threat of a court case will change their mind."

Ria looked doubtful. "He will say we didn't live together."

"His word against yours; and you *are* pregnant."

"And when they find out I'm not?"

"We'll be in Italy."

He started the engine again, giving her a challenging smile.

"And this time I want cash."

Arthur gazed in consternation at Ria. "Very well; give me until this time tomorrow," he said abruptly.

Ria looked at her watch. "Three o'clock tomorrow. Last chance," she warned, turning on her heel and marching to the hall, where she let herself out, slamming the front door behind her.

Arthur was waiting in the drive the following day.

"My wife doesn't wish you in our home; we will conduct our business in the barn."

Ria shrugged and strode along the pebble path leading to the barn. Peter was tending a nearby flower bed and touched his cap, as Arthur took his time, fumbling noisily with the door, before allowing her to precede him into the barn, where she jumped violently and stamped her foot when he suddenly banged the door shut.

"Stop doddering about and get on with it," she said, swivelling sharply as a voice from the stage asked, "Get on with what, Ria? What are you doing bothering my grandfather? Does Andrew know?"

CHAPTER FIFTEEN

With wedding plans well in hand, Clare was able to spend time on herself. The wedding dress had just been delivered and they were in Clare's bedroom where Laura was eagerly helping to unpack it from its zipped, white nylon cover.

"I'm so looking forward to wearing my lavender lace dress, again. I couldn't possibly find anything lovelier, or that I would enjoy wearing as much." Her eyes filled with happy tears. "Thank you for that lovely present."

Hardly able to believe how her mother had blossomed under Alan's love, Clare gave her a quick hug, before whipping her top and trousers off.

"Let's make sure it still fits."

"Since two days ago?" Laura laughed, slipping the dress over Clare's head.

It was an afternoon they would both remember. Admiring the slim fitting silk gown and holding the frothy veil against it, as Laura laughingly quoted the superstition of it being unlucky to put the whole outfit on before the day.

"Just a silly superstition," she said with a dismissive wave.

"Mm. Even so, I think I'll wait."

"Surely you don't believe in those old wives' tales?"

"No, of course not."

She quickly slipped out of the dress. "Let's have a cup of tea."

"You seem to drink more tea than you used to, dear."

"Something I picked up in Cornwall, I expect." Clare smiled thinking of Connie.

Laura put the dress back into its cover, and was about to hang it on the outside of the fitted wardrobe when she caught sight of the 'Bluebell woods', still partly covered by its brown paper wrapping, half hidden behind the bedroom chair.

"That looks interesting. Can I have a proper look?"

At that moment the doorbell rang and Clare hastily covered it up. "I'll show it to you later. That will be Alan to pick you up."

Attention distracted, Laura hurried to answer the door and Clare gave a 'Phew!'

Her mother's birthday wasn't until June.

Left alone, she waited for Andrew's telephone call, picturing him in his sitting room, living for the day when she could be with him.

He was late calling. Probably busy in the surgery, she thought. Only another three weeks to go and she would be Mrs Andrew Davenport. She had worked the month required for her resignation and said her goodbyes today, so she was ready to start moving her things down to Andrew's cottage.

She stretched her arms wide above her head, a habit she had developed of late from sheer joy. She had never imagined life could be so wonderful.

Andrew's phone call eventually came an hour later than usual and she answered it with a breathless "Hello, darling," expecting him to answer in his usual yearning voice, knowing immediately something was wrong when he greeted her with, "I can't make it this weekend; something has cropped up and I need to be here."

"Shall I come down?"

"Best not," he answered briefly. Then without any of their usual loving exchanges, the line went dead, and she barely slept that night.

CHAPTER SIXTEEN

Ria stared at Mark and turned angrily on Arthur. "You said a private matter between us."

"And so it is, but with such a large sum involved, it occurred to me I should have a witness and I know I can trust Mark, so if you will just repeat your request?"

Ria decided to bluff. "What are you on about? This was your idea. You said I would do well to listen to what you have to say. Well here I am. Say away."

Mark looked puzzled. "What's this about, Gramps?"

"She has obviously changed her mind. Nothing more to be said. Sorry to waste your time, son. See her off the premises will you?"

Ria strode to the door, narrowing her eyes at Arthur, as Mark regarded her disappearing figure curiously.

"Am I seeing things or is she pregnant?"

"She says Andrew is the father and is threatening to denounce him at the wedding."

Mark's jaw dropped. "That would cause a bit of a stir. What are we going to do?"

"She doesn't want Andrew to know about the child. For two hundred thousand pounds, she will disappear."

"Who wouldn't? What does Grandmother say?"

"Pay her off. Reputation is more important."

"Mm; tell me," Mark muttered, reminded of his own severe reprimands from Grace.

"She also says I shouldn't tell Andrew and Clare; it will spoil their day."

They heard Ria's car rev up and Mark started for the door.

"Don't worry. She's gone. Perhaps that didn't go quite to plan, but she left without the money, so she'll be back. In the meantime, my old opposite number is keeping tabs on her. Are you going to wait and see your grandmother? She won't be down until sixteen hundred hours."

Mark shook his head. "Can't stay; I left Kathy looking after the office and said I would pick Luke up from school on the way back." He looked at his watch. "In fact I must dash."

Arthur gave a satisfied smile. "Yes, you run along son. Thank you for your help."

Mark looked worried. "I'll give you a ring from the office. Are you sure you and Grandmother are all right?"

"We will be now."

Mark looked puzzled as they walked to his car. "Not sure how I helped."

"I just know I can rely on you."

Mark drove away thinking about his grandfather's comments, debating with himself. His grandparents definitely needed help, and the one person who should definitely be told was Andrew, in spite of what Grandmother said.

Arthur returned to the house chuckling confidently. Two birds with one stone, he congratulated himself, seeing the gardening tools lying unattended by the flower bed and no sign of Peter, knowing he would be following Ria and sending S.O.S messages to Laurie.

After running Kathy and the children home, Mark called Arthur from his office. It only rang once before Arthur answered, sounding as if he was standing to attention.

"Nothing to report as yet. Will make contact when it's all systems go."

Mark replaced the receiver, even more worried because his grandfather sounded as if he thought he was in charge of a Naval operation.

He decided to close the office and go straight home to speak to Andrew, convinced that his grandfather was close to a break down.

Andrew was in his surgery, tending a black and white spaniel with an ear infection and Jim was helping by holding the dog. Unable to wait a moment longer, Mark barged in and unburdened himself, ending with, "I think he's losing the plot; I really do."

Andrew finished putting drops into the dog's ears, lifted him off the table, and handed Jim his lead and a phial. "Take Dexter to Mrs Morris, will you Jim? Tell her to put the drops in twice a day and be sure to bring him back next week. Right now, it sounds as if my grandfather needs help. Oh, and Jim, lets keep it to ourselves for now."

Once they were alone, Andrew sat Mark down with a whisky. "Now, tell me why Ria was there, and why you were there at the same time."

"Gramps called. Said he wanted me to wait behind the stage in the barn until he slammed the door. I thought it must be a surprise he had in mind, you know how he loves giving surprises; and did I get the surprise of my life when I saw Ria. She actually had me believing her until she was silhouetted in the doorway and I saw she was pregnant. Gramps told me then why she had really come. Is it really yours?"

"No, and that's one thing you can be absolutely certain of."

"She doesn't want you to know about the baby."

"Of course she doesn't, she knows it's not possible, but she can certainly put a spanner in the works at the wedding. I can't let Grandfather deal with this alone. Coming with me?"

"Afraid not, I rescheduled a viewing to this evening, when Gramps asked me to go over this afternoon. It was strange. I didn't do anything, but he kept thanking me. Apparently, Grandmother said he wasn't to tell you and Clare, because it would spoil your day, but I think you both need to know."

Andrew gave a knowing smile. "Of course. And don't worry, Grandfather isn't losing it; in fact he's way ahead. That's why he sent for you and I'm really glad he did. Clever thinking," Andrew chuckled admiringly.

"You've lost me."

"Got to dash right now, but remind me to enlighten you about his Naval tactics one day."

Arthur welcomed Andrew with relief, satisfied that his plan had worked, when his grandson turned up at the house less than two hours later. Grace however looked accusingly at Arthur when Andrew made the reason for his unexpected visit clear.

"She would have gone abroad and we would have seen the last of her, if we had just given her the money. Andrew need never have known. Why did you tell him?"

Andrew jumped to his defence. "Gramps didn't tell me. I heard on the grapevine."

"I find that extremely hard to believe when she doesn't even want *you* to know she is having your child."

"Of course she doesn't, because it isn't possible."

Grace and Arthur looked bewildered. "How can you be

sure, when you have," Grace looked disapproving, "cohabited for a year."

"You wouldn't allow her name to be mentioned, or I could have explained that she lived in the cottage and I lived in the flat over the surgery. All perfectly respectable, Grandmother. I was nicely surprised when she wanted to wait. Old fashioned by today's standards, so not what I expected from her, but it's very clear why, now."

Arthur looked delighted, but Grace asked, with heightened colour, "Are you saying that you never actually ... bedded that dreadful woman?"

Andrew hid a smile."That is exactly what I am saying, Grandmother."

Grace relaxed visibly. "So she has nothing to blackmail us with or cause any scandal."

She nodded happily. "Clare need not know about this. The wedding can go ahead as planned and just to make certain, we will let Ria think she'll get the money after the wedding ceremony, as arranged, providing she doesn't cause a scene. We will deal with her and her little games, when you and Clare are safely married."

Andrew stood up preparing to leave and Arthur followed him to the hall.

"I shall tell Clare, Gramps, or she'll take it badly when she does find out."

"I agree, son. Grandmother is only looking out for you both. This marriage means everything to her."

Andrew grinned. "Me too."

"Unanimous then." Arthur gripped his hand. "Glad you came. There will be a phone call from her any time now."

"I'll stay if you're worried."

"No, we're fine. Peter's nearby."

"Okay, but don't stand any nonsense and call if you are the least bit worried."

It was gone nine by the time Andrew got home, and as he opened the front door the phone was ringing. Expecting it to be Clare, he quickly picked it up, nerves jarring as he heard the stress in his grandfather's brief, staccato sentences.

"Had a call after you left. Changed her mind. Common law wife. Taking you to court. Half of everything you own. Wish I'd just given her the money. Grandmother is close to a break down."

"Calm down, or you will both have a break down. This is my problem and I will deal with it. First thing in the morning, I'll hire a solicitor. Both of you get some sleep please and I will be in touch as soon as possible."

Andrew stood for a moment, wishing he felt as confident as he pretended, dreading Clare's reaction to the only possible solution he could think of until this mess was sorted.

CHAPTER SEVENTEEN

Jason looked up from his newspaper as Ria put her phone down.

She had phoned to tell Arthur she wasn't prepared to wait any longer, after the trick he pulled yesterday, but then she heard Grace whisper, 'For goodness sake just give her the money,' and she was sure he would pay up, just to keep Grace happy.

"Give them a day to stew?" Jason sipped his whisky, looking bored.

Ria held her stomach. "Not sure I can." She screwed her face up, swallowing hard.

"Not like you to let nerves get the better... of..." he broke off and stared as Ria made a dash for the bathroom.

Clare sat staring into space. Andrew had phoned an hour ago, this time sounding completely distracted, saying he would have to cancel the wedding until he cleared things up with Ria. And he sounded hurt as he asked, "What did I do to make her hate me so much?"

Was he hoping she would come back to him? Questions teemed through her mind. Should she take the flat off the market? Withdraw her resignation; even supposing she could? Send her wedding dress back? With no answers and devastated by the thought that she was losing Andrew she ran sobbing from the flat.

Laura gazed in disbelief as Clare threw herself into her arms sobbing uncontrollably, disbelief that turned to shocked dismay as Andrew's phone call cancelling the wedding was repeated.

A long silence followed until Laura said shakily, "I need to speak to Alan."

Alan was in the garden, but came when Laura called, expecting it to be the phone call he was waiting for, but on seeing her face he quickly kicked off his muddy shoes and hurried towards her, then on seeing Clare sitting at the kitchen table sobbing, he whispered, "Andrew?"

Pale-faced he dropped heavily onto a chair as Laura hastily assured him that Andrew was all right. "Sorry, dear, I didn't mean to frighten you."

Laura caught his trembling hands in her own and Clare saw the look that Connie and Jim shared. Would she ever have that? With an effort she pulled herself together.

"I'll go. I shouldn't be upsetting you. Andrew must have realised he still loves Ria," she said despairingly.

Alan looked up in amazement. "Nonsense! He's never been happier than he is with you."

"That's what I needed to talk to you about, dear. Andrew has cancelled the wedding without any explanation. Do you know anything about it?"

Alan's mouth dropped open and it was obvious he didn't.

"He must have said something." He looked at Clare. "Have you quarrelled?"

She shook her head. "He just said he had to sort things out with Ria and didn't want me involved."

Alan gave a big sigh. "So you assumed the worst? Really, Clare!"

"Well wouldn't you?" she demanded tearfully.

"No. Something has obviously happened. I'll ring him right now and find out what."

He shuffled into the hallway in his stocking feet and they heard him say, after listening for several minutes, "Well, tell him to ring me the minute he comes back. The poor girl is beside herself."

Alan returned to the kitchen. "Arthur says Andrew is hiring a solicitor, as we speak, and doesn't want you involved." He looked serious. "Think I might pop down; see if I can help. All right with you my love?"

"Of course."

Clare stood up. "I'm coming too. I'll go home and pack an overnight bag."

About to object, Alan changed his mind. "Right! We will leave in the morning."

He arranged to pick her up at seven o'clock the following morning, so she set her alarm for six o'clock, but at six thirty she received a text message from him:

Sorry Clare. Don't hate me. Best I go alone until we know the problem. Will ring the minute I know anything. x

She tried to ring him but his phone was switched off, so she drove round to see her mother.

"Did you know he was going without me?" she asked tearfully.

"I sort of guessed, when he left at five o'clock," Laura confessed.

"Why didn't you stop him?" Clare demanded.

"I think it might be for the best, dear. Let Andrew deal with this in his own way. He obviously needs to."

"But *I* need to know what's going on," Clare insisted.

"Alan will ring as soon as he finds out anything. Please be patient."

Hearing Clare's familiar stubborn tone, Laura gave a despairing sigh.

She was a devout Christian and not for the first time, the proverb, 'Honour thy mother and father', rang in her mind. She had paid dearly for the lie she had been living all these years. But with the happiness she had found lately, she thought God might have finally forgiven her... or perhaps not.

CHAPTER EIGHTEEN

Laurie watched Ria walk swiftly up the path of a semi detached house and ring the bell, before running back to her 4×4, to wait for the young blonde girl slipping into a warm coat to join her.

It was raining hard and the girl hurried, head down, so a clear picture of her was not possible, but he quickly took one of the house before following them.

After a fifteen minute journey they pulled into the hospital car park, and walked to the automatic doors. Laurie debated whether to follow, but deciding he would look conspicuous, waited in the car and was glad he did when Ria came out quickly, got into her car and started talking angrily on her mobile phone.

Half an hour later, the blonde girl came out and Ria appeared to be having angry words with her as well, as he followed them back to the house, where Ria hardly gave the girl time to close the car door before pulling away.

Following her back to her flat, he watched her let herself in and slam the door hard behind her and shortly after that, the man came out and he followed him to a Chinese Takeaway in town.

It was getting dark, storm clouds were gathering and they were obviously planning to settle in for the night, so Laurie decided to call it a day and go back to his hotel.

It had been a satisfying day discovering where Ria lived

and that the dark haired, olive skinned man lived with her, but he was curious about the girl. Was she part of the set up, and if so, how?

Ria slammed the phone down and scowled at Jason.

"I can't even get to speak to the old man. I knew I should have rung sooner. Why do I listen to you? The maid keeps answering. Just says contact Mr Davenport and puts the phone down. All he says is, see you in court. Suddenly they aren't worried about scandal. It wasn't supposed to be like this." She thumped the arm of the chair. "If everything had gone to plan we would be in Italy now."

"We can still go to Italy and have a good life," Jason said quietly.

Ria raised her eyebrows. "On a television engineer's pay?"

He looked resigned. "What do you actually want from life, Ria?"

"I thought you knew. You did when we planned this together."

"That was when you were happy with fifty odd thousand from Davenport. Now suddenly it's not enough; you want hundreds of thousands from the old folk; since you dreamt up this pregnancy nonsense?"

"It won't be nonsense if it works," Ria snapped.

"Well you can't have it both ways. Davenport obviously intends taking *you* to court now."

"And *who* came up with that idea?" She glared at him accusingly, then in a shrill voice said, "And *just to top it all; Monica comes up with the brilliant news that Daddy* wants her to go and live in France with them to have her baby. *She is ecstatic.* It upsets my plans, of course; but hurrah! *She is over the moon* – and expects *me to be thrilled for her. Great!*"

Jason picked up his newspaper and shrugged. "It was a mad idea anyway."

Ria suddenly put her hand over her mouth and dashed to the bathroom.

"You're making yourself ill; you need to go and get something for that," he called as she disappeared.

Over the next two days, Ria couldn't keep anything down and Jason insisted on her seeing a doctor.

Having examined her the doctor smiled. "Absolutely fine. Roughly two months I would say. Make an appointment with the maternity clinic for more ..."

Ria came to in a green curtained cubicle with a cool flannel on her forehead and an elderly nurse calmly taking her pulse.

"No. No," she wept as memory came flooding back.

The nurse gave a resigned sigh. "Will you girls *never* learn that if you play with fire you *will* get burnt?"

Jason took her home and as instructed made her comfortable, with a warm drink. Her shocked silence panicked him.

This staring into space was freaking him out. Why wasn't she screaming and shouting? He could handle that; he was used to it. He dithered whether to call her father, but having left him in the lurch, he wasn't at all sure how John would take the news that he had got his daughter pregnant and planned to run away with her, especially when he didn't even know they had been seeing one another for eighteen months. Ria had insisted on keeping it secret, so that John would believe she was going to marry Davenport.

CHAPTER NINETEEN

Alan arrived at the cottage to find Andrew deep in conversation with Simon Dunbar, from the firm, Dunbar and Blake.

In his mid thirties, Simon was well versed in the financial problems of couples splitting up, and more than a little puzzled by Andrew's reluctance to sue his ex fiancée for fraud, even though the bank confirmed regular, large sums of cash had been transferred from his business account, into her private one.

It left him wondering why Andrew had hired him and was relieved when Alan turned up. But even when his father suggested taking out a restraining order to protect the grandparents, he murmured, "Is that really necessary, Dad?"

"Yes, it is, Andrew. I don't know the whole story yet, but Arthur says she has already tried blackmailing them. We can't allow her to upset *them; it isn't fair.*"

"But that's exactly what I am trying to avoid. She knows how they hate scandal; that will be why she went to them. I called her bluff when she started threatening *me*. I just said see you in court, thinking that if Mr Dunbar wrote a warning letter, it would make her see sense. She knows the baby isn't mine."

Alan looked shocked. "She's pregnant? And you're sure it isn't yours?"

"Absolutely." Andrew looked his father straight in the eye,

knowing that it was hard to believe, when she had lived in his cottage for a year.

"So actually, she paid herself a salary, and lived free for the year. A good point to raise in court?" Alan asked.

Simon nodded. "And, it would appear, cheated you from the very beginning as well as trying to run off with all of your possessions."

"That's what Clare said, and would have succeeded if it hadn't been for the snow – and Connie's phone call. Clare was amazing too."

Simon Dunbar collected his brief case and stood up. He took Andrew's word for it that he wasn't the father of the child, but a jury would want proof. It was a strange case.

"Have a good talk with your father. I'll get a letter in the post today. This Victoria Kirby is obviously a law unto herself. Doesn't realise the penalty for perjury. She will find out though if she persists."

"Oh, you can be sure she'll have a plausible story ready," Alan said disparagingly.

Andrew shrugged. "Thought Grandfather would just pay up, rather than have Grandmother upset. And of course he would have, if Mark hadn't told me what was going on – as Grandfather intended of course."

Simon Dunbar looked thoughtful. Not as gullible as the Kirby woman thought perhaps but it was obviously making her more determined.

Soon after Simon Dunbar's car disappeared out of the drive, Connie made her way along the walkway. "Saw ye come, Alan. Ye must've started out early. Breakfast's nearly done. Don't s'pose you've eaten either, Andrew," she tutted.

"Not now you mention it." Andrew put his arm around her shoulders. "Thanks, Connie. Have you had yours?"

"Jim thought we should wait."

Alan gave her a knowing smile. "Sure it was Jim?"

"None of ye cheek now. Don't be long; it'll be ready dreckly."

She bustled out and they heard her singing to herself. "Ding dong the bells are gonna chime."

Andrew looked sad. "She and Jim are going to be really upset about cancelling the wedding, but I can't go ahead, even if Clare still wants me, with all this sordid mess hanging over my head."

"Speaking of which, we need to ring her. She is going to be mad enough with me, but you had better be ready to eat a very large plate of humble pie."

He explained on their way and over breakfast faces were long, as Andrew also explained why he would have to cancel the wedding.

After a long silence Arthur asked tentatively, "Mind if I make a suggestion?"

"Any are welcome," Andrew agreed forlornly.

"Don't say cancel. It sounds too final. Postpone sounds hopeful and after all, that is what you mean, isn't it?"

Andrew sagged, then got up and rushed out. "Must speak to Clare. Why didn't I think of that?"

"Why didn't we all?" Alan said, closing his eyes, remembering Clare's tear stained face.

Connie gave a grim nod. "Thought she was bein' left high an dry agen."

Ten minutes later Andrew returned and sat down looking miserable. "No answer and her mobile's switched off. I rang Laura. She was worried too. Said Clare was distraught and just dashed out. How could I have been so stupid and thoughtless? I should have explained instead of trying to keep it to myself. I've been a complete fool. She's obviously taken off again."

On her way to the kitchen, Connie raised her eyebrows to Jim, and he glanced at the big clock. It was eleven o'clock. Connie indicated 'soon', in their own sign language.

Since his stroke, they had found a comforting way of communicating without words and their awareness of what the other one was thinking was quite uncanny.

Engrossed in their own thoughts Andrew and Alan missed the signals and Andrew stood up again.

"I must go. Can't afford to miss a call from Simon Dunbar. You should sleep, Dad. Use the cottage."

"My mind is too busy to sleep. Think I'll go over and see Arthur and Grace, for a couple of hours."

"If you wait until this evening I'll drive. You've driven far enough today."

"I think I need to speak to them alone, Son. I haven't seen them for a long time. Not sure how they feel about me marrying again. Don't mind do you?"

"Course not; and don't worry. They adore Clare, and will love Laura. Who wouldn't?"

Jim put another log on the fire and settled in his chair, where he could see the clock.

"Sit a while, Alan. Rest for an hour before you drive again."

It was cold and blustery outside and Alan gladly sat in the other chair; the one that Clare always sat in, Jim thought, happy that she must be on her way, as Connie said.

Watching him, Alan saw the anxiety on his face and, knowing how he had always loved Andrew like the son he never had, his heart went out to him. He had obviously set *his* heart on Clare being the only girl for Andrew.

He had known Jim for a good many years; since Connie first took pity on him, in fact.

She found him sitting by the wayside, having been knocked off his motorbike by a hit and run driver. He was not badly hurt, just bruised, badly shaken and suffering from shock; certainly not fit to travel on to St Ives where he was booked in at a camp site.

Being Connie, she arranged for his bike to be picked up by a local garage and took him home to her cottage. It was high summer, so by the time he was fit enough to travel, his booking had been taken and she asked what he planned to do. He said he had come down intending to look for a cottage near the coast and was delighted when she offered him her spare room until he found something suitable.

Then she spent time driving him to view cottages, but when he did eventually find something – six months later, they were enjoying each other's company too much to part and decided to get married.

A marriage made in heaven, Rosemary had said. That was when Andrew was twelve and he and Mark and Kathy spent long summer days together, whilst staying at 'Tamarisks'. He and Rosemary always thought Kathy would choose Andrew, and he knew Andrew had a soft spot for her, but there was never anyone but Mark for Kathy, even though he treated her like one of the lads. How different her life was now, with two lovely children and an adoring husband. How many times had he wished though, that she had chosen Andrew when that awful woman had him wrapped around her little finger.

He looked across at Jim again. His head was nodding with the warmth of the fire. Please God don't take him for a long time, he prayed.

He rose quietly and walked out to the kitchen where Connie was ironing. "See you later, Connie. Thank you for the breakfast. It was wonderful, as always."

Arthur and Grace greeted Alan fondly. "Far too long since we last saw you, old chap." "We've missed you, Alan," they said as Alan shook Arthur's hand and kissed Grace's cheek. "Wasn't sure I would still be welcome."

Grace looked sad. "Could you ever not be? You were our lovely girl's soul mate. She loved you dearly and so do we. You will always be part of our family."

"Andrew says how much you like Clare, I hope you will like her mother as well."

"Rosemary spoke very fondly of her and if she is anything like her daughter..." Grace touched his arm reassuringly.

About to agree, Alan changed his mind and smiled. "Not quite so forthright perhaps, but Clare is just what Andrew needs."

Arthur and Grace nodded. "Not like that useless, conniving hussy who is causing so much trouble. And what kind of a name is Ria for goodness sake?" Grace said irritably.

"Short for Victoria, I learnt from the solicitor this morning."

Alan sank gratefully into a comfy chair by the fire, his early morning catching up on him.

"Trust her to take a perfectly good name and ruin it." Grace tutted as Hannah entered, pushing a well filled tea trolley.

Glad of the interruption, Alan complimented her on the delicious array of cake and scones. "And you must be thrilled to have another grand-child. I'm still waiting for a first."

Hannah handed them all tea plates and napkins and pushed the trolley close.

"I'm sure it won't be long now, Mr Alan. I've never seen a happier couple than your Andrew and his Clare."

On her way to the door, she gave Grace a tentative look before smiling at him. "Every happiness to you and your new wife."

"Thank you, Hannah. Much appreciated."

Arthur looked concerned. "You must bring Laura down as soon as possible. Squash any doubts that we mind you marrying again, Alan."

Grace nodded, before asking, "So what happened with the solicitor this morning?"

"That is the main reason I travelled down. Andrew must tell you what he intends doing, but I think a restraining order is needed. She can't be allowed to come here when ever it suits her. Do I have your permission to insist? Andrew won't agree, because he is afraid she will retaliate and upset you."

"Gossip must be avoided at all costs," Grace said quickly.

"But he must do whatever he has to," Arthur argued sternly. "Laurie contacted me this morning. He has located where she is living and has sent the address."

He left them and went to a small room leading off the big hall. Ostensibly commandeered for his computer and paper work, he referred to it as his cabin, and if, as he sometimes did, miss the comradeship of his fellow officers, he would retire to its comforting solitude, to relive Naval days and imbibe freely on Navy Rum, fondly believing Grace to be unaware of his self indulgent walk down memory lane, when in actual fact she sympathetically made sure he never ran out of rum, and quite often had her own trip down memory lane by going through her wardrobes, reminding herself of memorable occasions and dresses she had worn to them.

He shut the door, sighing heavily, knowing Grace was going to be inconsolable about Andrew's decision to cancel the wedding.

Returning with an envelope, he gave it to Alan. "The solicitor will need to see this, there are photographs as well as two addresses. Laurie is coming to stay for a few days next week, but in the meantime he will continue watching them."

"I had no idea you were this involved. Does Andrew know?"

"Probably not; there hasn't been much to report until now."

Arthur spoke casually but there was a hint of amusement in his voice.

Alan looked at him with undisguised admiration. "And here am I thinking you need protection." He laughed out loud. "Wait until I tell Andrew. And to think Mark thought you were losing the plot."

Grace looked curious and Arthur said quickly, "Oh yes, we got our wires crossed; not hard to do with Mark as you know. Always one step behind. Bless him."

Alan laughingly agreed and the subject was dropped, as Hannah came to take the trolley.

"Think I'll get back before dark. Not used to the narrow roads now and it's been a long day."

They stood and waved him off. "I will bring Laura, soon."

"Please do," they choroused, sorry to see him go. He brought back such endearing memories of Rosemary.

On the familiar drive back to Andrew's cottage, Alan also

reminisced sadly. Rosemary would always be in his heart, but how fortunate he was to have someone as loving as Laura, knowing their union was blessed by Rosemary. Her last words rang in his ears. "I'm leaving you in good hands my darling. Take care of her."

Tears blurred his vision and he pulled over. After sitting for half an hour, he took his mobile phone out and rang home, desperate just to hear Laura's voice, but there was no reply.

Coming back to Cornwall was a mistake. Too much heartache to bear. He didn't stop to think when he came rushing down, how raw his feelings still were. Everything happening so quickly of late had taken the edge off his grief, but seeing the old folk brought it all back and Laura was the only one who could soothe his heartache, as only she had been able to ease Rosemary's pain and suffering with her ability to make her smile, even on the bad days.

Rain started to hit the windscreen. Bodmin Moor was fast becoming shrouded in mist, blotting out wonderful landscape that on a fine day stretched as far as the eye could see. But that was Cornwall; the Cornwall that once in the blood, kept calling you back.

He closed his mind with a determined effort. That was all behind him. Laura was just a few hours away.

The small hump-backed bridge on the outskirts of the picturesque village came in sight and he drove over it, to where the 'Three Feathers' pub, with its colourful window boxes and planters, vied for domination with the large wood built community hall, set back in the trees nearby; both providing the only source of entertainment for residents of the quaint cottages and the surrounding area for miles around.

He sighed, remembering balmy summer nights, sitting with a motley crew of friends, at the wooden tables in the well kept pub gardens, listening to the lively entertainment in the nearby hall, knowing the youngsters were safe and enjoying themselves.

They had always come down for a month during Andrew's school holidays, again at Easter and always for Christmas and New Year. As a teacher, Rosemary had the same holidays as Andrew, but his own time off had depended on his partner Kevin, who, with five children to support, was always glad of the extra cash.

Driving on through the village and up the hill, in the gathering dusk and heavy rain, the welcome sight of the five bar gate came into view, and he was grateful that Andrew had thought to leave it open for him.

Lights from the sitting room and hallway said Andrew was home, and making a dash for the front door, he let himself in, calling "Its only me."

In the throes of taking his wet coat off, Clare appeared leaning nonchalantly against the kitchen doorway, watching in silence as he hung his damp waterproof on a carved wooden coat peg and slowly turned to look at her, holding on to the peg for support.

"I can only apologise. I don't expect you to forgive me. I thought I could help. I thought it was for the best. I was mistaken. I should never have come. There is nothing I can do, so I've just come to pick up my things. I'm going home." His voice broke. "I really, really need to be with your mother."

Clare moved aside and Laura walked quickly towards him, arms outstretched.

Clare walked away as he buried his face in Laura's

shoulder and after she heard them go upstairs, all was quiet except for the faint murmur of her mother's voice.

Left alone, she decided to go along and let Connie and Jim know they were here.

She looked at her watch. Four o'clock. It had taken longer than she anticipated to drive down, because they got lost several times once they left the motorway.

The Sat Nav hadn't helped, it kept telling her to turn right; taking them back to the same spot in the middle of nowhere. *It* appeared to be as bewildered as her mother, who kept repeating that all the roads looked the same.

Anticipating the warm welcome awaiting her and picturing their surprise, she hurried along the walkway. Later she would bring her mother to meet Connie and Jim. They would get along famously.

About to knock, Connie opened the door.

"Come on in, me lovely. Yer late an' Jim's worried."

"But..." Clare protested as Connie ushered her into the sitting room, where Jim was getting out of his chair. "Thought you'd never get here, lass."

"But you didn't know I was coming."

"Course we did," Connie laughed. "Now sit an' tell what ye 'ave in mind."

She sat in her usual chair and they waited expectantly.

"I don't know. Andrew phoned, saying he was cancelling the wedding and I haven't heard from him since, then Alan came rushing down after speaking to Mark, so something is obviously wrong, but all he said just now was that he can't help and it was a mistake for him to come. He was too upset to make much sense and Mum is at the cottage with him. Has Andrew decided that he wants Ria after all?"

Her eyes searched theirs desperately, and they stared

187

back incredulously, just as the door burst open and Andrew rushed in to catch her in a bear hug.

"Talk about good timing," Jim whispered, as he and Connie sighed with relief.

Clare allowed the pent up tears to flow as Andrew kept a firm hold, mumbling emotionally, "I'm sorry. I'm so sorry sweetheart. I didn't want you involved. I still don't. This whole thing is so sordid."

He held her shoulders so that he could see her face and she angrily wiped the tears away with the back of her hand, pushing him away to stand hands on hips, regarding him with flashing dark blue eyes.

"For heavens sake, tell me what all the fuss is about. Explain, what can possibly prevent our wedding in three weeks time. Surely you..." She petered off as he gave a resigned smile and guided her backwards into the chair. "Best sit down."

"Now you've really got me worried," she said, calming down, but still bristling with impatience.

"I'll put kettle on."

"Thanks Connie." Andrew sat and took Clare's hand as doubt began to show in her eyes.

"Start with delay, not cancel," Jim advised, getting up and following Connie.

"What was that about?" Clare demanded, beginning to get impatient again, and Andrew grinned in spite of himself.

"I was clumsy. Delay, not cancel our wedding."

"That remains to be seen if you don't hurry up."

She gave him a warning flash, but as he revealed the worry of the last few days, she touched his cheek sympathetically.

"Grandmother insists we should go ahead, but it would

be nice to get married without this awful business hanging over our heads; and I wasn't even sure you would still want to marry me, until I prove that I'm not a rapist or the father of the child."

Clare looked sad. "Your word is good enough for me, but I can see your point. We will just wait until the horizon is clear. Nothing must spoil our wedding day."

He kissed her tenderly. "And nothing will. I promise you."

Clare pursed her lips. "And no more sparing my feelings."

Connie and Jim came back with the tea, and Connie invited Laura along to dinner.

"Alan was comin' anyway and there's plenty to go round." She beamed at Clare, obviously delighted that she was back. "So when you comin' down fer good?"

"I'm ready. Only bringing personal bits. I'm selling the flat furnished." She looked at Andrew. "When do you think?"

He gave a teasing grin. "I thought you and Grandmother had it sewn up already," he said dodging a pillow.

"We should get back and see if Mum and your Dad are okay."

Wandering back hand in hand they were content to put their plans aside for the time being and concentrate on the problem in hand, together.

There was no sign of Alan or Laura as they let themselves in, and assuming they were still resting, made themselves comfortable by the sitting room fire. But when there was no sound by half past five, Clare went upstairs to knock on the bedroom door. Her mother was a light sleeper, so surprised at no answer, she quietly turned the handle and peeped in.

Andrew looked up as Clare returned to the sitting room. She was looking puzzled.

"They aren't there."

"Perhaps they've gone to see Gramps and Grandmother. I know Dad was keen for them to meet your mum."

"Surely they would have said?"

"I didn't see them when I came home. Saw your case in the hall and guessed you would be at Connie's. Didn't know your mum was here until you said. Dad usually leaves a note if I'm out and he's going anywhere. Have a look on the kitchen table."

Clare went and returned waving a sheet of note paper. It was written by Laura and they read it together.

Hello Dears.

I'm taking Dad home. Returning to old haunts can be very traumatic and he was not prepared for the emotion it caused him. You probably aren't aware, Andrew, that Dad has been having help for his grief. He asked me not to worry you and I agreed because I thought he was coping. I will be taking him to see the therapist, so don't worry.

He is also upset to realise there is nothing practical he can do to help with your problems, but asks me to say that if financial help is needed, don't hesitate to come to him. Sorry to run off like this. Need to get Dad home. I will be driving, so if necessary will stop overnight at an hotel I know in Bournemouth. Will ring from home.

All our love Mum and Dad.

After the initial surprise, Clare said her mother shouldn't be driving all that way, so late at night. "Why didn't she say?"

"Probably thought you would stop her?"

"I jolly well would have."

Andrew pulled a face. "There you go then."

"There I go then, what?" Clare asked indignantly.

"There you go then, *why she didn't say.*"

Clare pouted. "Stop being so logical. That's my job."

Andrew caught her to him and tickled her until she begged for mercy and then, long mesmerising kisses took them to a world of their own, where problems vanished like magic and dreams lived on.

CHAPTER TWENTY

Laurie sat opposite Grace and Arthur at the breakfast table. Sprightly and alert for his seventy-two years, he looked questioningly, first at Arthur then Grace.

"You are actually prepared to just hand over this large sum of money?"

Arthur looked worried and remained silent, but Grace replied quickly, "If it means the wedding can go ahead and we never see her again."

"No guarantees there. She looks a pretty hard case to me. Could come back for more. Not sure about the younger woman. Think I might call on her."

The telephone rang in the hall and Hannah entered to say Andrew would be over at about twelve o'clock.

Arthur gave a sigh of relief. Laurie was right and Grace might listen to Andrew.

"Haven't seen Andrew since he was a boy," Laurie said reminiscently.

Grace pursed her lips. "Too soft," she said, adding acerbically, "Thank heavens his taste in women has improved."

"Considerably," Arthur agreed.

Laurie studied Grace curiously. She was usually so strong. He remembered how she kept the Navy wives in order with her high standards and fought for their rights, so fiercely.

So why was she insisting on giving in to these outrageous demands? It didn't make sense.

Seeing his look and knowing he would ferret until he got answers, Grace excused herself. "I'll just remind Hannah there will be four for lunch."

She was relying on Clare marrying Andrew, because she was sure she was right about her recent convictions.

Andrew didn't say Clare would be with him as he wanted to surprise them and they were delighted to be able to introduce her to Laurie.

Andew remembered Laurie as a frequent visitor at 'Tamerisks', and Gramps referring to him as his opposite number. At ten years old, that made Laurie extremely important.

Looking at him now, he saw the well toned physique of a man who could easily pass for ten years younger than he was, whereas Gramps, on his own admission, having succumbed to easy living, Hannah's cooking and Cornish cream teas since retiring, looked his age.

Over lunch, Andrew started to say the wedding was to be postponed until any problems were dealt with, but Grace interrupted, as if the matter was entirely out of his hands.

"No, Andrew. We will just give her the money. You and Clare will have your day."

"Sorry, Grandmother." Clare spoke up quietly but firmly. "Andrew and I have already decided to wait until such claims as the child being his, or her being his common law wife, have been disproved. No tenterhooks. No disruptions. Just harmony, on what is going to be an amazing day."

Taken by surprise, Grace looked about to demur, but instead just murmured, "Oh! Of course, dear."

Later when the three men were playing snooker, and Arthur was taking his turn, Laurie said to Andrew, "Never thought I'd see anyone dissuade your grandmother from something she'd set her heart on. She's quite a girl, that Clare of yours."

"Isn't she though?" Andrew rubbed chalk on his cue.

Laurie laughed. "Very *like* your grandmother, in fact."

Andrew stopped chalking. "Oh dear!"

"Count your blessings, boy."

"Did you ever get married?"

"No."

Hearing Laurie's last comment Arthur chuckled, "Not for the lack of offers."

"Ah! As the old fisherman's tale goes, I was the one who got away."

"Any regrets?" Andrew asked out of curiosity, purposely missing the blue ball.

"That the only woman I was ever able to love, married someone else. Oh yes!"

Laurie sent the white ball in after the blue, leaving Arthur to clear the table with a triumphant flourish. "You can't win them all, Shipmate."

"No, you lucky old sea dog," Laurie said with rueful good humour.

Excluded from what was obviously a private joke, Andrew focused intently on replacing his cue on the rack, his mind filled with worrying suspicions.

On their way home, Clare remarked what a nice man Laurie was, and Andrew looked worried. "He certainly took a shine to you."

"Grace mentioned that he has never married. Wonder why?"

"Apparently the only woman he ever loved, married someone else."

Clare looked thoughtful. "How romantic. Wonder what she was like?"

"Much like you apparently, and I don't trust him, especially with Grandmother," Andrew commented shortly, as he stopped the car and got out to open the gate.

Obviously watching for them, Mark hurried towards the car, holding Emma.

"Simon Dunbar phoned. Needs to speak to you urgently. Got to go."

He hurried back, and they heard Emma crying loudly as they let themselves into the cottage.

"Teething," Clare said sympathetically.

Andrew looked surprised. "And you would know because?"

She twinkled her eyes at him. "Connie told me, for future advice."

Andrew caught her to him, his grey eyes searching her face.

"Future advice for us?"

"Of course," she reassured him gently, hating to see his uncertainty. They should have been getting married in nine days' time. She pushed him gently away.

"Go and make your phone call to Simon Dunbar. Maybe it's good news."

Twenty minutes later, Andrew came into the kitchen looking pleased.

"Apparently, when Simon called on her, Ria was totally shocked that he knew her address and wouldn't let him in. She spoke to him by opening the door six inches and was interestingly considering waiving all rights as my common law wife. He thinks she just said it to get rid of him though, because when he got back to his office she phoned saying it would cost me two hundred thousand pounds. I could live with that."

Clare jerked into business mode. "You most certainly couldn't. I bet the solicitor didn't advise it either."

"Well, no, but we could go ahead and get married, couldn't we?"

"Yes, but at what cost? It's as good as admitting she is right."

Andrew looked downcast. "Never thought of that."

Clare gave an exasperated groan. "Dear lord give me patience, but please hurry. Well you can be certain she has. Phone Simon back and give a definite thumbs down."

She banged the kettle down and jerked the switch on. "I need a cup of tea."

"I need a whisky," Andrew said on his way to the phone in the hall.

"Even better," she agreed, promptly switching the kettle off.

When he returned, tail between legs, she put her arms around his waist and rested her head against his chest. She could hear the steady beat of his heart. It was comforting, dependable, trustworthy.

"Don't ever change," she whispered, hugging him closer.

He pulled her down onto the settee. "Are you sure you mean that?"

"Yes. The insurance world taught me to doubt; that's why I'm the way I am."

"Lucky for me you are, and that we met when we did. Quite a day wasn't it? And did I ever tell you it was my birthday?"

She pulled away from him in surprise. "No you never did. Why not?"

He gave a mischievous grin. "Assumed you would know. You complained, contradicted or said I know, to everything I said or did, but it *was* 30th November."

She gave him a questioning look. "And?"

"The reason I'm called Andrew?"

Clare gave a long suffering sigh. "And your point is?"

"You must've heard of *Saint* Andrew's day?" He laughed, pulling her back into his arms, kissing her until she pulled away.

"Was getting married on your birthday important to you?"

"No. Ria said it was so that her mother would be able to come after the holiday season was over. She runs a hotel in Malta." He shrugged. "She didn't even remember it was my birthday."

Andrew heaved himself off the settee. "How about that whisky?"

Watching him pour the amber coloured liquid into two cut glass tumblers, Clare came to a decision.

"I'll go home on Monday and spend the week packing and clearing up loose ends."

Andrew placed a glass beside her. "You will come back won't you?"

"Before the weekend; I promise," she said softly.

He sat down beside her, staring unhappily into his drink. "I wouldn't blame you if you didn't. I've made such a mess of things."

"Don't even think that. I could happily strangle the woman, but I'm grateful she left you. Now. Why don't we invite Connie and Jim here for a change this evening?"

Andrew pulled her closer. "Nice idea. By the way, Grandmother's invited us over for Gramps' eightieth birthday on Sunday. Just us, Mark, Kathy and the children." Looking thoughtful he added, "And Laurie."

For a while they talked about how much of her home

would fit into the cottage, until a comfortable silence enveloped them as daylight faded and twilight fell, sending dancing shadows from the log fire, around the room.

Aware of an inner peace she had never known before, she asked herself, as she had many times lately, what it was that gave her that inexplicable, almost magical feeling of coming home. As if Andrew and this place had been waiting for her.

Andrew stirred beside her. "You look comfortable. Shall I go and invite Connie and Jim?"

"I'll go." She turned her head and kissed him lightly. "Won't be long. Don't move."

At the end of the walkway, she wandered past Connie's door to stand by the dry stone wall and marvel at the wondrous view down though the meadow, to where it met the narrow, tumbling river bordering the two acre property. It was a beautiful still evening and only the soft rush of the river, meandering its way on through the village, broke the encompassing silence, until a bird, disturbed by Clare's presence, called from a nearby pine tree.

"Sorry to disturb you," Clare called back softly, becoming aware of a breathtaking scent drifting towards her, which disappointingly she was unable to put a name to.

One day she would know the names of all the birds – and the trees, she promised herself.

CHAPTER TWENTY ONE

Having spent a whole month ranting and raving at Jason for being stupid enough to get her pregnant, Ria was now in icy control and even more determined to use whatever means necessary, to extract enough money from Andrew – or his wealthy family, to enable her to live in what she considered a style befitting her person.

"No. I have spent over a year planning this," she assured Jason as once again he wearily suggested giving up the whole idea and moving to Italy.

She narrowed her eyes at him. "Can't you see? They are afraid enough to cancel the wedding so a few more calls, and they *will* pay. You'll see."

Lips set in a determined line, she picked up her mobile phone.

Waiting for Andrew's mobile to be picked up, she frowned with disgust at her rounded belly, as a woman's voice said, "Mr Davenport is driving and unable to take your call."

"Tell him to pull over and speak to me. *Right now*," Ria demanded as she heard Andrew saying, "Tell the caller to leave a name and number and I'll call back."

The woman's voice came back on the line and started to speak but Ria rang off.

"He knew damned well who was calling," she shouted at Jason.

"Of course he did. Now calm down before you make yourself ill again."

"You don't care about what I want."

Jason sighed as she flung herself into the armchair.

"I do. I love you. I'm just sure we can be happy without all this aggravation."

"Well I didn't spend all that time buried in the country, to give in now."

She stared at him sulkily. "I was bored out of my mind. No shops, theatres, cinemas, restaurants or entertainment of any sort," she grumbled.

"Your choice. No one made you," Jason reminded her. "And don't forget I went on working for your dad, when I could have been in partnership with my brother in Italy."

"On a rubbish wage," Ria scoffed.

"Better than running around in circles as I am now. Heaven only knows what your father will think when he knows *why* I left him in the lurch like I did."

Jason looked depressed. He hadn't liked doing that. John had always been good to him. No good denying it though. He had willingly gone along with her plan, in a mad moment of passion, but all he really wanted was to work with his brother in Italy; there was a baby to think about now.

He pictured the joy on his mother's face, just as Ria's voice broke harshly into his thoughts, saying quickly, "Don't worry. He won't find out until we've gone," as she snatched her mobile phone up.

He watched her face contort with anger as she read out the short text: 'Contact my solicitor with anything further'.

"We'll see about that, *Mr Davenport*."

Jason didn't like her look as she stared into space.

"Whatever you're thinking," he said apprehensively,

"don't forget the money you stole from the business hasn't even been mentioned. I'd quit while you're ahead?"

"What? Oh do be quiet. I'm thinking. Twelve thousand is nothing to that family."

Face set in hard lines she continued to stare across the room before saying slowly, "If I'm right, and I know I am, those cottages are worth far more than what I was asking from the old folk. You were right about the common law wife."

Jason closed his eyes in dismay, knowing nothing he said would stop her.

"Are you sure they are his? Wish I'd never suggested it."

"They were his father's wedding present. The deeds are in his safe. Yes!" She punched the air gleefully, as Jason frowned disapprovingly. It was a gesture he hated.

Arthur's birthday lunch was in full swing, with balloons tied to his armchair and a pile of presents waiting to be opened. "Come and help me, Luke. I'll never get all that sticky tape off."

Arthur made room beside him in the big armchair and Luke enthusiastically ripped paper off and handed presents to Arthur, whose eyes lit up at the box of Havana cigars from Mark and Kathy and six bottles of Navy Rum from Laurie. Andrew held out a large rectangular parcel, wrapped in blue paper, covered with gold anchors.

"This was Clare's idea, Gramps. She thought you would like a framed map of the world, tracing all the routes you travelled during your time in the Navy. Your second in command helped, of course."

Andrew bowed to Grace, and everyone laughed.

"And Jim painted the routes in," Clare added.

Laurie got up and looked over Arthur's shoulder. "Well done, Clare! A perfect gift."

He turned to Andrew. "Your future wife obviously has your grandmother's knack of choosing a present to fit the occasion, as well."

Clare looked amused until Andrew asked sharply, "As well as what?"

"Quite a few ways," Laurie called back glibly as he opened a bottle of the Navy Rum and poured Arthur a large tot.

Clare and Andrew's eyes met over Arthur's head, and Clare sidled past the presents to reach him.

"Just too much wine talking," she assured him.

"Mm, I wonder," Andrew said, watching Laurie suspiciously.

"Well don't go putting two and two together and making six," Clare murmured, glancing across at Grace, sitting elegantly upright, in her gold velvet armchair, watching Arthur examine his picture, her love for him still showing plainly after their fifty years together.

"Well she certainly gives every appearance of living up to her name."

"I'm learning that appearances can be deceptive and it's well known that Naval parties got... quite... a bit... well you know."

"As do most parties – so I'm told," she added quickly as his eyes opened wide.

They laughed the moment off, and it wasn't until they were home and sitting on the settee together that he brought the subject up again, voicing his suspicions strongly.

"You obviously had office parties. Will you miss them?"

"I went to one but their idea of *fun* wasn't mine, and the only other one was when I went with Paul, just after we got engaged. So the answer is no I won't miss them."

Andrew gave a sigh of relief. "Unlike Grandmother, who apparently loved them."

Clare gave an exasperated tut. "Just organising them, I would imagine."

"I still need to know."

Clare tutted. "I'm sure there's nothing to know."

Andrew looked obstinate."We'll see."

"Forget it. He goes home tomorrow and you won't see him again until our wedding."

"Not even then if he's cheated on Gramps. I've asked him to drop in tomorrow, on his way home."

Clare looked horrified. "If your grandmother gets to hear she will be furious."

"I don't care. I won't have them cheating Gramps."

"But you don't know they have," Clare insisted heatedly.

Andrew spoke calmly but firmly. "No; but I intend to find out."

"I wish you'd get this angry about Ria cheating you."

He pulled her to him, and she snuggled against his chest, loving his warm muskiness as her thoughts went off at a tangent.

Andrew was so adamant about morality, how was he going to react if Grace had cheated on Arthur after instilling such high morals in them? What if she hadn't practised what she preached? It was a long way to fall, from that pedestal she was on.

She sighed, afraid happy family days could end if his suspicions were right.

"Penny for them," Andrew said softly.

"This time tomorrow, I'll be at the flat," she murmured, reluctant to reveal her thoughts.

"Don't go. You don't have to."

"I must, I need to clear the flat, plus it's mum's birthday on Saturday and Alan is taking us out to dinner."

Andrew looked hurt. "And I'm not invited?"

Taken off guard, Clare sat up and put her hand to her lips. "I wasn't supposed to say, in case you felt duty bound. They really don't expect you to travel all that way for a birthday."

"Laura's first birthday as my step mum, and soon to be mother in law? I'm coming. And not out of duty."

Clare settled down again with a contented sigh. "Wonderful!"

Laurie arrived at eleven o'clock the following morning, looking prosperous and relaxed in his Jaguar XE.

Clare showed him into the sitting room, where Andrew was opening his morning mail and excused herself before any awkward questions could be asked.

"Sorry to dash, Laurie, got to finish packing."

Sensing nothing amiss, Laurie smiled agreeably. "Of course, dear girl. No problem."

Listening from upstairs, expecting to hear raised voices, she eventually ventured down into the kitchen, set the tray and carried it though to the sitting room.

To her surprise the room was empty, but the French doors were open and she could hear faint voices, so curious as to what was happening, she followed the voices through the connecting door leading into the office.

Andrew and Laurie were leaning over the desk, looking at a letter that had arrived that morning from the solicitor, and Andrew was saying, "She is claiming her rights as a common law wife, so I need to prove we never lived together. What's this fellow like that she's living with?"

"Ah! Meant to show you yesterday."

Clare watched as Laurie produced his mobile phone.

"I took this one evening. He was all wrapped up in a duffel coat and the light isn't very good, but I managed to get his face."

Clare leant forward curiously, saying disappointedly, "It's only her cousin. The photo in the briefcase, Andrew? You remember; you said you were to meet him at the wedding?"

"Yes. How odd." Andrew stared at the hooded figure in the photo. "And I distinctly remember a hooded figure, waiting for her the night she returned my furniture. Just a silhouette, so I can't be absolutely certain, but it could be him."

Laurie touched the screen. "And this is a girl she picked up and took to the hospital. Thought I might take a closer look at her. You've got both addresses."

They returned to the sitting room and while Clare poured the coffee, Laurie arranged to phone Andrew when he had any news.

"Let's not worry Arthur. He's doing his best, but Grace is making it difficult for him to make rational decisions, because she is so set on this wedding. Personally, I think you are right in waiting for a day without problems."

He got to his feet. "And now I must be going. If I can possibly help in any way, just say the word."

"Actually, there is a small favour. Clare doesn't know the roads very well yet. Could she follow you until you reach the motorway, perhaps?"

"With pleasure."

Clare smiled gratefully. "I'm all ready."

Andrew gave her a bear hug. "See you next Saturday, and we'll drive back together on Sunday. Don't tell Mum and Dad I'm coming."

Laurie started to walk away but turned back. "If you are

driving up anyway, why don't I take Clare? It's a shame to let her drive all that way alone, when I nearly pass her door. Plus, you can drive back in one car?"

Andrew waited for Clare to refuse, knowing how she disliked decisions being made for her, and, surprised when she agreed, had a moment of disquiet as he watched her slide into the luxurious interior of the grey Jaguar XE.

Mulling over the trouble it could cause by opening up such a can of worms and the fact that Laurie had a very honest and forthright way, that according to reputation earned him trust and reassurance from clients, he had refrained from asking pertinent questions. He could well imagine him defending strongly in court, but then again there was the very charismatic, charming streak, not to mention the daredevil one that women were attracted to. Andrew shook his head. Gramps would be devastated and he actually didn't want to think him capable of deceiving him.

Connie and Jim came along to see Clare off, interrupting his thoughts.

"Don't be long," they called, waving until the grey car snaked out of sight.

"They have all certainly taken to you," Laurie commented.

"And I to them."

"That bodes good for the future. Of course winning Grace's approval was always going to be your biggest hurdle; but you have, with flying colours."

"I'm glad. I've never had a family before. It's just been mother and me. And its really rather lovely."

"How about Andrew? You are perfect for him. Is he right for you?"

Clare thought the questions were getting too personal on such a short acquaintance, and answered shortly, "Absolutely."

"And you believe this baby isn't his?"

"Without a single doubt," Clare snapped, glaring at him.

Laurie gave her a sidelong glance. "Why?"

"Because he says so," she answered, clutching her hair back tightly into its pony tail.

Laurie gave another sidelong glance. "Lucky man."

Clare sat bolt upright and twisted sideways in her seat, to face him. "I think you mean truthful and sincere."

To her astonishment Laurie burst out laughing. "You are right of course and so was Grace. She said you have a short fuse. Just *one* of the things she likes. You'll do for Andrew."

He continued chuckling to himself as she settled back in her seat and they travelled in silence for a while, as he watched her admiring the dove grey leather seats and thick pile carpets.

"Lovely isn't she?"

Clare took a chance. "Who, Grace? Is she the only woman you ever fell in love with?"

"Touche. Too much wine loosens one's tongue."

"That's roughly what I said. So does Grace have feelings for you?"

Laurie hesitated. "Let's say we understand each other."

Clare had the feeling he was toying with her again. "Time to change the subject I think. How do you intend finding out about this girl?"

"She lives in a house with three other students. I shall call with an official looking clip board and say I am checking student lodgings for problems."

"Very clever! What do you expect to learn?"

"Oh, how long she has lived there. Family, if any. Which college she belongs to; anything that will tell me her background. Why do you ask?"

"Just interested."

Laurie narrowed his eyes."I don't like the way you say that. What are you planning? Damn! I've just missed the pub where I intended us to have lunch."

He did a U turn in a convenient lay-by and drove back fifty yards to 'The Travellers Rest'.

Having parked the car he turned to her. "I repeat, what are you planning? And I'm not moving until you tell me. Andrew will never forgive me if you get hurt."

Clare opened the car door. "Let's talk while we eat. I'm starving."

"Very well, but I shall phone Andrew and leave you here, if you don't tell me."

Without a word she got out of the car, stood to attention and saluted him.

Looking sceptically amused, he led the way, opened the door, and followed as she made straight for a table by the window. After taking her coat, he held a chair, smiling to himself when she sat in another.

A waiter came with the wine list and she chose a Spritzer and he ordered a fresh orange juice for himself.

Given the difference in time, he decided, she and Grace *were* absolutely alike. Women of their time. Minds of their own. Aah, if only he was forty years younger. He sighed sadly. But then even if he was... he had learnt to live with that a long time ago.

Clearing his mind of useless regrets, he picked up a menu and passed it to Clare, only to see she was already studying one, and noting what he took to be indecision, recommended the duck.

"Mm?"

The waiter came to ask if they were ready to order, and she put the menu down. "The sea bass please."

He ordered the duck, realising that if he had said sea bass she would have chosen duck. What a girl! God help Andrew, he chuckled to himself.

Clare calmly sipped her Spritzer and put the glass down. "You've obviously been here before."

"In passing," he agreed briefly, offering no further information; playing her game. He had also been on training courses.

Their meal came and neither of them spoke, until Clare broke the uneasy silence by saying she should have driven herself and he felt shamed into apologising.

"I'm sorry, I shouldn't have asked such blunt questions. I was just trying to make sure you were confident about the situation you find yourself in. It's a difficult one, not of your making and will take a while to disprove her allegations. Lets hope it isn't too long. The main thing I wanted to know, was that you trust Andrew, and I was happy to hear you do, because he will never let you down."

Clare looked at him steadily, liking his sincerity. "I'm sorry too. I thought you were trying to put me off marrying Andrew."

He looked aghast. "What! And risk the wrath of Grace? Have you never seen her on the warpath?"

They laughed and by the time the journey was resumed they were relaxed and enjoying each other's company.

The high speed, luxurious Jaguar ate up the miles, and even after stopping an hour for lunch, they still arrived at Clare's flat in less than four and a half hours. Her first thought was to let Andrew know, and while she was on the phone Laurie wandered around with a speculative look.

She kept the call brief, saying she would call again later, and went to put the kettle on, while Laurie sat in one of the cream leather armchairs, deep in thought with his fingers steepled together.

"Is the flat on the market?" he asked absently.

"That is top of my 'to do' list."

She waved her hands, encompassing the living and kitchen area with its granite breakfast bar and modern appliances, taking a deep breath, and letting it out with a long sigh.

"The furniture's staying, so apart from packing personal bits, I'm done here."

"Do I detect regret?" Laurie asked.

"It's my very own, first home; there has got to be some I suppose, and I never dreamt I could fall for old furniture – but I have," she admitted, sounding surprised at herself.

"Ah, but there is old and then there is antique. A world of difference." A far away sadness filled his eyes. "With Andrew you will have the very best of both worlds. Children, family, country life, etcetera, etcetera."

It was his turn to take a deep breath and shake his head sharply as if to clear unwanted thoughts, saying abruptly, "I would like to buy your flat."

Taken by surprise, Clare's jaw dropped. "Really?"

"It will make a splendid Pied-a-terre, for when I visit my godson and his thespian friends at the Festival Theatre. Let me have the name of your solicitor. It will go through very quickly and relieve you of any added anxiety."

"But you haven't even asked how much," Clare murmured, incredulously.

Laurie shrugged and named a figure that made her gasp.

"That's settled then." He looked around approvingly, obviously happy with what he saw as Clare recovered enough to write the name and address of her solicitor on a postcard.

"I'll be off then and you will hear from my solicitor tomorrow."

He kissed her on both cheeks before stepping into the lift, and she wiggled her fingers at him as the doors closed.

Back in the flat, wandering around in a dreamlike state, it was hard to take in how meeting Andrew had changed her life so completely.

CHAPTER TWENTY TWO

Laurie stood in Monica's bedsit, making notes on the official looking clip board resting on his arm.

"To make sure you students have safe living accommodation, we have to check for dampness, and faulty gas or electric fittings."

"I won't be living here much longer, but the other girls will be glad." Monica moved a cardboard box from a chair as she spoke.

"On the move are you?"

Monica's hazel eyes lit up and her long blonde pony tail danced as she nodded.

"I'm going to live with my dad and his family in France, to have my baby."

She was obviously excited and her innocent eyes, set in a make-up free face, convinced Laurie she was unlikely to be guilty of what he had suspected. But at least it had eliminated his fear of something more organised. Must be getting suspicious in my old age, he thought as an idea came to him.

"You don't by any chance know a mature student, by the name of Victoria Kirby do you? She has gone missing and her parents want to contact her."

Monica frowned and shook her head slowly. "Don't think so."

He tried again. "She calls herself Ria, I believe?"

Monica's face cleared. "Ria? Oh yes, we met a few weeks ago at the maternity clinic."

"Quite a new friend then?"

"Well she was, until I told her I was going to live in France. Then she got really angry and said she wouldn't be giving me a lift to the clinic any more. I wouldn't have kept in touch though. I found out she took one of my baby X-rays. I didn't trust her after that."

Laurie looked sympathetic. "I'm glad. She actually isn't a very nice person. You take care of yourself."

He let himself out of the front door, happily convinced that Ria stole Monica's X-ray to pretend she was pregnant. Andrew must be informed straight away.

On the Wednesday evening Andrew passed the good news to Clare and when the call ended, she began to wonder how Ria could be made to give herself away.

When nothing practical came to mind, she decided to ring Laurie, but disappointingly his only advice was to wait, as it would be obvious soon anyway and the really pressing problem was the common law wife claim. Then he asked if there was a chance of meeting up with Andrew when he came on Saturday but Clare had to say she wasn't sure because she didn't know what time he was arriving and they were going to the Festival Theatre restaurant for her mother's birthday that evening.

"It won't take long, but it is very important and I can't make the Sunday. Not something I want to talk about on the phone though. Coincidentally, I'm meeting friends at the theatre for seven fifteen. How would in the bar at six suit?"

In the end, Alan and Laura joined them and it became a meeting of old friends, because Laurie and Alan hadn't seen each other for a good many years.

Laurie kissed Laura's hand, asking, "Where did you find these beautiful women, Alan?"

Alan chuckled, knowing how women loved Laurie's old world charm, but introductions and frivolity over, Laurie became serious, anxious to have a private word with Andrew; coming straight to the point when he followed him to the bar to help with drinks.

"Don't want to spoil your evening but can you dispose of some assets somehow? You may have a job proving you didn't share a home."

"That's my biggest worry; she knows Dad gave me the deeds to the cottages."

Laurie pulled a long face. "Sorry to hear that. You could be in for a trip to the cleaners."

"I'll just have to pay up. As long as I don't lose Clare..."

"That won't happen."

They took the drinks back to the table where Laurie and Alan talked over old times and amusing conversation flowed easily, until Laurie left, saying friends would be waiting.

Their table was booked for eight o'clock and while they were waiting, Clare's eyes shone as she told her mother and Alan about Laurie buying the flat.

"He loved it, but I feel a bit embarrassed because he has been too generous and won't take no for an answer."

"Don't be," Alan said as he and Laura looked happy for her. "Laurie was never one to quibble and will enjoy helping you. His family were mega rich and as the only child, he inherited 'Smythe House', a country estate in the Lake District. His father's family home. His name is actually double barrelled. Laurence Willerby-Smythe. Had quite a nice ring to it, I thought, but he dropped Smythe. Thought it sounded ostentatious. Apparently it will all go to his godson. Shame really. You'd think he would have married to carry the line on, wouldn't you? Bit late to start a family now I suppose."

Eyes still shining, Clare laughed, "I don't know. Some young women like older men; especially wealthy ones."

Andrew got up, saying abruptly, "Let's go in shall we?"

When they were settled at the table, Clare laid her hand over Alan's. "On this special day I want to tell you how happy I am that Mum has got you. And is it all right if I call you Dad?"

He looked at her softly. "Thank you, dear. I can't think of anything I would like better."

Laura's eyes filled with tears and Andrew proposed a toast. "Happy birthday – Mum."

"One of the best birthdays I've ever had," Laura said as they were making their way to the car park.

"Your present is in the car. I was going to bring it round earlier but Andrew arrived and then we arranged to meet Laurie and time slipped away. Sorry, Mum."

"I've got the best present I could have. We are a family now."

"I'll ring in the morning and you can tell me if you love it as much as I do."

On the way back to Clare's flat she asked about Laurie. "Was it important?"

"Very! He advised disposing of some assets, but unfortunately Dad transferred the cottages and land over to me as a wedding present. It seems she can take at least half of everything. I might have to sell."

"That's hard to take."

"Yes, they have been in my family for a long time. The grandparents gave them to Mum and Dad as their wedding present, that's why Dad was giving them to me as a wedding present and I was supposed to pass them on to my children. I've made a right mess of everything haven't I? Dad will be devastated."

"I don't know what to say. If it was just money, we would get by."

"I can't burden you. If you want to call it a day I'll understand."

"I'll pretend you didn't say that; please don't ever say it again."

The evening ended on a sad note and instead of Andrew going back to Alan's flat, they curled up on the big leather settee and slept till morning.

Andrew was quiet over breakfast and eventually said he needed to see his father before returning to Cornwall.

"I must tell him. If I could only transfer them back," he groaned.

Clare started to clear the dishes. "Well you can't and we must just deal with it. I'm sure a mortgage can be arranged."

She raised a hand as he said, "But..."

"I'll come with you and *we will deal with it*. Telling Dad is the hardest bit. We are all packed, so we'll do it on the way home."

She stood and looked around the flat for the last time.

"Regrets?" Andrew asked anxiously.

"How could there be? Pride maybe, knowing I did it all by myself." She smiled and hugged him. "But I'm not alone any more."

Alan was in the garden when they arrived, and Laura was preparing Sunday dinner.

Her face fell when she saw Andrew. "What is it, Andrew? You look dreadful."

"I need to talk to Dad."

Laura ran to the back door. "Alan, come quickly, Andrew is here."

Alan came in, his smile disappearing as he saw their long faces. "What?"

"Let's go in the garden, Mum. Andrew needs to talk to Dad, alone."

Laura followed her into the garden and they sat on the garden seat.

"I hope Alan won't get too upset," Laura said. "He's not properly over the Cornwall trip."

"Are *you* all right, Mum? You don't look as well as you did last night."

"I'm fine. Just worried about Alan. If there was just something he could do to help Andrew, he would feel better."

"I'm afraid Andrew hasn't come with good news. This woman is causing so much trouble in her determination to get easy money."

The back door opened and Alan appeared. "Come in. Come in. You must hear this."

They both hurried in, to see Andrew slumped at the kitchen table, head in hands and Alan looking beside himself with joy.

"You'll never guess. What was I worried about, before we went on the cruise?"

"Just about everything," Laura laughed, relieved to see him so happy.

"Will one of you *please* say what's going on?" Clare begged.

Andrew raised his head and relaxed back in the chair, relief written all over him.

"Dad had arranged to actually sign the cottages over to me, while I was on honeymoon. They are still in his name."

Clare suddenly needed to sit down but got up again. "I'll put the kettle on."

They all laughed and Laura suddenly remembered that her present was still in the car.

"I'll get it for you, dear."

With renewed energy, Alan left and returned a few minutes later carrying the wrapped 'Bluebell Woods' picture.

Clare watched her mother's face light up as she looked at the picture.

"It's absolutely beautiful, dear. It..." She went very still, looking stunned.

Clare put her arm round her. "Thought you would like it."

Transfixed by the picture, Laura just nodded.

"Really glad you like it, Mum; let me know where you decide to hang it."

Arms linked they went out to the car, where Andrew was already saying goodbye, clapping his father gently on the back, both looking as if the weight of the world had been lifted from their shoulders.

Clare settled herself in the well-laden car and as they were about to drive away, Laura asked, "Who did you say painted my picture?"

"Not sure I did, but it was Jim. A really lovely man who's teaching me to paint."

"How nice!" Laura said faintly, as they drove away.

They travelled in silence while Andrew concentrated on driving. Living in Cornwall, he was accustomed to queueing nose to tail, but once off Hayling island and on the motorway, he glanced across.

"Happy?"

"Mm. You?"

"Mmmm."

CHAPTER TWENTY THREE

Clare poured herself another cup of coffee and took it into the sitting-room to sit by the bay window and read her mother's letter. They seldom wrote to each other, so it was a nice surprise to see the pale blue, Basildon Bond envelope on the door mat; a dead give away, even if she hadn't recognised the handwriting.

Andrew had just left to keep his regular appointment close to Crackington Haven, where his grandparents lived, so he would stay for lunch and bring them up to date with what was happening; which at the moment was waiting for what Ria would come up with next.

Glancing out of the window overlooking the drive she saw Connie's car leaving.

On her way to the monthly Farmer's Market, she would have been up since four o'clock, baking cakes and pies. Clare gave a satisfied grin, picturing the array of bread and rolls she had helped to make the previous evening.

At eight o'clock in the morning, the cottage was quiet and peaceful, so looking forward to reading her letter, she slit the envelope open with Andrew's silver letter opener and made herself comfortable.

Engrossed in the surprising contents of the letter she missed hearing the front door open but heard the barely audible click as it closed, and knowing Jim was the only one with a key she got up quickly and went to the sitting room door, just in time to see a stealthy figure about to climb the stairs, give a startled intake of breath and bolt, leaving the front door wide open.

Momentarily rooted to the spot, Clare saw a car drive off quickly. But there was no mistaking who it was, in spite of the head scarf and dark glasses.

Feeling shaken she closed and locked the door, wondering what Ria would risk breaking in for. She obviously saw Andrew leave, thought the cottage was empty, and with Mark at work and Connie out of the way, took a chance that, this early, neither Kathy or Jim would notice.

Unsettled, she forgot about the letter as she realised Ria must have a key. The catch was definitely down, because she hadn't yet got into the country way of leaving doors unlocked, and Andrew had used the conservatory entrance to come and go.

Unwilling to leave the cottage in case Ria returned, she bolted the door and went upstairs to unpack her cases. The box containing her wedding dress reminded her of the afternoon with her mother and she was half tempted to try it on again, but restlessly remembering the half read letter, she hung it in the wardrobe and wandered back to the sitting room, the image of Ria with her foot on the bottom tread of the stairs uppermost in her mind.

If only Andrew was within phoning distance, but he would be with the client by now on the remote farm, without reception. Should she phone Arthur and let him know of Ria's latest move? No, she mustn't worry them.

Desperate to tell someone, she phoned Laurie, but frustratingly there was no answer. Then just as she was wandering despondently into the kitchen to put the kettle on, Laurie called her back to explain he was driving.

"Anything the matter? You sound upset."

"Andrew and Connie are out and I really need to tell someone that I had an unwelcome visitor just after eight this morning."

"I'm glad you phoned; no need to ask who. I've been following them since early morning. Wondered what she was up to when I saw them speed away from your place. Sorry I didn't call in but I had just caught up with them again. Didn't know you were alone; should have checked but didn't realise they were making for your place when I lost them for ten minutes at traffic lights. Thought they were making for 'Tamerisks' again." He paused.

"At the moment, I'm sitting in a pub called 'The Three Bells'. They appear to be having heated words about something, with an indignant looking young fellow. I rather suspect she paid him to tell her when the coast was clear and he let her down; so she's refusing to pay him."

"Obviously wanted to be sure Andrew was keeping his regular Wednesday appointment and that Connie was going to the market, as usual. The worrying thing is, she must have a key and could have broken in on the weekend while we were both away. She obviously didn't know I came back with Andrew, but why risk breaking in?"

"For the deeds to the cottages, I imagine. According to Simon Dunbar, her solicitor is saying she doesn't believe they are still in Alan's name. You need new locks but in the meantime make sure to bolt the doors. She is one very determined lady."

"You are really rather good at this, aren't you?" Clare said admiringly.

"Part of my training with..." He broke off. "Full ahead. They're leaving. Batten down the hatches until Andrew's back on board and I'll phone when there is anything to report." The phone went dead and Clare couldn't help smiling, realising that Laurie was really rather enjoying himself.

Feeling better for having got things off her mind, she made sure all doors and windows were locked and went back to continue reading her mother's rather puzzling letter; wondering how the painting of the 'Bluebell Woods' could have anything to do with her past. The letter ended with:

It is really, really important that I come to see you as soon as possible; this week-end if possible, to confirm whether what I suspect is true. All my love, your truly, truly devoted Mum. x

Clare sat holding the letter, staring at her mother's well formed handwriting.

It was clear she needed to get something off her mind. Clare picked up the phone and it rang several times before Laura's breathless voice answered.

"Sorry I was down the garden." She broke off. "It's all right Alan, it's for me."

She came back on the line. "Sorry again, dear, Alan just came in."

Clare thought she sounded nervous. "Just ringing to say I got your letter and of course you must come."

"What a lovely surprise. Yes of course we would love to come, wouldn't we Alan? This weekend you say? Perfect! All right dear, I won't keep you, as you're busy; see you on the weekend."

The phone went dead and Clare sat staring at it, trying to figure out what had just happened, murmuring to herself, "Think I'll put the kettle on. This is turning into a very weird day."

Andrew arrived home later to find all doors locked and Clare in a jumpy mood, waiting to tell him about Ria.

He promptly rang a local locksmith, who arrived twenty minutes later to fit new locks, and security latches on all doors and windows.

"Feel better now?" Andrew asked, placing a glass of wine on the table beside her armchair.

She nodded. "Could she have taken the deeds? She obviously knows where you keep them."

"Not without a safe cracker. Stupid I suppose, but it never occurred to me to conceal the combination, until she took the log book for Dad's car. I changed it the same day."

Clare looked at him fondly. "If only people were as nice as you expect them to be."

"Most are," he said defensively.

"I have to agree there."

"You what! I definitely have to note today in my diary."

He dodged a cushion, pulled her gently out of the chair and took her in his arms. "Why don't we just pop off and get married? No worry about her turning up. What's the worst that could happen?"

"Our families would never forgive us and your grandmother would disown you."

"I could just about live with that, but I can't live another week without you."

"There is something I haven't told you." She leant back to watch his face as he relaxed his hold apprehensively.

"Ye-es?"

"Mum and Dad are coming on Friday for the weekend."

He caught her firmly again. "Don't do that. I thought it was more bad news."

"Well it still might be, I'm not sure what to make of Mum's letter – or the phone call."

"Nothing terrible, or I'd have heard from Dad."

"Just to change the subject, I was talking to Connie yesterday. She says if you were the father, the baby would have to be born, at the very latest, first week in September; Oh, and a DNA test will prove you aren't. So at the very worst we can get married after that," Clare finished triumphantly

"But that's four months away." Andrew groaned.

"At least it will prove she is lying about that, so could be lying about everything else," she said sympathetically.

"Most women would have doubts," he said ruefully, hugging her to him.

"Not if they knew you like I do."

Her deep blue eyes looked unwaveringly up into his troubled gaze as he asked, "Do you know how totally amazing you are?"

She gave a light laugh and squirmed out of his arms.

"Of course. And with you as their father, we will have four amazing children."

His face lit up in joyful astonishment. "*Four?*"

"For a start."

"*For a start*?"

She put her head on one side, looking thoughtful. "Twin boys would be nice."

"*Twin boys*?"

She looked thoughtful. "Twin girls would be just as nice. A set of each, perhaps."

Andrew collapsed in the nearby armchair, looking dazed. "I had no idea you were so... so..." He fumbled for words before asking faintly, "Do I get to say?"

She gave a dismissive frown. "Do you have other ideas then?"

He laughed. "Are you *sure* you're not related to grandmother?"

Clare sat on the floor beside his chair and rested her head on his knee. "That's better. Why don't we tell the grandparents it's definitely a September wedding. They need cheering up, bless them."

Andrew stroked her hair, glad to see she wore it loose so often these days. He hadn't dared hope she would settle so quickly into a life so different to the one she had known.

"I must tell Grandmother to expect two more for dinner on Sunday," he said gently.

"And I will tell mum to pack her best frock," Clare said contentedly.

Late on Saturday afternoon, Laura telephoned to say there had been a bad accident and they had been stuck in traffic for nearly three hours, so they had decided to stay overnight at a bed and breakfast.

"Are you all right?" Clare shrieked, as Andrew snatched the receiver from her and after listening briefly assured her they were fine.

"Still two hours away but too tired to travel any further. Forgot how heavy bank holiday traffic would be. Nothing to worry about and they will be here early tomorrow morning." He looked at her shakily, forcing his hand to replace the receiver. "No problem. No problem at all. I'll put the kettle on."

He escaped to the kitchen and leant against the sink, closing his eyes with relief, asking himself, while he filled the kettle, why he automatically assumed the worst lately.

A little while later, he went along to tell Connie why Laura and Alan wouldn't be coming to dinner and she guessed his thoughts.

"I know a lot's 'appened, but you won' 'elp by meeting trouble 'alf way."

"They could have been in the accident though?"

Connie stuck her chin out. "But they weren't. And what's got inta Clare? *She* don't usually tek on so."

Andrew looked depressed. "Ria breaking in, shook her more than she will admit."

Connie tutted. "Course, but everywhere is safe now and if *you* don't panic, she'll cope. Level 'eaded, she is."

"Meaning I'm not?"

"Ruled by 'eart, not 'ead," Connie comforted, smiling fondly. "What we love about ye."

"Connie's right," Jim agreed.

"Then *I* need to change."

"No need. You've got Clare. She wouldn't want you to change," Jim said placidly.

Andrew gave a worried frown. "Mm, but I would hate her to get fed up with me."

"She won't." Connie gave him a push. "Go tell 'er dinner's ready ta dish."

Early next morning, Alan telephoned Andrew to say traffic was already nose to tail and it would be better if they made straight for 'Tamarisks'.

"It means they won't have to come here and get back in the car for another hour," Andrew explained to Clare, over breakfast.

It was a warm, sunny morning as they set out. Everyone was in a happy mood, especially Kathy, who was looking forward to spending the afternoon on the beach with the children, so the boot of Andrew's 4×4 was full.

"Imagine what it will be like when you have children as well," Kathy said as Clare helped her settle Luke and Emma into their seats.

"It will have to be a bus, for what Clare has in mind," Andrew said in a loud aside to Mark; and the rest of the journey was spent laughing at Clare's plans, which grew bigger by the moment.

On arriving at the house, Emma was fractious on being woken from a deep sleep when the car stopped and Luke was lively after being restricted. So even though Grace smiled, when conversation was constantly interrupted, Kathy was sure she meant keep them quiet when she suggested taking them to Hannah for a cool drink.

Once in the kitchen, she said adamantly, "We aren't welcome. I'm taking them to the beach."

"Bad manners," Hannah said disapprovingly.

"Bad manners or not, my main concern is the children – they need fresh air and freedom. I'm also in no doubt *whatsoever* that Her Grace will welcome their absence at her luncheon party. Don't bother to deny it, Mum."

Kathy looked hurt as Hannah turned away tutting and started to pack chicken and salad into a picnic basket.

Kathy went back into the sitting room to tell Mark she needed the pushchair and beach things and he went out to the car immediately, knowing he should offer to go down to the beach with them, but Laurie had just turned up and the conversation was interesting.

He returned to the sitting room in time to hear Kathy say, "That's the television repair man."

She was leaning over Arthur, who was going through a folder of papers on his lap, and had just held up an enlarged photograph that Laurie had sent him of Jason.

Clare looked. "Are you sure? Only it's the same man that Ria had a picture of in her brief case, isn't it, Andrew?"

"Yes. She said it was her cousin."

"Well whatever he is, they are living together now," Laurie said with a speculative look at Andrew. "Think I might look into who he really is. Thanks, Kathy."

"He came every Wednesday. Ria said you were having trouble with the television and didn't want to bother you; so I never mentioned it."

"Well it's the first I've heard of it," Andrew said.

"And it was always on a Wednesday, when she knew Andrew would be out for the day and so would Connie," Clare said triumphantly. "Just like she did last Wednesday."

"Well done, Kathy," Grace said quietly.

Kathy turned to her, hearing approval for what she saw as the first time.

"Thank you. I'm going to take the children to the cove now and leave you to have lunch in peace. You don't mind do you?"

"They will be much happier, dear."

Kathy could never remember Grace calling her 'dear' before and her eyes filled with tears as she hurried from the room.

During the afternoon, Andrew told Clare there was something he wanted to show her in the garden, while Grace and Laura got to know each other.

It was a beautiful day and he took her to the garden at the back of the house, where the lawn swept down to a shallow river, babbling over a rocky bed, with a small wooden bridge crossing over to a private path leading down to the cove. What he had brought her to see was the screen of tamarisk trees on the far bank, where frothy pink fronds waved enchantingly in the breeze.

"The house is named after them," he said with a sentimental smile.

"I wondered where the name came from," Clare murmured, completely captivated by the magical setting. "It's so serene; I can see why you love it."

"Mm, and it's good to know it will always be in the family," Andrew said contentedly.

"Was there ever any doubt, then?" Clare asked curiously.

"I did wonder what would happen if it was left to Jacqueline. I'm pretty sure she would have sold it, but Mark will inherit 'Tamarisks' now. Kathy will, no doubt, make changes, but it will always be a wonderful home; just as it is now and hopefully they will carry on with *some* of the Carlyon traditions."

"I'm sure they will, and hopefully make a few of their own. I know I would."

Andrew took her hand to lead her over the bridge to the cliff top.

"There's Kathy and the children."

He waved back as Kathy caught sight of them and pointed them out to Luke, busy making his sandcastle, in the shade of the high cliff.

Obviously Kathy's idea of a perfect day, Clare thought, picturing her bringing her children here every day when she lived in the house, doubting her own ability to idle the days in that way. Lovely as it was.

Kathy was relieved when Mark offered to drive Andrew's car, to save Alan driving home.

It meant they were alone. She felt inexplicably emotional about the change of heart Grace had shown, even accepting she was wrong to be resentful about her mother's well paid, housekeeping job, which gave her not only a safe and comfortable place to live, but a quality of life exceeding most peoples.

Deep in soul searching, she travelled in silence, but as the children fell asleep on the journey home, Mark put her quietness down to the long day on the beach, and it wasn't until they were settled in the darkness of their bedroom that she shed tears and unburdened herself. Mark just held her close, relieved that, at last, there could be a truce to the bad feeling he was in the middle of.

Once she was calm, they made love and fell asleep, contented and blissfully unaware of the new life that would be stirring soon.

On their way home, Clare was concerned at how unusually quiet her mother was, and how when she did speak, it was brief and edgy.

"Almost as if she's nervous about something," she confided to Andrew, while they were preparing supper together.

"Grandmother does have that affect on people on first meetings; or don't you remember?"Andrew laughed.

Clare had to admit he was probably right, but it didn't entirely explain her mother's distracted behaviour, especially when very early the next morning, awoken by a door slamming, she went downstairs to find Laura up and dressed, having already taken Alan a cup of tea.

Only half awake, she ambled downstairs and half laughingly asked, "What are you doing up at this unearthly hour? Even Connie doesn't get up at five o'clock."

"Speaking of which," Laura asked abruptly, "when am I to meet these people who have stolen your affections?"

Jerked wide awake, Clare showed concern. "They are lovely, but they could never take your place, Mum. That isn't what you are worried about is it?"

"I'm not worried; just curious to meet them. That's all."
She changed quickly. "I'll pour you a cup of tea?"

"If you don't mind I think I'll take it back to bed. Why
don't you go back for a couple of hours? You must be tired
after the last two hectic days."

"Perhaps you're right. I'll just finish my tea. You go
ahead."

"I wish you would tell me what *is* worrying you," Clare
said with a resigned sigh.

"I will when I know for sure myself."

Clare picked up her mug of tea. "And that cryptic remark
is supposed to make me feel better?" she asked with a
despairing look.

"Sorry, it's the best I can do right now," Laura said to her
retreating figure.

An hour and a half later when Clare went downstairs again,
she assumed Laura was in their bedroom, as she had seen Alan
on his way back from the bathroom, so it wasn't until he
arrived downstairs and showed surprise at Laura's absence,
that they discovered she wasn't anywhere in the cottage.

"Gone next door to see Andrew, I expect," Alan said
unperturbed, until Andrew appeared and said he hadn't
seen Laura.

"Now I'm really worried," Clare said anxiously.

"Why? It's a lovely morning; she will have just gone to
have a look around."

As he spoke, Andrew put two slices of bread in the toaster.
"I need to hurry. I have an appointment at nine and another
at ten. I should be home by twelve."

"I could come with you," Alan offered.

Andrew grinned and popped two more slices in the
toaster. "Great!"

It was all so homely and relaxed that Clare began to think she was making too much of her mother's unusual behaviour. There was going to be a perfectly simple explanation, she told herself, as she put the toast on two plates and placed butter and marmalade on the table.

After she had seen Andrew and Alan off, she set the table, expecting her mother to return for breakfast at any moment, but when there was still no sign of her by quarter past nine, she decided to go and see if she had been waylaid by Connie with a cup of tea, or even more likely a full English breakfast.

It was a fine morning and, as always, captured by the beauty she strolled to the dry stone wall to view the riot of colour in the wild flower meadow. Stretching down to the river it reminded her of the tamarisk trees and lost in thought she was unaware of Connie until she touched her arm, when she turned, with a smile that quickly faded on hearing Connie say she had caught sight of her mother earlier.

"She should a come in for a cup o' tea; thought it too early I 'spect. Jim was in his studio; 'ad an idea 'e couldn't wait to paint."

She smiled cheerfully, never happier than when Jim was happy.

Clare smiled back, hiding her apprehension. "I was sure she would be with you; must be home by now. I'll bring her to see you later?"

"Right ya are my lovely." Connie went back indoors humming to herself and Clare hurried home, anxiously telling herself she was fussing too much, but when she arrived back at the cottage, Laura was sitting at the kitchen table, looking pale and distraught.

CHAPTER TWENTY FOUR

Ria faced her solicitor angrily. "I insist you demand to see those deeds. I saw the letter from his father, telling him the cottages were his wedding present to us."

"Yes, Miss Kirby, but apparently the deeds were never actually transferred," Norman Taylor patiently explained.

"I understand Mr Davenport Senior intended to, whilst you and Mr Davenport Junior were on honeymoon, but as you failed to appear and Mr Davenport Senior went on the cruise instead, the transaction never took place."

"I don't believe that for a moment," Ria insisted, raising her chin obstinately.

"Very well, I will pass on your instructions, but in my opinion you are running up needless expense for yourself, Miss Kirby."

Ria looked sharply at him. "I only have to pay if you win."

Norman Blake gave her a pitying look. "I don't know who is advising you, but I'm afraid any work my firm does has to be paid for."

Ria was shocked into silence for a moment. "But... it says on television..."

"Not this firm, Miss Kirby. And your chance of coming out of this claim with the kind of money you are hoping for is most unlikely, if not impossible. Mr Davenport isn't the wealthy man you suppose him to be. All you can realistically expect is a share from the home, and half of any limited capital, plus child support until the child is eighteen."

Ria looked at him with thunderous disbelief. "He has put you up to this. I shall go to another solicitor." She stormed to the door and turned. "And don't bother sending me a bill." With that she slammed the heavy door until the room shook.

Sitting at his large, flat topped desk, Norman gave a sigh of relief as his secretary entered.

"Oh dear! I think I have just lost a dissatisfied client, Jean."

"Really, sir? Would that be the paternity case you took on whilst I was on holiday? She looked very determined. Woe betide her husband."

"Davenport isn't her husband and denies he is the father, so only time will tell. In the meantime, she will be going after anything and everything she can get her hands on. She emptied his house illegally once before, but this time she will make sure the law is on her side, if I'm any judge of character."

"Davenport? Not Andrew Davenport?" Jean asked in a surprised voice.

Norman leant back in his swivel chair. "You know him?"

"His mother came from our village; he and I are much the same age. We partied together as a group of teenagers and if he says he isn't the father, he isn't."

"Really." Norman looked thoughtful.

Ria knocked loudly on the big oak door of 'Tamarisks', and when it opened, walked straight in and made for the sitting room.

"I have been told by Mr Davenport to call the police if you come here making a nuisance of yourself," Hannah warned, as Ria ignored her and barged into the sitting room.

Startled by the disturbance and about to open the door,

Arthur was forced to step back quickly to avoid being knocked over.

"She can put the phone down. I'll say what I want before the police get here anyway."

Hands on hips, Ria stood looking first at Arthur and then Grace and, still holding the receiver, Hannah hovered uncertainly in the doorway, until Arthur asked her to wait in the hall, before turning to face Ria.

"I'm sure the police have got better things to do with their time, so say what you have to and go."

Ria turned to Grace, who was sitting very upright, surveying her with disdain.

"My story will make good headlines and I know you really don't want that."

"What do you suppose will happen when the newspaper finds out Andrew isn't the father?" Grace asked calmly.

Ria stamped her foot. "Just pay me and I'll go miles away. Out of your hair forever. That's what you want isn't it?"

"Most certainly but Andrew denies the child is his," Grace continued calmly.

Ria bluffed brazenly, "Well he would wouldn't he?"

"So we will just wait until the baby is born. And now, Hannah will show you out."

"You won't like the publicity," Ria threatened.

"Slander will be expensive," Arthur warned, returning to his chair and picking up his newspaper.

Ria stomped out. "Don't say I didn't warn you," she shouted as the big front door shut behind her.

Grace gave a weary look. "Why not just give her the money, dear?"

"Certainly not." Arthur folded his paper briskly and went quickly to the door leading to the garden.

They rarely disagreed but with strong reasons clouding her usual sound judgement, Grace watched him leave the room. She hadn't liked the wild look in Ria's huge, dark brown eyes and whatever previous doubts there had been, she certainly looked pregnant now.

She heard Arthur speaking to Peter and went to the window in time to see the 4×4 drive out of the gates and Arthur return to the house.

She heard him go into his cabin, then half an hour later he entered the sitting room wearing a grim smile.

"Andrew and Alan will be here for lunch and Laurie is on his way with news. Apparently he has discovered the identity and whereabouts of Ria's father."

It was much later than expected when Andrew and Alan arrived home, fully expecting that Clare and Laura had enjoyed their day, eager to tell them Laurie's latest news.

One look at Laura's distraught face though, as she sat at the kitchen table, said this wasn't the right time, and Alan went straight to comfort her, as Clare said sharply, "I've just been told that Jim is my father."

Dead silence reigned, as Alan looked at Laura for confirmation.

"It's not a part of my life I'm proud of, but I hope you will understand that I felt I had no option, I leave it to you, Andrew, whether to tell James, or Jim, as you know him. This will obviously come as a shock to both him and his wife."

Andrew stared uncomprehendingly, until reminded of Jim's behaviour over the last two weeks, he managed to say, "Maybe not as much as you imagine,"

Alan was at a loss as to what to say and just sat looking at Laura, until Clare suddenly burst out accusingly, "You've lied to me all of my life; deprived me of the love of a wonderful father. I can't forgive you for that, Mother."

Gathering his thoughts, Alan jumped to Laura's defence. "Wow! Steady on! This is a shock to all of us; even more so your mother, I imagine."

"Absolutely. So just curb that short fuse of yours and let's talk about it calmly. Shall we?" Eyebrows raised questioningly, Andrew stared sternly at her and, completely taken aback, Clare remained silent.

Alan took Laura's hand, stopping her from twisting her handkerchief. "Take your time, dear, and just tell us how this has come about."

Squeezing his hand tightly, Laura nodded nervously.

"As I've already told Clare, it was the painting of 'The Bluebell Woods'. The moment I saw it I thought what a coincidence it was that she had chosen a picture of a very favourite walk of ours. Then I recognised his signature; the way he does his Js, and I had to make sure it was her father. It is. I saw him in the conservatory this morning."

Andrew looked at her intently. "Can you be certain after all these years? We don't want to cause unnecessary distress."

Laura nodded. "I'm certain."

"Give me time to prepare Connie and Jim and then come along."

Andrew left, mulling over the situation. He knew they both loved Clare like a daughter, but when it came out of the blue that she actually was... well!

He found Connie in the sitting room, sorting her diary for the following week.

"You okay m'love? All alone? Where's Clare then?"

"She'll be along in a while."

"Whatsup? I know that face o' yours." She snapped her diary shut.

"Something unexpected has come to light. I think Jim has been having suspicions of late, so it might not come as a complete surprise to him, but I need to prepare you both."

Connie looked at him with exaggerated patience, and grinned. "Not much surprises old Connie these days."

"Well..." He hesitated and Connie waited with an encouraging, "Yes?"

"Jim is actually Clare's father."

The words came in a rush and Andrew waited with bated breath for her reaction, which came falteringly as her demeanour changed from curious to open mouthed astonishment. The only sound in the room was rain spattering on the windows.

"Well I never," she murmured, getting up and wandering to the door. "I bes' put kettle on."

Giving her time to compose herself, Andrew waited before following. He found her standing, very still, beside the table, staring vacantly. Looking up at him, she said simply, "Never did know what 'e did afore 'e met me. Never mattered. Still don'," she added gruffly.

He put his arm around her, groaning as a knock came too soon, and Clare's voice called, "Can we come in?"

She appeared in the doorway and seeing Andrew comforting Connie, hung back.

Connie pulled herself together. "There, there me lovely, don' upset yersel. I'm okay."

Jim appeared in the doorway. "What's all the fuss about? You all right my love?" he asked anxiously, seeing Andrew and Clare's concerned looks, but before Connie could answer, he staggered back, his face dropping as he caught sight of Laura in the kitchen doorway. "Clare?" he said hoarsely.

Caught unawares he staggered again and would have fallen, but Andrew and Connie ran and helped him to a chair.

Clare knelt beside him. "I'm here, Jim."

"He means me," Laura said quietly.

CHAPTER TWENTY FIVE

Laurie wandered into John Kirby's television showrooms and John came towards him smiling hopefully. "Can I help, Sir?"

"Well that depends on how much control you have over your daughter Victoria."

A look of desperation replaced John's eagerness. "What has she done now?"

"Well, where shall I begin? Oh yes! Currently blackmailing an elderly couple for the sum of two hundred thousand pounds. Suing the man she ran out on for half of everything he owns, as his common law wife, which she never was. Claiming the child she is carrying is his, which incidentally we know is a lie. Stealing the keys and log book to a Daimler with the intention of stealing it, and in my opinion she must be very close to a mental breakdown, because she actually broke into his cottage to raid his safe. She says you have disowned her but if she isn't restrained she *will* be taken to court."

John closed his eyes in despair.

"I've never been able to control her. Her mother left us when Ria was twelve, because she couldn't take her tantrums and lies any more, but Ria blames me for the break up. I'll do what I can, but I'm not certain if she is still living where I left her."

"I can tell you," Laurie said quietly, allowing that perhaps the man was more to be pitied than blamed, after all.

John looked surprised and Laurie explained, "They aren't aware but we have followed them from day one. We know their every move."

"They?"

Laurie looked surprised. "Yes. The man she is living with. Jason Donelli? But surely you knew that. He is one of your employees."

"Ungrateful little toe rag," John thundered, suddenly full of indignant rage.

"Treated him like a son I did. Let him live above the shop. Made him head engineer."

His anger disappeared. "He left me in the lurch. Customers waiting. I thought he must have had an accident. I phoned hospitals. The police. Nothing. Not a word."

He sat down at a nearby desk, looking hurt. "Can't believe he would do that to me. Ria, yes, but not Jason."

Laurie wrote the address on the back of one of John's own business cards; one of a pile sitting on the desk, and handed it to him.

"You could have a job to catch them there; she is constantly in Cornwall, threatening the Carlyon's. I would advise contacting Mr and Mrs Carlyon immediately if you don't want to be accused of helping your daughter."

John gave a start. "This is exactly why I washed my hands of her. I'll phone them straight away and put a stop to this lunacy." Panicking, he picked up the receiver. "This is all because she thinks she's entitled to the high life. Well enough is enough. This time, she's gone too far."

Mission accomplished, Laurie made for the door.

Jason switched his mobile phone off and gave Ria a despairing look. "My brother says, if I don't join him soon, he will have to find another partner. His offer is too good for me to turn down so I'm going on my own, if you won't come with me. Please give this idea up. You are making yourself ill. For the baby's sake if not for your own."

She gave an impatient wave.

"Stop worrying. The baby's fine. After my visit yesterday they *are ready to* give in. She won't let this reach the papers. I know her." Ria gave a grim smile. "I can read Grace Carlyon like a book. You'll see."

"But we don't need all of this pressure. You are just fooling yourself. I don't want to leave you on your own but I want this partnership with my brother." At the end of his tether, he paced the hotel room.

Hands on her hips, she glowered at him. "Go then. Just go. *I know what I'm doing* and I'm certainly not giving up now I'm winning."

Jason gave a hopeless shrug. "I'll leave this afternoon then."

Ria gave a sharp look. "No need to be in *such* a hurry."

Her mobile phone rang before he had time to answer, and she snatched it from the dressing table. "Aha! Told you so. It's Carlyon."

She let it ring three times before answering lazily, and heard Grace's defeated voice say, "Be here by two thirty this afternoon," before the line went dead.

Ria threw her arms around Jason. "I told you so."

Eyes shining she drew away and looked up into his unresponsive face.

"Aren't you pleased? We can be on our way this evening."

"Give it up, Ria. I don't want to be part of this any more."

"Then leave it to me." She walked swiftly to the wardrobe

and retrieved the old dress. "Won't be sorry to ditch this," she laughed as Jason closed his eyes wearily.

At two thirty exactly, Ria drove the old red car through the wrought iron gates and came to a halt with a triumphant toot on the horn.

Hannah opened the door immediately and stood holding it, head averted, as Ria entered confidently and made her way to the closed sitting room door.

Without knocking, she walked straight in and came to an immediate halt, facing both Arthur and Grace, standing, as she thought, stiff with hostility at finally having to give way.

She gave a triumphant smile. "I knew you would see sense and do it my way eventually."

"Sense is the last word I would use for blackmail," Arthur said angrily. "If I had my way the police would be handling the matter."

"Ah! But that would upset dear Grace. Thank you, Grace. Now I hate to rush you but I have an important appointment, so if we can just get on with things I'll be on my way."

"I wonder what your father thinks about this little scheme of yours?" Grace asked.

Ria looked sharply at her and Grace continued. "Only, we thought he should hear it from you."

As she spoke, she and Arthur stood aside to reveal John sitting on the settee, his face a picture of disbelief.

He rose and spoke quietly, controlling his anger with an effort. "I didn't think even you would stoop to this, and was it absolutely necessary to involve Jason?"

Shocked into silence Ria just stared for a moment before saying defensively, "He didn't take much persuading."

John looked stern. "This wasn't his idea. You wheedled him."

"It wasn't like that. He loves me."

John gave a pitying look. "Poor Jason!"

"Don't be sorry for him," Ria snapped angrily. "All he can think about is this baby and getting it born in Italy, because 'mamma loves Bambinos'," she mimicked. "It doesn't matter that I don't want it, oh no; I don't matter."

Her feelings appeared to get the better of her and she ran sobbing to her father, burying her face into his shoulder.

John stood motionless, waiting for her to quieten down, before asking sharply, "I take it you and Jason intend to get married?"

She gave a tearful nod. "In Italy, as soon as we get the money. I told *them* that." She shot an accusing look at Grace and Arthur.

"Stop this nonsense and pull yourself together. I must speak to Jason. No grandchild of mine will be born out of wedlock. Plus, we have upset these good people long enough."

John eased her away, looking anxiously across at Arthur and Grace who were exchanging hopeful looks.

They were looking very tired and it suddenly came home to him just what serious effects Ria's behaviour could have on them at their age.

"I can't apologise enough for the stress my daughter has caused you. If I can compensate, please let me know how." He held his hand out to Ria. "Come."

"There is something," Grace said quickly, looking straight at Ria.

"A *written* statement saying the child is not Andrew's, and also disclaiming any rights as a common law wife."

"My solicitor will deal with that straight away."

"But that means I won't get anything from him either," Ria complained petulantly, forgetting her play acting.

Lips set firmly, John ushered her into the hall. "And why are you wearing that disgusting dress?"

And then he saw the red car. "What on earth? Why are you driving that wreck? Where is the 4×4 I bought you?"

John's estate car had been parked out of sight, but having driven it round, Peter emerged from the driving seat and promptly informed him that Jason was waiting in a nearby lay-by with it, where the red car was kept ready for visits.

"Mind your own business," Ria hissed.

Red faced with embarrassment, John motioned Ria to get in his car as he extracted his wallet and handed Peter a fifty pound note.

"If you would dispose of that wreck; keep whatever you get for your trouble."

He turned as Grace called to him and beckoned. Walking back to her his heart was in his mouth, dreading what else there was to come, but after a few words he shook her hand, walked back to his car, and with a final wave, drove off.

Peter touched his cap and watched the car out of sight, vowing never to underestimate the older generation again, while Arthur sighed wearily and watched Grace return to sit bolt upright in her chair, obviously having got something off her chest, asking himself if it was relief or pity he saw in her eyes?

"I must tell Andrew," he said briskly.

"Yes, dear."

"Laurie will be pleased with himself."

"He will."

There was no answer at the cottage and Andrew's mobile was switched off, so after leaving a message and sending Laurie a text inviting him for the weekend to discuss their successful manoeuvre, they sat, Arthur wearing a satisfied smile and Grace holding back tears of relief.

When Hannah took a tray of tea in a short while later, she found them both sound asleep; Grace looking serene, obviously dreaming of the wedding she could now go ahead and plan.

CHAPTER TWENTY SIX

It was late afternoon by the time they gathered in Connie's sitting room: Connie holding Jim's hand, looking anxiously at his drawn, set expression; Andrew puzzled by the reproach in his eyes; Clare wondering why both her mother and Jim were looking so accusingly at each other, while Alan pressed Laura to tell her story.

"I don't know where to start," she whispered.

"At the beginning is always a good place," Clare said curtly.

Andrew frowned deeply. "Be quiet," he whispered urgently and once again taken aback by the way he was speaking to her, she retaliated with, "I need answers."

"Your feelings are not the only ones to be considered. Give your mother time."

Unable to contain himself any longer, Jim suddenly burst out, "Why did you accuse me of forcing myself on you?"

"I did no such thing," Laura gasped.

"So why was I called to the headmaster's study and given instant dismissal without references. I lost my job, accommodation, not to mention my reputation. I had to sleep on a friend's settee for weeks. Your father said you didn't want to see or speak to me, and shut the door in my face when I called at your home trying to contact you."

Silence reigned until Laura murmured with disbelief, "He said you couldn't get away fast enough when you heard I was pregnant."

"But I heard nothing. He said nothing. You said nothing. How was I supposed to know?"

"How could you, Mother?" Clare demanded.

"I had no idea."

"That doesn't explain who the man in the photograph is on your dressing table. Obviously not my father, as you have always said. Just another lie!"

"That was my brother." Laura looked at Alan. "When Rosemary saw the photo and assumed it was my dead husband because Clare was so like him, I went along with it because I didn't have any photos of her real father, whereas I had some of my brother and myself together. It saved awkward explanations." She shrugged sadly and looked at Clare. "As you say, another lie."

"So where is this uncle I never knew I had?"

For a moment Laura couldn't speak; then emotionally she whispered, "He was my brother, my idol. I adored him. He was a naval officer; the absolute pride and joy of my parents. Up for promotion; father's dearest ambition. Engaged to the beautiful daughter of their best friends. A perfect match. Mother's dearest ambition."

Tears ran down Laura's face and she wiped them away angrily. "He was injured in the Falklands war. Spine damaged by shrapnel and his beautiful face scarred beyond recognition. He shut himself away in a wheelchair. Wouldn't even let his fiancée *see* him; said he couldn't condemn her to a life with him. What lunacy wars are. Just four years older than me, he died within months. And their whole life ended when my mother had a complete breakdown and went into a nursing home. So we lost my mother and my brother and I'm afraid the added shame of my pregnancy was just too much for my father."

"So where are they now?" Connie asked sympathetically.

"Why change your name?" Jim interrupted. "I had no way of finding you. They said at the school you just didn't turn up. I was astounded by your accusation, even more so by your refusal to see or talk to me, but when the headmaster dismissed me on the spot, after teaching at that school for seven years without a blemish, I was so completely mortified, I just gave up teaching."

Laura hesitated, looking aghast. "My father was determined on me having an abortion and locked me in my bedroom when I refused. He even made an appointment with a private doctor to come to the house. I climbed out of the window and went to your room at the school, but the porter told me you had left suddenly and hadn't left a forwarding address. It confirmed my father's words, so thinking I was on my own, I drove all day to get as far away as possible. Changed my name to Laura James, to keep a part of you. It must tell you something, that I gave Clare both of our names.

"I was lucky enough to find a room to let and get a teaching post in the local school until she was born, then I took pupils at home, in need of extra tuition until she started school."

She looked at Connie. "Both of my parents are dead, I took Clare to see them just once when she was six months old, but she was so like my brother, my mother went into a frenzy. She never did fully recover from the tragedy of my brother's death, and sad to say, my father took the easy way out for them both. I read about it in the newspaper, otherwise I wouldn't have known. I went to their funeral." Laura gave a cynical little grimace. "Commander Bellingham and his Lady were buried together."

"So you were Clare Bellingham. Would you ever have told me? Would I have ever known if I hadn't come to Cornwall?" Clare accused.

"When would have been the right time?" Laura whispered unhappily.

"When wouldn't?" Clare demanded.

Andrew stood up. "I think it's time we left."

"But was it fair not to have told me all these years?"

"You've had your say. Now give them time to talk. We will go back to the cottage."

Clare looked at Jim. "Say something to me."

"Later!" He smiled sadly and she ran from the room sobbing.

Andrew followed with a heavy heart, allowing that her attitude could be forgiven to a point, but not liking it.

When he reached the cottage, she was already sitting taut and upright in the armchair, staring belligerently out of the window. "You obviously think I'm being unreasonable," she said, without looking at him.

"No. I think you are being heartless. Your mother has been through enough."

"She should have told me."

"What? That you wouldn't even be here if your grandfather had had his way?"

Clare swung round, ashen-faced, collapsing back into the chair, as the truth went home.

"I'm sorry but you wanted the truth and the way I see it your mother took the only course open to her."

"She could still have told me," Clare insisted.

"And what would you have done?"

"I would have searched for my father until I found him."

"Where would you have started? She actually saved you

a lot of frustration, not to mention heartache if, as she believed, he didn't want to know."

"At least I would have known who my real father was."

Andrew lost patience. "For goodness sake, at least give her credit for trying to protect you from what she thought would be a lot of unhappiness and rejection. You really need to see this from her point and not just your own."

The telephone rang in the hall and he went quickly to answer it, leaving her indignantly searching for an answer.

A lengthy silence followed as Andrew listened and when he did speak, there was a lift to his voice as he explained that he had only just come in and hadn't picked up the earlier message, before thanking his grandfather for calling back with such great news.

Clare waited wondering what the great news could be and was curious when Andrew dialled a number straight away to thank who was on the receiving end for an amazing effort. She waited for him to come back, but infuriatingly he went straight to the kitchen and she heard him filling the kettle. Why was he being so difficult? A few minutes later he came and placed a cup of tea beside her, and in answer to her enquiring look, satisfied her curiosity without elaborating. "Laurie contacted Ria's father. She won't be a problem any more."

Clare waited for him to mention renewing wedding plans and when he didn't, tentatively asked, "So we can set a date now?" And was shaken by his answer.

"I need you to sort this other problem first."

"What are you saying?"

"If you carry on blaming your mother, you will cause a rift between the four of them – and us, and I won't be part of that."

Clare looked at him indignantly. "So it's them or me?"

"If that is how you see it, I'm disappointed in you."

He walked from the room and she heard the front door close.

Left alone, she drew a shocked, deep breath to collect her thoughts. Andrew had just given her an ultimatum. It had never been her intention to create a rift, but surely she was entitled to voice her opinion. Feelings with her mother very often ran high, but they always made up. Her mother knew that. But Andrew had actually... A sob escaped her as she ran from the cottage and flung herself into her car, desperate to get away.

Fumbling with the keys, she careered recklessly out of the open five bar gate and drove fast, heedless of direction until the engine spluttered and the car slowed to a standstill and stopped. The petrol tank registered empty and she had left without not only her handbag, but her mobile phone.

The road rose steeply and she allowed the car to roll back into a pull in. Trying not to panic she applied the hand brake, telling herself as she looked along the deserted narrow country road, bordered by high hedges either side, that she stood little chance of seeing a landmark, even if she knew of any. Her mouth went dry. Someone would come along soon she assured herself, looking at her wrist watch. Half past six on a Saturday evening? Perhaps not. If only she knew where she was, she could leave the car and walk, but as far as she knew, she was in the middle of nowhere and wouldn't find the car again. No, she would just wait and hope. Andrew was bound to come looking for her.

A cyclist whizzed silently by as she was about to recline the seat and she waved frantically out of the window to receive a cheery, answering, thumbs up. Looking hopefully back certain there would be others because they always rode in clubs. But not this one, she admitted an hour later, reclining the passenger seat and laying back to wait for the inky blackness of the countryside to engulf her.

Laurie changed down to a lower gear to pass the car parked at the side of the steep, narrow road, glancing into the car as he drew level. A woman curled up in the passenger seat looked as if she was sleeping and for a moment he thought his eyes were deceiving him. "Clare!"

Coming to an abrupt halt, he ran back and yanked on the passenger door but it was locked and the driver's door was parked too close to the verge to get to.

"Open the door," he shouted urgently.

She didn't stir and he panicked. She looked blue with cold, he must get her into his car. She needed warmth.

"Unlock the car so that I can help you?"

Clare's eyes flickered, but she seemed incapable of moving.

He rang Peter's mobile but it was switched off and in desperation, picked up a rock to break the back window and unlock the passenger door.

Catching her under the arms he dragged her out of the door. She was a dead weight and very cold and it took all of his strength, but he finally managed to get her into his car and cover her with a blanket.

Putting his foot down on the accelerator, he sped along, anxiously asking himself what she was doing out there, on her own, at five o'clock on a Sunday morning?

Luckily he had driven down early to avoid the traffic, intending to watch the dawn break over the Cornish coast until a suitable hour to arrive at 'Tamarisks'.

Within ten minutes he drove through the wrought iron gates and tooted the horn loudly several times, relieved to see, a minute later, both Peter hurrying from his cottage, pulling a T-shirt over his dark head and Hannah standing at the front door in her dressing gown.

"Be quick, Peter. Carry Miss James into the house. She needs something warm, Hannah. And let Mr and Mrs Carlyon know, will you?"

Peter picked Clare up easily and carried her into the sitting room while Hannah went quickly to fetch a warm blanket and inform Grace and Arthur, before going to make a warm drink.

Comfortable on the settee Clare responded to the warmth and opened her eyes.

"How long had you been there and how did you come to be stranded?" Laurie asked curiously, just as Grace came rushing in, in her dressing gown, followed seconds later by Arthur, also in his dressing gown, then Hannah with a strong cup of tea.

Seeing Clare looking so pale and exhausted, Grace sunk down beside her on the settee looking aghast. "What happened, my dear?

Clare closed her eyes and shook her head, and Laurie volunteered, "I found her in her car, ten minutes away. She must have been on her way to see you when she ran out of petrol. Heaven knows how long she'd been there; she was absolutely freezing."

Grace looked stern. "What was Andrew thinking of allowing her to run out of petrol?"

Clare tried to protest, but didn't have the strength.

"Women always run on an empty tank, so they say," Laurie added quickly as Grace frowned.

With the strong, hot tea doing its job, Clare managed to say, "I got lost, and had to spend the night in the car."

"Why didn't you phone?" Arthur asked, sinking into his chair yawning.

Just when he thought he had sorted one problem, his family seemed to find ways of inventing new ones.

"I left my mobile at home," Clare admitted sheepishly.

"It's a good idea to keep a blanket in the car for emergencies," Laurie pointed out.

"I usually do but the car is due its M.O.T on Monday so I emptied it. I'm not usually so ill prepared," Clare defended herself hotly.

"Ah well. All's well that ends well," Arthur said, getting out of his chair. I'm going back to bed. You know where your room is, old chap. Have a snooze until breakfast."

Laurie turned to Grace. "There's something I need to do first, but then I might just do that." Adding in an aside, "You just might get to the bottom of this on your own. Shout if you need me."

Grace nodded and went to sit in her comfortable chair as the door closed.

"Now, start at the beginning and tell me why you were out driving on your own, in a thin, cotton dress, no coat, no phone, no handbag. It's just not you."

"Like I said. I emptied the car for it to go into the garage."

Grace pursed her lips and raised her eyebrows. "Now the truth please?"

A moment passed before Clare admitted, "We had words and I just got in the car and drove without thinking. I ran out of petrol." Her eyes filled with tears. "I was so cold and scared because I didn't know where I was. I was sure Andrew would come and find me – but he didn't." Her voice rose shrilly and tears ran unchecked down her face. "He doesn't care any more. He doesn't want to marry me now."

Shocked with disappointed indignation, Grace managed to demand, "Why?"

She listened in silence as the whole story came, out then rose and went into the hall.

Clare could hear her on the telephone, but the door was shut and the words were muffled. Then she heard her go upstairs and return half an hour later fully dressed.

"Hannah is bringing you breakfast on a tray. When did you eat last?"

Clare looked uncertain. "Breakfast probably. Everything went haywire after that, but I'm not really hungry."

Grace frowned sternly. "Of course you are. That's why you feel so weak."

Hannah arrived with a loaded tray and Clare ate obediently, under Grace's watchful eye, admitting afterwards that she did feel better for it.

"There is something I need to do. Try and sleep."

Grace left the room abruptly and left alone Clare worried about her car; she was supposed to take it into the garage in the morning. If only she hadn't driven off in a temper. Where would she go now that Andrew didn't want her? Worrying thoughts filled her head. She shouldn't have been in such a hurry to sell her flat.

Her heart sank at the thought of asking for her job back and worse still, leaving Jim when she had only just found out he was her father. And Connie, Grace and Arthur. They were like her family now. What must it have been like, having to run away from parents? And how awful to be told your baby was unwanted?

Tears ran down her face again, but this time they were for

her mother, who must have been as much in love with Jim, as she was with Andrew.

With her face buried in her hands and sobbing quietly, she was unaware of Andrew until he took her in his arms.

"Thank goodness you're safe. We have all been going out of our minds with worry."

"I ran out of petrol," she sobbed loudly. "And I didn't have my phone, or even know where I was. I was cold and scared and sure you would come. *Where were you? Why didn't you come and find me?*" she thumped his chest with both fists.

"You can come in, she's perfectly normal," he called, hugging her to him, as the sitting room was invaded with relieved laughter and Laura came and hugged her before beckoning to Jim.

"Come and tell this daughter of yours never to do that to us again, will you?"

"I promise," she said sheepishly, as Connie and Jim hugged her.

"I wan' it in writin' this time mind," Connie warned seriously.

"And we'll frame it and hang it on the wall," Jim added.

Laurie and Arthur joined them, and the whole story had to be told again.

Laurie was thanked endlessly for his part and as they drifted apart he unexpectedly came up with the answer to Laura and Jim's sad saga, by cornering Jim and asking, "This Commander Bellingham, where was he stationed?"

"I don't know for certain, but they had a house in Maidstone. Chatham, maybe? Laura would know."

"Your story of instant dismissal rings a bell. What did you teach?"

"History and geography," Jim answered ruefully. "It was

the end of my career. Should have changed my name like Clare did."

"And your headmaster was ex Navy?"

"Yes. Clive Henderson." Jim looked curious.

"Thought so. Henderson served under Frank Bellingham, before he retired. Clare, or Laura, as you know her now, was earmarked for the headmaster's son, Lieutenant John Henderson. Hence, her father arranged the teaching job for her but her relationship with you will have upset their plans, so I think we can pretty much guess the reason for your ignominious dismissal, which incidentally made an opening for yet another retired Naval officer.

"There were six of them, all from Naval backgrounds, all married, all with children earmarked to marry each other. They considered themselves *The Elite,* and sons were signed up from the day they were born. I served under Bellingham for a time. Didn't fit in with his lot, so he got me transferred."

Jim held out his hand. "I owe you a huge debt of gratitude. Shame has prevented me from revealing my past, even to those I hold dear."

Laurie looked sympathetic. "Laura is obviously embarrassed by the lie she has lived as well. Tell her how right she was. She would have had no chance of keeping her baby if she'd stayed."

Jim looked at him admiringly. "I will; and thank you for your concern. Her brother was badly injured in The Falklands war and died from his wounds. She was heart broken."

"Really? How tragic! Lovely young man. Not a bit like his father. Must have been after I was transferred."

At that moment, Hannah announced brunch was ready and they all wandered through to the dining room.

Once seated at each end of the long table, Grace returned

Arthur's happy smile with a seductive tilt of her head, and catching the exchange, Laurie smiled to himself, wondering what bomb shell Grace had in store for Arthur. He knew that look well; it was one that said she was biding her time for the right moment to suggest something not to his liking.

Poor old Arthur. But what I wouldn't give to be in his shoes, he thought, as for the last time in several weeks to come, peace reigned, while the ladies discussed a possible wedding date and the men aired their opinions on Match of the Day.

CHAPTER TWENTY SEVEN

With all the excitement, Clare had completely forgotten about her car, so it came as a surprise the following morning when she saw it coming through the gate, driven by the mechanic from the garage.

She went out and was handed an envelope and greeted cheerily with, "All done, Miss; passed with flying colours, and the petrol tank's full."

"Thank you. I didn't know you had my car. I was supposed to bring it in today."

"No problem, Miss. We picked it up yesterday, as instructed." He tipped his cap and started to walk towards the gate, where a motor cyclist was waiting.

"Just a minute, I'll pay you now." She went to go indoors but he carried on, calling over his shoulder, "All paid for. Receipt's in the envelope."

Wandering back indoors she wondered why Andrew hadn't mentioned it that morning. But then he wouldn't, she thought fondly.

Laura was in the kitchen making the mid-morning coffee. "Thought we might sit in the garden, dear. It's a beautiful day."

"Good idea, Mum." She gave Laura a hug and for a moment they clung together without speaking, both glad that they had made their peace.

Alan had just finished cutting the lawn and he joined them to sit at the table on the patio.

"I'll cut the edges next. I take it you still want to go home tomorrow?"

Laura smiled affectionately at him. "If you do." She turned to Clare. "Is that all right with you, dear?"

Clare gave her an enquiring look. "Only if everything is sorted with you and Jim."

"It is. We spent the evening with him and Connie on Saturday, thinking you and Andrew were together, but Andrew and Mark had a drink together after you had words, and when he passed the cottage on his way back to his flat, intending to come in and smooth things over, all the lights were out and he thought you were in bed," Laura explained.

Clare nodded. "He did say."

"He nearly had a heart attack when Grace phoned to say you were recovering from spending a night in your car and what the devil did he mean by letting you?" Alan interrupted, with a rueful smile.

"Sorry!"

"Extremely out of character for my oh so sensible daughter."

Laura laughed as Clare pursed her lips. "Well it was!"

"I know. I know," Clare admitted huffily.

"Think I'll just get on and cut the lawn," Alan said, rising quickly as Laura said, "In answer to your question: James and I realise now that neither of us was to blame and Connie assures me I did the right thing too. I'm so glad he met Connie. She's amazing."

"You're pretty amazing yourself, Mum."

The gentle words were spoken softly, and looking across, Alan sighed contentedly. One day he might even understand their relationship.

After planning an early start, Alan changed his mind and

suggested that if they left in the evening, the traffic would be quieter and he and Jim could spend the day helping Andrew with his full day of surgery appointments.

Laura was more than happy with the arrangement, and Connie immediately took the chance to introduce her to Kathy.

"Never thought I'd see the day!" Laura said, cutting chunks of home made bread, as Connie dished big bowls of soup for lunch and Clare dumbfounded her by feeding Emma.

Clare stood staring out of the window. Andrew had just left to keep his Wednesday appointment and the house felt quiet and lonely now her mother and Alan had gone.

It was only eight thirty and the whole day stretched endlessly before her.

Wandering out into the garden she sat on the wooden bench. She would walk along to see Jim, later. He might tell her about himself while they painted together. It was good that everything had been sorted. She smiled, thinking of Jim's happy face, when her mother, seeing how attached they were, left Chloe with him.

Wandering restlessly back into the cottage, she sat down in the armchair by the window. She wanted to speak to Jim. Watching him glow with pride when her mother asked him how he felt about giving his daughter away on her wedding day, had told her how pleased he was to be her father. Yet another unselfish act on her mother's part, because they had decided *she* would do the honour.

She got up and wandered into the kitchen, automatically put the kettle on, then switched it off again. Tea wasn't the answer. Why wasn't she doing something useful instead of mooning about like this? She would go and see Jim right now.

About to close the front door she saw Kathy pushing the pram towards the gate.

"Hi, Kathy. Thought I'd go and keep Jim company."

"I saw them both go out in the car, about five minutes ago. Got to dash. Baby clinic."

She waved and hurried on and Clare waved back, suddenly filled with doubt as to whether she could live with the remoteness and slow pace of life.

Returning to the sitting room she sat down again asking herself what she would be doing if she still lived in the flat?

Silly question; she would be at work. Saturday afternoon was the only time she actually went anywhere. Lunch with Mother, then shopping in Chichester. That was why the theatre tickets had seemed a good idea.

What if she hadn't met Andrew? She couldn't imagine life without him now.

Laurie's car pulled into the courtyard and, filled with relief to know she wasn't entirely alone in this remote part of the world, she went out to welcome him, feeling foolish about how absurd she was being.

Vaguely curious at how long he was taking to switch the engine off, she walked to the car to find him just sitting and staring, apparently deep in thought, unaware of her. She tapped the window gently and taken aback by the startled, unseeing expression in his usually alert blue eyes, she opened the car door.

"Lovely to see you, Laurie."

He got out of the car and, worried by his unusual manner, she slipped her arm through his as they walked towards the cottage.

He nodded towards her car.

"Glad to see your car was returned safely."

"They brought it back the very next day."

"They promised they would."

She looked at him, wide eyed with surprise.

"You did that?"

"Least I could do after breaking the window."

A touch of his usual humour returned. "I would have got a right dressing down from Grace if I hadn't."

"So you paid the bill and filled it with petrol as well?"

"My pleasure." He patted her hand absently.

Glancing at him, as she filled the percolator and set out two cups and saucers, she realised he obviously had something on his mind and asked, "Anything I can help with?"

He raised his eyebrows.

"*Something* is obviously worrying you."

He pulled a face. "Should have known nothing would escape you."

"So?"

He looked at her for a long moment. "I needed to get away. Arthur and Grace are exchanging broadsides at the moment."

"What about?"

"I'm not at liberty to say, but Arthur shut himself in his cabin all day yesterday and the last I saw, he was half way through a bottle of rum. Grace and I had a long talk and I have to say I agree with her... and I didn't tell you that," he added quickly.

"Arthur will wave the white flag some time today, as he always does, and Grace will go ahead with her plan... as she always does."

"Sounds intriguing."

"You will all be told in good time. Grace will get her way."

"Because she always does?"

He gave a small indulgent smile. "And why not?"

"You seem more than a little enamoured," Clare observed, tilting her head to one side.

"I fell head over heels on the first day we met."

"Does she know?"

Laurie gave a resigned laugh."Oh yes. And Arthur, lucky old sea dog."

Clare frowned.

"Strange friendship you think? Not really. Arthur and I met in our early days in the Navy. Grace and I actually got engaged when we were both twenty-two, but she broke it off after a year; said she wasn't convinced. We remained friends and I introduced her to Arthur, at a party in the Mess. He was smitten, but completely out of his depth. He only had his Naval pay, so would never even consider proposing to a wealthy, landowner's daughter. The three of us spent a lot of time together and it became obvious that Grace really liked Arthur, but he always insisted on me joining them." He gave a hollow laugh. "He has admitted to me since that he found her intimidating."

Picking up the tray, Clare led the way into the sitting room and he followed.

"Sorry if it sounds patronising but Arthur and I grew up in different worlds. He was a miner's son; that's what makes him so admirably down to earth and steady. He rose from the ranks, you know. Far more impressive than me."

By now, Clare was intrigued and asked, "So how did they eventually get together?"

"Being the only child of a rich family, patience was never one of her virtues and true to character, she proposed to

Arthur; and as you probably realise by now, she never takes no for an answer."

He spread his hands theatrically. "C'est la vie."

"Were you upset?" Clare asked curiously.

"Of course, and like Arthur, wondered why she chose him, over what I could offer. In the long talk I had with her yesterday, when Arthur shut himself away, she finally told me she chose Arthur because he needed her more – and she needs to be needed." He gave a hollow laugh. "If she only knew."

He got up from where he was sitting beside her on the settee and wandered to the patio doors to stare out at the garden.

"I saw Andrew before I left 'Tamarisks', so I hoped you would be on your own. I need to talk and feel I can, to you. Perhaps because you are so like Grace. I have never told her but it was for the best we didn't marry."

Clare remained silent, concerned but also curious. This was a side to him she had never seen.

Laurie returned to sit beside her and for a long moment, just looked into her eyes. Then realising he was making her uncomfortable, got up again and went back to the patio doors to say haltingly, "There is something I've never told anyone; not even Grace and Arthur, but I have come to a crossroads and the time has come to set my affairs in order."

Clare drew a sharp breath. "Are you ill?"

"No. Just weary and lonely, having no one to share my thoughts with."

Clare frowned deeply. "Have you never married because of Grace? Surely there was…"

Laurie interrupted her. "There you go again, sounding just like her. Let me finish."

"Well make it something I can help with, after all you have..."

Laurie stared hard and she folded her hands in her lap, pursing her lips impatiently.

He closed his eyes in silent despair. "How can you possibly get any more like her?"

He held his hand up as she was about to speak and his eyes lost their smile.

"Edith and Thomas have looked after my family house ever since I can remember, but Edith died recently and Thomas can't stay there on his own. He's ninety."

"So you need to decide what to do with your home?"

"I've already decided. I should have done it years ago."

"So how can I help, if you have it sorted already?"

His answer was strangely staccato. "I just need to tell someone. We seem to think in the same language. Am I making sense? Assuming too much?"

Clare had only ever seen him in control and she was getting worried.

"Not assuming too much, and I'm more than happy to listen but wouldn't Andrew be the obvious one to confide in?"

"Andrew sees me as his granddad's wealthy, Naval opposite number; a playboy without a worry in the world, and it has suited my purpose to keep it that way. I can talk to you because I don't feel I have to live up to that false image."

Clare kicked her shoes off and tucked her feet up under her. "Fire away then."

He sat hunched, elbows on knees. Altogether unlike himself.

"Don't quite know where to begin?"

267

Clare uncurled, went to the drinks cabinet, poured him a stiff whisky and curled herself up on the settee again. "Start with what you plan to do with your home."

"Ah! Yes. Well I've transferred the house to my godson. It should be lived in. It has eight bedrooms. Morgan and his wife Donna have a family of three boys and a girl, all under fourteen. They will love it and the house will come alive again. What do you think?"

He looked at her with an almost boyish need for approval and she smiled back.

"I think it's absolutely wonderful and you will still be able to go and stay."

His face dropped. "Not sure about that."

"I'm sure you will," she said encouragingly.

"Time will tell," he said shortly. "Morgan is a playwright and frequently works at Chichester theatre, so now I have your flat as my permanent home, he stays over. It's good to have his company."

He finished his whisky and settled back, but sat forward again, regarding her restlessly before apparently making up his mind.

"There has always been speculation as to why I've never married and I've never told anyone the real reason; not even Arthur."

"So why now and why me?"

He shook his head. "I don't know."

"Start from the beginning," she suggested gently.

He took a deep breath and began with a far away look in his eyes.

"My mother died when I was ten. She was only thirty-three and my father was twelve years older. No one ever told me exactly what her illness was, just that she needed to be confined to her bedroom. To me, she was a fairy princess living in a blue and gold world. Long ash blonde hair, big lavender blue eyes, skin like porcelain. Very beautiful. Very fragile. Her room was all powder blue and gold, with rococo furniture and white satin bed linen. When she died, father had the room locked and it has remained so. Once a year on her birthday I put her favourite flowers, forget me nots and lily of the valley on her bedside table, as he did, but other than that, the curtains remain drawn and the door locked." He shuddered.

"On the day after her funeral my father sent me to Naval boarding school in Ipswich. I understand my mother's father, an ex Navy Captain, took responsibility for my education. I can only assume, to make up for keeping his family history from my father. I was homesick and hated it. Missed my mother. Cried myself to sleep for months. It turned out for the best though. I quickly learnt, if I did well, I could control my own future. I was lucky enough to pass everything with honours and went on to study law."

He spoke without vanity, wearing an amused, rueful smile.

"I understand there is a very fine line between insanity and genius."

He took a black and white photograph from his left, inside breast pocket and handed it to her. A beautiful young woman and a small boy stared back.

"My mother and me. I was eight years old. My resemblance was one of the reasons my father couldn't bear to have me around. He adored her and went into deep depression after her death; in fact he became a complete recluse. When I went home for the holidays, I never saw him, not even at Christmas. He gave orders that I was never to enter his part of the house. Edith and Thomas cared for me, but when I finished my education and went into the Navy, I never went home again."

A third person had been carefully cut out of the photograph. Obviously his father, telling of his hurt.

She handed it back, fighting tears, then swallowing hard, remarked on his mother's beauty and asked her name.

"Alice Lauren. I'm named after her," he said proudly. "Alice Lauren." His voice caressed her names as he took the photograph and replaced it next to his heart.

"I spent every leave travelling, but Cornwall was always my favourite place; where I first met Grace. My father died when I was twenty-eight. He never spoke to me after my mother died, but sent for me when he was on his deathbed. Needless to say I didn't recognise him. He was very bitter and could hardly speak, but with his very last breath he said I killed my mother and he wished I'd never been born because it was giving birth to me that sent her insane."

Clare held her breath in horror. "What did you say?" she managed to gasp.

"Nothing. However cruel, what can one say to a heartbroken, dying old man?"

"It can't be true, surely?"

"Not entirely. But apparently it was something I could pass on to my children and in his Will, he said I would have to live with that, as my punishment."

He gave a humourless laugh. "I investigated and discovered that my mother had two siblings; a brother and a sister, both severely mentally handicapped and placed in an asylum at birth. There were a number of cases, in other generations on my grandfather's side, so I suppose you could say my mother was lucky, in that she did have a few years of normal happiness. My father cut me out of his Will. Left everything to Edith and Thomas, but they refused, even before the doctor declared him of unsound mind."

"One *could* argue it was your father who killed her, by making her pregnant in the first place," Clare argued indignantly.

Laurie gave a resigned sigh and answered the challenge in her eyes, which seemed an even deeper blue, with her intensity.

"And in *his* defence, I would have to argue that my mother's family probably kept the insanity from him to protect their family name."

He raised one eyebrow quizzically. "What say you, Counsellor?"

"I say, you don't know that for a fact. He could have blamed you, to hide his own feeling of guilt," Clare returned spiritedly.

"And I would have to say that you've missed your calling, Miss James."

"Why on earth didn't he tell you sooner?" Clare asked seriously.

"What if you had already had children... and?" She spread her hands expressively.

He sighed. "Thankfully, I hadn't and I've made sure the line ends with me."

"Quite a burden to keep to yourself for so long."

Laurie looked her straight in the eyes.

"Bad things happen in all families – even the, so called, good ones. I'm glad your mother's burden has been lifted and she's found happiness with a good man."

Clare leant over slowly and kissed his cheek.

"Can you stay until Andrew comes home?"

"No, I need to be on my way."

"Then I'm going to make you lunch."

He followed her out to the kitchen. "I'll be back for your wedding. I'm going straight up to Cumbria, to clear Mother's room and bring Thomas back with me. I've found a private nursing home, close to the flat, where I'll be able to visit him frequently."

"That will be amazing for him," Clare said softly.

"And for me. He's more of a father to me than mine ever was."

He turned abruptly to hide his emotion and she covered the silence by taking chicken and fresh salad from the fridge, while he recovered.

"Something light to travel on," she said, ignoring his forlorn look and inviting him to help himself as they sat opposite one another.

"Perfect. Thank you."

With lunch barely over, she was concerned at how quickly he wanted to leave, and said so as she walked to the car with him.

"Sorry, I don't mean to eat and run, but I'm really anxious to get things started."

He was looking very agitated again, and she said quickly, "Please wait for Andrew. Then perhaps I could come and help you with your mother's room."

Once again he looked at her for a long moment. "Thank you. I really can't think of anything I would like better, but it's something I need to do alone."

His sadness touched her and reaching up to kiss his cheek, she was startled by the fierceness of the hug he gave her, before letting go so abruptly that she had to steady herself by holding onto the car door.

"Sorry! Sorry! Didn't mean... Forgive me. Can't think what came over me."

Shaking visibly, he got quickly into the car, shut the door and turning the engine on, was about to drive off as she tapped the window.

"Wait. Please wait."

He wound the window down, overcome with embarrassment and she reached in to touch his shoulder.

"Don't go like this. You're too upset to drive. Please wait and talk to Andrew."

He shook his head and put the car in gear. "I must go."

Clare's eyes swam with tears, just as a car pulled up blocking his way, and to her relief it was Connie.

One look and Connie said, "You're upset."

Laurie tipped his head back and closed his eyes in despair.

"Laurie really shouldn't drive, Connie."

Connie looked at him and he shook his head. "I need to go. I'm all right."

"Mm, can't say ye look it. I'm about to put kettle on and I'm not movin me car, so come on in ta mine. You too me lovely. Stop ye blubbin'."

Jim wandered over looking curious.

"Put kettle on, Jim."

Connie went back to fetch a bag of shopping and Clare looked at Laurie.

"You might as well," she said tearfully.

He got out of the car and handed her a man-sized tissue to wipe her eyes, while he straightened his blazer and took several deep breaths before starting to stride slowly across the courtyard, sternly telling Clare to stop crying or she would have everyone at it.

The midday sun was warm, and the coolness of the cottage welcome, as they stepped inside to find Connie and Jim in the kitchen, where Jim was making tea while Connie put the shopping away.

When the tea was poured, Jim calmly put two of the cups and saucers onto a small tray and said he was taking Laurie into his studio.

Connie said nothing, but Clare could see she was delighted at him taking charge.

"Stay with Connie," he told Clare, beckoning Laurie to follow him.

"Jus like 'is old self," Connie beamed, when they were alone. "'E really likes you bein' is daughter, me lovely."

An hour later Jim joined them in the sitting room. "He's resting," was all he said.

"What did he tell you?" Clare asked anxiously after a short silence.

"Enough!"

Connie nodded proudly. "You did 'im good then."

"One good turn deserves another," Jim answered, adding as they both looked curious, "He restored my integrity, the other day."

Seized with curiosity, Clare asked, "How?"

After a moment's hesitation Jim said, "By explaining something that has shamed me for years; stopped me from being myself."

And with that Jim refused to be drawn further. If Laura wanted Clare to know the full extent of her grandfather's duplicity, she would tell her.

Andrew arrived home to find a very subdued Clare and was very moved, but also curious about Laurie's story.

"How has he managed to support such a false image for

so long? Gramps always jokes about him having a girl in every port, and he never denies it."

"How he has wanted to be seen, for the sake of his pride," Clare sympathised.

"Like Grandmother and her fear of scandal, you mean?"

"Exactly!"

"Laurie's car's still there. Think I'll nip along and make sure Jim and Connie are all right."

He was back in ten minutes.

"Jim says Laurie is still sleeping. Connie says to leave him."

Busy dishing their meal, Clare nodded. "Connie will know best."

Half expecting Connie to let them know when Laurie was awake, they were surprised to see the cottage in darkness when they looked along the walkway later.

"Must be staying the night," Andrew murmured.

"I feel so sorry for him," Clare said, sliding her arms around his waist and burying her head against his chest, as he drew her close.

"Pity won't help. This stays between us. No one else need know."

"Not even your grandparents?"

"Especially them. If he wanted them to know, he would have told them."

In the morning Laurie's car had gone and Jim said he heard him leave at four o'clock.

"He'll be in touch when he's ready. He has big changes in mind."

Connie came in with the tea tray and they all nodded as Jim said, "Goes without saying this stays between the four of us."

Andrew nodded. "Agreed. Let him know that, Jim."

Thankful to see Jim looking so alert, they were all pleased when he said confidently, "I'll write. It will come easier for him in a letter. He's been in a lonely place for a very long time, in spite of appearances."

"No more ta say then."

Connie planted the big willow pattern tea pot down with a bang, and they drank their tea in silence, except for Chloe's soft snore coming from under the table, beside Jim's feet.

CHAPTER TWENTY EIGHT

It was a Tuesday evening and Clare was helping Connie make bread for the market when Kathy joined them. She could hardly wait to tell them her news as, smiling excitedly, she eased herself onto a kitchen chair, looking radiant and pregnant.

"You'll never guess what. Mum and Peter only went'n got married yesterday. Didn't tell *anyone*. Granma Grace is right put out. Said she would have made the day special for them. That'll be why they never said. You know mum," she chortled. "She's giving them a fortnight off, to go away, but Mum says Peter wants to spend some of it moving her into the cottage with him. Won't that be lovely? A place of her own again. Taken her time hasn't she? I thought she'd never say yes." She laughed happily and Connie smiled fondly as she continued kneading.

Perhaps they would settle down and resolve their differences at last. It was the one thing she hadn't been able to help Kathy with, because her one wish, after her father died, was for her mother to have a life of her own. She blamed Grace for her mother's situation, without realising how worrying life could have been for Hannah, without the security of her housekeeping job.

Finding Kathy's exuberance touching, Clare asked how she and Mark were going to celebrate with them.

"Mum won't want a fuss, so we'll, most likely, just invite

them over for a day. As long as she's happy, that's all that matters."

Kathy glowed with happiness, and Clare couldn't help comparing the simplicity with the elaborate arrangements for their wedding day.

As usual, Connie guessed her thoughts and after Kathy had gone, she said, "Me an' Jim 'ad a quiet day. Wouldn't 'ave 'ad it any other way if you'd paid us, but we're all lookin' forward ta your big day, me lovely. Different when yer young. Yer going to be the prettiest bride ever."

Dumping a fresh lump of dough onto the board, she gave a deep chuckle.

"Granma Grace'll be in 'er element."

Sitting upright at her bureau, consulting her well filled diary, Grace glanced across at Arthur, puffing agitatedly at the cigar between his fingers, staring morosely at the newspaper across his knees; obviously not reading.

She hated seeing him upset, but she was convinced she was right. It was an important decision; but the only one that made sense. Hopefully she would be able to prove that to him. Not quite seven weeks to Andrew and Clare's wedding.

Laying her pen down, she asked quietly, "So when shall we arrange this meeting for?"

"Entirely up to you, my dear. You know my feelings, but I've said I'll go along with your wishes. I just hope you know what you're doing."

He folded his newspaper noisily, pushed himself out of the armchair and left the room.

Hearing him go into his cabin and shut the door, Grace sighed. She couldn't remember a time when they had disagreed so strongly, but she was sure she was right.

Andrew would be dropping in for lunch shortly and she would arrange a meeting for Sunday week, when the family would be coming anyway.

She looked at the date in her diary, glad that Laurie could make it. Arthur valued his advice but didn't know yet that she had told him her plan – that was playing on her mind; she must tell him. It was good to know Laurie thought it a sound decision.

Alan looked up from reading a letter at the breakfast table and tutted.

"Grace wants us to visit them next weekend. Says it's very important. It's an awful long drive though when we'll be going down in six week's time, anyway. Surely we can just phone. The wedding's all arranged isn't it? Or do you want to go?"

He handed the letter over and after reading it, Laura passed it back.

"Not really, but she says a family meeting. Doesn't actually mention the wedding. Why not give Andrew a ring?"

"Mm. Think I will."

Ten minutes later he was none the wiser.

"Says he'll try and find out what the problem is today. They always go for lunch on a Sunday. Apparently Arthur's been behaving very oddly for a few weeks. Keeps shutting himself in his cabin, and clams up when Andrew asks why. Can't see what we can do about it."

"How odd! If they need help though, we must go."

"Of course, but wait and see what Andrew comes up with first."

Later that evening, Grace phoned. "I really need you here. Please come?"

"If it means that much to you, of course we will." Alan put the phone down, not knowing what to think.

Andrew drove home in silence, at a complete loss to understand his grandmother's insistence on, not only Alan and Laura joining them the following Sunday, but Jim and Connie as well.

"There is to be a meeting, was all she would say."

Curled up beside him on the settee, Clare recalled Laurie saying Arthur always protested before giving way and murmured lazily, "Something he doesn't agree with, I expect."

"That can't account for why he wouldn't even play snooker, surely."

"Don't worry. He'll get over it by next week."

She snuggled closer. "Six weeks from now, we will have been married thirty-three hours!"

"Well I never! 'oe'd 'av thought we'd get an invite." Connie put the note let back in its envelope.

"Sounds formal. Wonder if Andrew's going? He hasn't mentioned it." Jim fingered the expensive stationery, suspiciously.

"It'll be ta do with weddin', that's fer sure."

"You think?" Jim wasn't convinced.

"Bound ta be. Best get me best frock out."

She went out to the kitchen chuckling.

Grace and Arthur sat next to one another at the head of the long dining table. Next to them, chairs were reserved for Andrew and Clare and Mark and Kathy. Alan, Laura, Hannah, Peter, Jim and Connie were invited to sit where they felt comfortable and Laurie sat at the other end with a blue folder on the table in front of him.

It was more formal than any of them had expected, except perhaps Jim, who had uneasily sensed that something out of the ordinary was afoot, when he and Connie were invited.

When they were seated, silence reigned as they all looked questioningly towards the head of the table, where Grace was sitting rigidly upright avoiding eye contact with anyone, while Arthur looked as if he would rather not be there.

All heads turned as Laurie spoke.

"If I have your attention, I would like to point out that Arthur and Grace have asked me to liaise on their behalf in what, to them, is not only an extremely important matter but also a very delicate and emotional one."

He opened the folder in front of him. "As you may or may not know, it has always been their intention to leave 'Tamarisks' to Mark. However, Grace feels very strongly about her convictions, and here I would like to add, on Arthur's behalf, that, although he will always support Grace, he has grave misgivings about her decision, because of the rift it could cause between two, much loved family members."

He paused and looked at Arthur, who just shrugged, and then at Grace, who nodded firmly.

"So after much heart searching, it has been decided that Andrew will now inherit the family home."

Gasps greeted his words, and Andrew's chair scraped back on the wood floor as he jumped up protesting.

"No, Grandmother. I won't accept Mark's inheritance. That just isn't fair."

Everyone else was speechless as Laurie said, "This must come from you, Grace."

He took the folder to her, and returned to his chair as all eyes turned to Grace.

Mark had his arms round Kathy and there were tears running down her face.

"If my instincts are wrong, 'Tamarisks' will stay with Mark. Sit down Andrew."

She tapped her stick twice, and Mark and Kathy drew apart, staring at her apprehensively.

"Surely you realised how hurt they would be?" Arthur accused.

Eyes full of tears, Kathy stared hopefully at Mark and he smiled and turned to Arthur.

"We couldn't be happier for Andrew to have 'Tamarisks', Gramps. We love our life at the cottage and don't want the responsibility of following in Grandmother's foot steps, with all the community work she does."

He looked at Andrew. "You two are so much better suited to this place, and Clare is simply cut out for the life."

Kathy laughed though her tears. "We like the beach though, so expect to see a lot of us."

Their relief was so genuine, that Arthur turned to Grace.

"Don't dare say I told you so."

"I wouldn't dream of it, dear."

Recovering from their dumbfounded silence, everyone started talking at once as an admiring chuckle came from the far end of the table.

Grace tapped her stick.

"I hope Clare and Andrew will take over soon," she said looking at Arthur. "Because in the unlikely event that I was wrong and you were right, I didn't mention that I have booked a world cruise for us, while a bungalow is being built in the field above the river. I know you miss being at sea and it's time we caught up with some old friends who will be joining us. We leave two weeks after the wedding."

Everyone looked first surprised, then anxious, as Arthur buried his head in his hands and started to shake, while Grace sat with an unperturbed expression, until Arthur raised his head to reveal tears of laughter as she gave him an angelic smile, and Laurie, knowing it to be their party piece, when she won, laughed out loud.

Hannah had prepared a cold spread on the table in the big hall, where Emma was sleeping soundly while Luke watched television, on a huge new set from John Kirby that had been installed that week. As she saw it, Grace was reminded of the letter of appreciation, thanking her for her timely advice in recommending professional help for Ria, who was now undergoing treatment, and thank goodness, already showing signs of more rational behaviour and hopefully looking forward to the baby in late September. The letter also mentioned the possibility of him and his wife getting back together and that he was selling his business and looking forward to going into partnership with Jason and his brother in Italy. Signing off: 'I can't thank you and your husband enough for your tolerance and understanding. Very warm regards, John.'

She smiled to herself and nodded. Today was really turning out rather well.

Just one more detail to go.

"Grace has certainly given you something to think about, hasn't she?" Alan remarked to Andrew, noting how quiet he was.

"Certainly has," Andrew replied, looking across at Clare, wondering how she felt about having her life planned for her, but most of all how Mark must really feel about losing his inheritance.

Alan paused in helping himself to new potatoes. "Must say you don't seem too pleased with your good fortune."

"Well, I'm worried that Mark is losing such a lot, but also, will Clare want such a demanding life?"

"Don't worry. Your grandmother will have something in mind. Mark won't lose out."

Andrew looked dubious as he helped himself to slices of chicken and ham.

"If it worries you that much, why not sign his cottage over to him?"

Andrew paused in putting coleslaw on his plate. "That's a wonderful idea, Dad. Sure you wouldn't mind?"

"Only seems fair to me. In fact why don't you turn the whole of 'The Haven' over to him? The cottage won't be enough, when the children are grown. He could knock through."

"You're a genius, Dad. That would certainly even things up. I need to ask Clare first though. She may not want to live at 'Tamarisks'. Grandmother hasn't considered that."

"Oh, she will have," Alan assured him.

"Then she knows her better than I do," Andrew scoffed.

"That is something else you can be sure of," Alan chuckled.

Andrew looked indignant."Dad, we're talking about the girl I'm about to marry."

"Yes, and as such, you *should* know, she will need more out of life than baking bread and keeping house. Grace has seen it all along; that's why she's so keen for Clare to be 'Lady of the House'."

"That can't be right; she wants half a dozen children."

Alan smiled. "And if that's what she wants, you can be sure she will have them, but take a few lessons from your grandfather's mistakes, Son. By all means take the line of least resistance, but now and then, when she puts her foot down, put yours firmly on top, because you have Grace the second on your hands. Clare is marvellous, and no one will even realise Grace isn't here when she runs this place."

About to say something, Andrew turned as Clare came over, eyes shining with excitement. It was as if he was seeing their future clearly for the first time, and his face broke into a confident smile. Grandmother was right. This *was* the perfect setting for her.

"Dad's just suggested that Mark and Kathy should have the cottages as we are having 'Tamarisks'. What do you think?"

"Perfect. Couldn't be better." She kissed Alan on the cheek. "Well done. Andrew will be a lot happier with that."

Grace joined them, looking intrigued. "You look as if you're scheming."

Andrew gave a satisfied sigh. "Dad's just suggested that Mark should have the cottages as we are having 'Tamarisks'. And we think it's a perfect idea, don't you?"

Grace looked surprised. "Absolutely marvellous, Alan."

Laurie joined them in time to catch the conversation.

"That will keep everyone happy, won't it, Laurie?"

The wide eyed innocent look on Grace's face made Laurie suspect that it didn't altogether come as a surprise and narrowing his eyes at her, knew he was right when she looked away quickly.

Highly amused, he wondered if there was any part of this operation she hadn't planned, down to the last letter.

"Sorry to interrupt but there's something I need to do. I'll be back shortly. Walk to the door with me, Grace?"

"How did you manage that?"

"Don't know what you mean."

"Yes you do."

Grace sighed. "I knew Alan would find a way to make the change acceptable to Andrew and I gambled on the obvious one."

Laurie chuckled. "You should back horses."

"Who's to say I don't?"

He left, laughing, promising to be back in less than an hour.

CHAPTER TWENTY NINE

Laurie drove along the narrow road, leading from the village of Boscastle. The hedgerow was ablaze with colour, and his thoughts were happier than they had been for some time, as he pictured the house he was heading for and a pair of soft brown eyes that would be waiting to greet him.

Settling Thomas into the care home had been the start of a new life for them both. Little did he realise the matron would be someone, from his past, that he could allow himself to fall in love with.

She was nothing like Grace. In fact the complete opposite. Well rounded, sunny natured, warm and comfortable, he had known immediately she was what was missing in his life. Thinking of all the reshuffling, he knew it had been worth it, even though it meant uprooting Thomas again.

As he drove into a wide, shingle driveway bordered by rhododendron bushes, he looked with pleasure at the square, stone-built house bathed in afternoon sunlight and his eyes softened as he saw her waiting at the front door. A real home at last. She *was* his home.

Simply dressed in a plain maroon silk dress, softened by a fashionably knotted pink scarf, Christine was curious to meet these interesting friends of his, that he thought it wiser to introduce her to after seeing how the meeting went. But he was smiling as he hurried towards her. "Full steam ahead. Let's go?"

"I'll get my jacket."

On the way to 'Tamerisks', he glanced at her anxiously. "I hope you will like my surprise."

She smiled fondly. "I'm sure I will. And if I don't, I promise they will never know. I've dealt with a lot of tenacious people in my job."

He pulled a face. "Surely I haven't made her out to be tenacious?"

Christine chuckled. "Really? I seem to remember you likening her to a bulldog, because once she gets her teeth into something she never lets go?"

They looked at each other and laughed. "Well perhaps; but don't tell her I said so."

The sitting room was abuzz with chatter as Laurie opened the door and pointed to Grace and Arthur, making Christine laugh and wag her finger at him. Then silence fell, as everyone turned to watch him lead her over to them.

"I would like you to meet my future wife," he said smiling broadly at their astonished expressions.

A murmur of surprise came from everyone, and Arthur clapped him on the back delightedly, while Grace just stood and stared in disbelief.

"You remember our friends, don't you, Christine?"

"I certainly do." Christine saluted Arthur.

"Permission to come aboard, Commander?"

"Good lord! Nurse Peters? I hardly recognised you out of uniform."

Arthur laughed loudly. "So you never lost touch all this time. You dark old horse."

Grace remained poker faced. "Why have you never told us?" she demanded, looking accusingly at Laurie.

"There was nothing to tell. We only met again a few weeks ago."

Christine laughed lightly. "And Laurie didn't really remember me, until we got talking. I recognised him straight away, of course. Proper love struck I was; like all the girls. I couldn't believe it when he walked into my Care Home with Thomas."

Laurie tucked her under his arm and kissed her forehead.

"I'll never forget you again. You're so wonderfully comfortable, and just the right size. I never want to be without you."

Her eyes filled with happy tears."I sound like a pair of old slippers."

Laurie turned to face everyone. "We are to be married at the local church, the week after Clare and Andrew, and you are all invited. We've bought a house between here and Boscastle, and the reception will be there. Nothing elaborate. Just special friends. Please be sure to come. I also want you to meet my dear friend and childhood guardian. Thomas is living in our annex. He's looking forward to meeting you all and hopes you will often find time to drop in for a chat, as he finds it difficult to get about now. I think you will find him particularly interesting, Jim. He enjoys painting, loves history and, like yourself, is a fountain of knowledge."

"You seem to have made quite a few changes of late," Grace murmured accusingly.

Laurie gave her a searching look."And every one for the better, Grace. I've taken a leaf out of your book and given 'Smythe House' to my godson."

He took her hand and kissed it but Grace drew her it away and turned to Arthur frowning. "Aren't you going to get our guests a drink, Arthur?"

Arthur slapped his own wrist playfully. "What am I

thinking. Come and choose your tipple, Christine. Don't mind if I steal her away do you, Laurie?"

They walked away, laughing together, leaving Laurie and Grace standing by the open French doors, Grace looking out at the garden, pretending indifference. Concerned that she seemed upset Laurie stepped outside, offering his hand.

"Show me where this bungalow is to be built?"

Without a word she allowed him to escort her to the end of the terrace, where a wooden bench overlooked the field leading down to the tamarisk trees.

Grace sat without speaking and when the silence lengthened, Laurie said, "What is it, Grace? Aren't you happy for me?"

She looked sharply at him. "Why wouldn't I be?"

"Perhaps, even after all this time, you still want to be the only one I could ever love?"

She gave a scornful laugh. "My goodness, how you flatter yourself."

Clare called out as she came towards them along the terrace. "Mum and Dad are leaving. Shall they come out?"

Grace got up and steadied herself with her stick. "No. I shall come and see them off."

Laurie offered her his arm, but she stiffly brushed him aside.

Clare waited until Grace had gone into the house and joined him. "You've told her?"

He shook his head.

"What is she upset about then?"

"Grace thought she would always be the only woman in my life, even though I could only worship her from afar."

"So why not tell her the truth?"

"I couldn't disillusion her. She will come around."

"What about Christine?"

"No secrets. I told her everything, straight away."

"I couldn't be happier for you."

She took his arm. "We'd better go and say goodbye. Everyone seems to be leaving."

"Yes. And you must come and see our home soon. You will love it. Ten minutes down the road from here." His eyes twinkled at her. "Even you can't get lost."

"Never going to live that down, am I?"

He laughed. "Nope."

Andrew appeared. "Ready to go home, love? Connie says Jim's had enough for one day. See you next week, Laurie. Christine and Connie are booking Thomas in with her and Jim, while you are on honeymoon." He disappeared again and Clare laughed at Laurie's glazed look.

"And there you were, thinking you were in charge."

Sitting on the wooden bench watching the sun disappear into the sea, Arthur wondered why Grace was so quiet, when her plan had worked out so well.

"Perfect end to a perfect day. How did you know Kathy and Mark were not looking forward to living here?"

"It wasn't hard. Kathy is the right wife for Mark, but she would never have coped with 'Tamarisks'. Clare will love it and make a perfect hostess. She will follow in our foot steps and keep up the traditions. I'm ready to hand the reins over to her. Time for us to relax and spend time cruising with our friends."

"So why aren't you happier? The day ended so well. Wasn't it good to see Laurie so happy? Without his help we could still be dealing with that awful woman. He worked hard. We must be glad he isn't lonely any more."

"He wasn't lonely. We were always here for him," Grace reproached.

"Not quite the same as having someone to go to bed with at the end of the day, sweetheart."

He put an understanding arm around her and they sat listening to a nightingale.

"Perfect spot for the bungalow."

"Yes it is. I think I'll ring and invite Laurie and Christine to dinner tomorrow."

"So soon? Just a quiet day or two?" Arthur begged.

"I want to tell them what we are giving them for their wedding present."

"Oh, well in that case." Arthur took a sip of rum, savouring it appreciatively. "Cheers, Laurie!"

"I'm booking them on a month's cruise with us and all of the old crew."

"What if they have other plans?"

"They haven't yet. That's why I need to make it tomorrow. I heard Christine telling Connie they could go ahead and plan something now she has offered to look after Thomas."

Arthur threw his head back laughing. "So you thought you would plan it for them."

"Of course. You don't object do you?"

"Of course not. Would I dare?"